AND THE SKY FULL OF STARS

SABINE BERLIN

IMMORTAL WORKS
SALT LAKE CITY

Immortal Works LLC
1505 Glenrose Drive
Salt Lake City, Utah 84104
Tel: (385) 202-0116

Cover Art by Rebecca Barney
barneydesign.com

ISBN 978-1-953491-45-9 (Paperback)
ASIN B0BHS5KP6D (Kindle)

To Dustin.
You will always be my sky full of stars.

1

"No," I said, glancing across the Pizza Palace at the small cluster of cheerleaders gathered around a booth on the opposite wall.

"Please, Caty?" Ryan begged.

I shook my head. "There's no way I'm going to *accidentally* bump into Valerie to see if she likes you."

Ryan leaned back against the red vinyl bench and sighed. "What's the use of having a best friend with superpowers if she won't use them to get me a date?"

I bit my bottom lip and shoved a breadstick into the cup of alfredo in the middle of the table. "I'm not a superhero," I said. "I don't even own a pair of tights." I turned to the trio who studied the menu plastered under the glass tabletop. Valerie Stephens, head cheerleader, and two other girls from the squad sat in full gear, from the confetti bows at the top of their ponytails all the way down to their perfect, white Skechers.

Ryan looked at the girls as well, but I could tell he wasn't wondering how they kept their shoes so clean.

"You have a gift." He tried puppy-dog eyes. "Use it. For me?"

"A gift?" I scoffed. "More like a curse." I'd been running from my so-called gift since it appeared five years earlier. I didn't care that Ryan thought my life deserved its own action movie. *He* wasn't a freak who had to keep his hands tucked in his pockets wherever he went. *He* never had to worry about picking up an object and seeing memories from a previous user or running into someone and knowing the most dominant thought on their mind. People always say you shouldn't touch things if you don't know where they've been. I can testify just how true that is.

"I'll buy you some chocolate." Ryan's pleading turned to bribery.

I rolled my eyes. "Extra dark?"

"Of course."

"I can't guarantee it will be about you." Just because he'd run into Valerie last night at Dairy Queen and just because she'd let him pay for her sundae and just because he insisted they'd had some sort of cosmic connection didn't mean he'd be the number one thought on her mind at the exact moment I touched her.

"I know," he said. "But you can *try*."

I wished that was the case. If I had any control over my memorysight—Ryan's name for it—then maybe I wouldn't have to worry about seeing what Wednesday's spaghetti surprise really contained, or worse, knowing the exact thoughts some teenage boy had about the semi-nude model on the cover of the magazine for sale at the grocery store.

"Fine," I said, tossing the breadstick back onto the plate. I glanced at Valerie. She scooted out of the booth and said something to her friends before walking toward the bathroom. I probably wouldn't find a better place to bump into her. At least I wouldn't have an audience.

I walked into the bathroom, and Valerie stood at the sink, shaking water from her hands. She looked up and waved. "Hi, Caty." Valerie was nice. Ryan could—and had—done worse, but that didn't mean I wanted to know the inner workings of her mind. Especially not if they concerned crushing on my best friend.

"Are you here with Ryan?" The look on her face made me fairly certain I could ensure him a date this weekend without having to actually touch her.

I smiled. Anytime I could avoid touching someone, I took it. "Yeah. We were at the pep rally." I stepped to the sink next to her and washed my hands as well. "It was really good." I didn't feel quite as awkward with Valerie as I usually did when I tried to be social. Ryan had my full support with this one.

"Thanks. I'm just glad it's finally spring break. We've been practicing nonstop. Do you have any exciting plans?" Her eyes assured me her real question concerned Ryan's plans for the upcoming week. I definitely did not need to have a memorysight to guarantee him a date.

"Just hanging around. Although Ryan has been pleading with me to go see that new baseball movie, and I really don't want to." I patted myself on the shoulder for already guessing what her reply would be.

"Oh, I've been wanting to see it." She looked more hopeful than she needed to.

"You should go with him." I tried to make it sound like the idea just occurred to me. Memorysight or not, I was earning my chocolate.

Valerie beamed. "Do you think he would mind?"

I shook my head. "No way, he'll just be happy to go with someone who doesn't complain during the whole show." I finished washing my hands and shook them off before drying them the rest of the way on my jeans—one of the many habits I'd developed over the years to avoid touching unnecessary objects. "Just leave it to me."

Who said you needed special powers to play matchmaker? This hadn't been too bad until Valerie decided to grab my arm and thank me. She started going on and on about how much she appreciated me doing this or something, but I didn't really hear. While she talked, I found myself inside her head, being her, feeling the things she felt, thinking the things she thought—all about Ryan.

He sat across from her, eating ice cream and talking about a test in Mr. Riggins' class. Valerie's feelings washed over me. I felt nervous, anxious, thinking about how hot Ryan looked in his black Hollister T-shirt, even if he did have a little bit of hat hair after he took off his ball cap. Then there were the thoughts I could have gone without. The way Ryan's chest muscles flexed through his shirt. The way I imagined nibbling on his bottom lip—

I stepped out of her reach—and right into the garbage can. I grabbed onto the hand dryer to keep from falling over, an act that caused a whole different memory—the waitress who served us earlier had been skimming cash from the register. I shook my head clear of that as well, steadying myself by a sheer balancing act. Valerie stopped talking, and the awkward moment when the person whose mind I'd just invaded looked at me like I might be crazy took over.

"Are you okay?" she asked.

"I'm fine," I mumbled. "Sorry, I just—" I hated explaining myself. So, I didn't. "Ryan is out there paying; I'll go get the movie set up."

Ryan looked up as we exited the bathroom. I gave him a small thumbs up. "Hey, Joe just texted me and asked if I could go get him a few things at Cranston's," I said. Which was somewhat true, except he'd texted me before school had even gotten out for the day. "Oh, and Valerie said she also wants to see that baseball movie." Valerie, who had followed me out, still gave me a strange look but smiled at my promised setup. "You should totally go with her."

Ryan grinned. Valerie grinned. I told Ryan to take his time and then made my way out of the restaurant toward the hardware store around the corner—not grinning. I really didn't want to see Ryan with lip nibbling still fresh on my mind. I shivered. Ryan and I had kissed once—at the ninth-grade dance. That was when I learned chemistry is a real thing—and just because you are best friends with someone doesn't mean you have it. We'd remained platonic friends since then, so Valerie's thoughts were a bit much for me to have to think about. But even so, they made me jealous. Not the Ryan part, of course, but that everything she imagined would come true. She'd get her guy. I never would.

I fiddled with the ring on my necklace as I turned the corner. The ring had been the anniversary present my dad had planned to give my mom, the anniversary they never celebrated. But even then, they'd been together until the end. I was never going to have a real relationship like that, true love—not even someone who I could consider lip nibbling with. Only Ryan knew what I could do, and even sweet, innocent Ryan, who had no secrets to hide from anyone, had been terrified of me for a good month before he'd decided my ability was screenplay worthy. Knowing how most people's minds worked, I wouldn't get lucky twice. I vowed I would never tell anyone else what I could do. I couldn't, not unless I found a way to control my memorysights. And that meant no falling in love.

I pulled out my phone and thumbed through the list of items Joe had requested, none of which seemed to have anything to do with the car restoration project he said he needed them for. Not terribly surprising. Joe moved us out to Kanab five years ago, just after my parents' accident and just before my memorysight showed up. Back then, he and Claire had just been my godparents, but now they were the only family I had. Joe could fix just about anything you asked him to, but never in a conventional way. He was a definite MacGyver. So the fact his current project involved restoring a '67 Dodge Charger but his list included items like twenty feet of copper wiring, a charcoal filter, duct tape, and a package of two five-foot-long industrial braid hoses with pre-installed washers and straight ends didn't really shock me much.

I walked to the back of the store where I knew they kept the wiring. I wasn't sure how long Ryan would be flirting with Valerie, but my goal, as always, was to get the stuff as fast as possible and get out without seeing too many unwanted memories. Luckily, objects weren't like people. I only had a memory from an object once—and I'd been to Cranston's enough to be safe as long as I didn't touch too much merchandise. Plus, spring break started tomorrow, which meant I could spend the entire week hiking through the red rock cliffs surrounding Kanab—another place I could guarantee would be mostly memory-free. Ryan might not be as keen to join me with Valerie now in the picture, but I needed to get used to being on my own before he left for college anyway.

I turned the final corner, still looking at my phone, lost in my thoughts, when a boy appeared out of nowhere. I caught the aroma of cinnamon and cloves, a different enough smell from Cranston's normal sawdust scent that his presence should have alerted me sooner. I reached out to keep from falling over and grabbed the first thing available–him. His mind invaded mine immediately, making me unsure of anything–except this memorysight wasn't like any I'd ever had.

I stood on the edge of a lake surrounded by mountains whose peaks reached high into the sky. The sky cued me in that something was different. A mass of colors swirled through the air—violet, red, green, orange—like a photoshopped version of the Northern Lights. Except memories couldn't be photoshopped, and real mountains didn't have two moons hanging just above them, the larger one almost shadowing the smaller. I wanted to be there more than anything. I wanted to be home.

My hand fell away from his, and, just as fast, the memory fell from my sight, but what I'd seen, what I'd felt, couldn't fall away as easily. I looked up into brilliant eyes, green like the crest of a wave shot through with sunlight. He was the most beautiful boy I'd ever seen—a strong jawline, a small scar near the corner of his left eye, and wavy, disheveled hair.

But he was definitely not from Earth.

2

He looked human enough, nothing little green man about him. He stood taller than my own 5'10"—at least 6'2" or 6'3". His hair was a sandy brown, his skin olive-toned. And those eyes. Those intense green eyes seemed to get darker the longer I stared into them.

"Are you okay?" he asked. His voice held a slight accent, but nothing I could place. Of course not, because he wasn't from Earth. People from Earth didn't have memories of wanting to be home on their two-mooned, multi-colored sky planet.

"I'm fine." I took a step farther back, biting my lip, but I couldn't take my eyes off him. Always one to overthink any situation, I found myself not being able to think much of anything at all. Was this even possible? Memorysights didn't lie. But an alien? Was there really an alien in front of me? No matter that I'd always been more into Asimov than Austen, I didn't believe in aliens. But there he was. "Sorry, I wasn't looking."

"No, the fault is all mine. I wasn't watching where I was going. I'm looking for the shovels?" he said questioningly.

"Aisle seven," I replied automatically. Why couldn't I look away? Shouldn't I have been running or something? And why, for the first time ever, did I find myself wanting to reach out and touch something —someone—again?

"Thanks."

Neither of us moved. I knew why I couldn't move, but what about him? Did he know I knew? Could he read my mind?

Can you read my mind?

No response.

"Caty, are you ready to go?" Ryan broke our trance. I couldn't be certain we would have moved on our own if he hadn't shown up. I for sure wouldn't have been able to. Now we both looked at Ryan.

"Um yeah, sorry." I looked back at the boy. "Good luck shoveling." *Good luck shoveling?* Had I really just said that?

He smiled. "Thanks."

Now I wanted to run, but not for any of the reasons I should be running. I took Ryan's hand and pulled him toward the door. I'd stopped having memorysights with Ryan two years earlier. We'd discovered in our quest for understanding why I could see memories that the closer I was to someone, the less I could see in their mind. I'd never even had a memorysight from Joe or Claire. But now, I wished I could see something in Ryan's head. Anything to make the memory fresh in my own head disappear.

"Okay Caty, we're not running a marathon." Ryan slowed down my retreat halfway across the parking lot. "And I'm parked over there." He nodded to the front of the store. "Want to tell me what's going on?"

"Nothing," I said. I always told Ryan everything. But this? How did I explain this memorysight to him? And why did I not want to? This was Ryan. And we were talking about aliens. In Kanab! I should have been talking a million miles a minute.

"Okay. So, where's Joe's stuff then?" Ryan, of course, didn't believe my *nothing* one bit.

"They didn't have the stuff." I started back toward his truck.

"They didn't have any of it?" he asked incredulously.

"No." I got to the passenger side and practically threw myself into the front seat.

Ryan slid next to me.

"They didn't have duct tape?"

Crap, I'd shown him the list earlier.

"They didn't have it," I said again, and then my eyes caught those of the boy who had turned me into a complete mess. He left the store, shovel in hand. He must have felt my gaze on him because he stopped and caught me staring.

"Drive," I said to Ryan. I knew I wouldn't be able to look away on my own.

Ryan turned on the truck, grinding the gears as he pulled into reverse and backed out of the space. "Who was that?" he asked as we turned onto Main Street.

"I don't know. He's not from around here." Understatement of the century.

"Caty Brown. You have the hots for the guy at the hardware store!"

My mouth dropped. Ryan's grin mirrored a crescent moon. "That is so not what's going on." Yes, he was breathtaking, but I didn't have the hots for him. He wasn't even from this solar system—at least, I assumed he wasn't.

"Whatever. I saw the way you were looking at him. You couldn't take your eyes off him. And it seemed he couldn't take his eyes off you, either."

"Ryan, you have no—"

"Caty, just admit it. It's okay."

I sighed. I could just tell Ryan the truth. I could tell him I wasn't staring at the boy because I was crushing on him but because he might turn into a lizard creature and eat me at any moment. But I didn't. I let him believe his theory. Because if the boy was an alien bent on Earth's destruction, how could I stop him? And also because the way he longed to be home lived in my head more intimately than any memorysight emotion I'd ever felt. I had no right to share it.

"Fine. He was...attractive." I went with what I could be honest about.

"Ha. I knew you liked him." Ryan tapped his fingers on the steering wheel.

"Too bad I'll never see him again." Strangely enough, the thought hurt.

"What do you mean?" Ryan turned toward me.

"Eyes on the road."

"Sorry. But why will you never see him again?"

"Did you recognize him?" I asked. In a town the size of Kanab, everyone pretty much knows everyone. Someone that looked like him couldn't have lived here and not been the talk of the town.

"No," Ryan said, and his tone implied he knew exactly what I meant. Still, I felt compelled to make it clear, if not to Ryan, then to myself.

"He was just another stranger passing through." *The galaxy.* I had to believe that because, if not, I had to start asking myself questions like: What was an alien doing here in Southern Utah? With a shovel? What did he plan on digging up? Or burying?

I let out a breath.

"It's okay." Ryan patted my hand again. "You'll find someone."

I half-laughed, half-scoffed. "In Kanab?"

"You don't need to stay here forever," he said as we pulled in front of my house.

"Yeah, because out there is so much safer."

"Caty, you have the ability to—"

"Be so much more. I know. I know." We'd had this conversation more than once. And more than once, I'd explained to Ryan the whole Spiderman-with-great-power speech did not work on me. Spiderman had powers he could use to protect himself. No matter how hard I had tried—from gloves to folded arms to refusing to leave my room for a whole week—I didn't know how to protect myself from things I couldn't unsee. And right now, the thing I couldn't unsee changed my entire perception of the universe. I wasn't going to get into that with Ryan. "I don't need the lecture right now."

"Okay, fine." He frowned.

"You know, you never asked me about my memorysight with Valerie."

His left eyebrow arched a little, and the corner of his mouth turned up. "What did you see?"

I opened the door and slid out of the truck. Reaching in my bag, I pulled out a pack of gum and threw a piece in his direction. "You probably will need this." I turned and started up the driveway.

"Wait, what?" he yelled through the open window. "What did you see?"

"Have fun on your date, hotshot!" I yelled without turning back.

Joe sat at the kitchen counter when I walked in, a newspaper sprawled across the island countertop in front of him. He looked up and smiled, and a stab of guilt found me. I'd gotten pretty good at justifying not telling Joe and Claire about my memorysight. I wasn't lying to them; I just spared them from the fear that would come if they believed I could see into their minds. Not that I could. I'd avoided touching them at first, but then as Ryan made me test out theories, we decided I must have been completely in sync with them since we were so close—hence no memorysights. This memory-free zone made home more of a haven than one could imagine. Another place where I could let go of my worries and not have to see a rush of memories.

"You get my stuff?" Joe asked.

Now I would need to lie. "I couldn't." I tried for semi-truth.

Joe gave me a questioning look.

"Ryan has a date and had to drop me off early. I can go back downtown and grab the parts now if you want." I feared going to the store and seeing the boy again. I also feared never seeing him again, never having all the questions swirling in my head answered.

"It's okay. I'll get them tomorrow," Joe said. I felt less relieved than I should be. "So, who's the lucky girl?"

I looked at him blankly.

Claire came into the kitchen and gave my shoulder a quick squeeze. "He means who is Ryan going out with?"

"Oh. Valerie Stephens."

"Mitch and Cami's girl?" Joe asked.

I nodded.

"You okay with that?"

I groaned. "Yes. Ryan and I will never get together. Never." This was another one of those constant conversations. Joe believed Ryan and I were meant to be.

"Never say never," he said, grinning. I stuck my tongue out at him.

"Leave her alone," Claire said. "Caty will know the right person when he comes along."

"How?" Joe asked. A good question.

"She won't be able to take her eyes off him—just like I couldn't with you." Claire leaned over the counter and kissed Joe on the cheek. His blush made me smile. An image of the boy popped into my head. The way I'd found myself mesmerized by him both times our gazes met. I shook my head. That was different. I couldn't take my eyes off of him because of what he was, not who.

"You're making Caty uncomfortable," Joe said, pulling Claire a little closer and giving her a kiss back. She giggled and swatted his arm playfully.

"Do I need to leave you two alone?"

"That might be best," Joe said with a smirk.

I rolled my eyes at them and snatched a couple of cookies off a plate by the stove before wandering up to my room. They were still giggling. I sank down on my bed with a sigh. Pining over something I could never have was pointless. I set my thoughts to what I did have—proof aliens existed. What did that mean?

And why was there one in the middle of nowhere buying a shovel? What if he was burying his human autopsy victims? What if he was planting noxious weeds meant to make our atmosphere breathable for his people before they invaded? If this boy fit into Hollywood's alien definition, I might be the only one who could stop him. Did I call the police? The FBI? Would they even believe me? Did I believe myself?

I leaned back against my pillows and closed my eyes, trying to recall everything I'd seen in his mind. Something that would let me know if the National Guard needed to be alerted or not. There was the color of the sky, the moons, even the mountains, more spiraling peaks than I'd seen on any *Planet Earth* special. None of that would be enough even to sell to the tabloids. The only thing that really stuck out was the longing he felt to be home. That kept me grounded. All I could remember was how he wanted to get back there. That made me believe he was not a threat. But if not burying something, then what?

Had his ship crashed? Had he gotten here on a ship? Were there more aliens than just him? These were all questions I should have been discussing with Ryan. But Ryan was getting ready for his date, and there was really no sense in telling him anything because we would never be able to get answers. The only time I'd ever see those green eyes again was when I closed my own.

I didn't even know his name.

THE FAMILIAR SOUND of crickets chirping woke me up. Ryan's ringtone. I glanced at the clock: 6:45. I rolled off the bed, then fumbled through my bag until I pulled out my phone and swiped across the screen sideways.

"Shouldn't you be leaving for your date?" I answered, stifling a yawn.

"I'm on my way to get her, but you're not answering your messages."

I fully yawned now. "I fell asleep. What's up?"

"What's up is that I got new neighbors." Ryan sounded a little too excited for the neighbors to be another old couple like the one who had moved out four months earlier. This must mean a family, and from Ryan's tone, they probably had a teenage daughter.

"Is she cute?" I asked, a little miffed he called me with this information while driving to pick up the girl he'd made such a big deal about earlier.

"No girls. Just a guy and his aunt and uncle. Look at the picture I sent you." Now he sounded even more excited. I knew why even before I pulled the phone away and opened my messages.

The picture wasn't great. Ryan probably used his phone through his front window. While blurry, I had no trouble making out the profile of the face that had just been occupying my dreams. He didn't belong here. Yet there he was, carrying a box he must have just gotten out of the moving van sitting in the background. I'd been certain I would never see him again. Now he was moving in next door to my best friend. I stared at the picture, a million more thoughts going through my head than I'd already had.

"Caty?" Ryan said loudly through the speaker. I pulled the phone back to my ear, still at a loss for words. "His name is Eri."

3

I dreamed about aliens. First, your typical Vulcans and Klingons with an Ewok or two thrown in, but then my dreams left the innocence of big-screen fantasy behind and became darker, more sinister.

Eri appeared in all of them.

Sometimes he played the whole rebel boy captain. Other times he ripped off his human suit to reveal scales and acid-dripping mucus. Always, his eyes seemed to bore into mine. Like in real life, I couldn't turn away from him in my dreams.

WHETHER OUT OF fear or curiosity, I found myself at Ryan's house far earlier than usual on a Saturday morning. His mom peeked her head out of the kitchen when I walked in. The scent of coffee and chocolate wafted through the air. "Hey, Caty," she called. "I just finished a shift. Ryan's still sleeping. You two going hiking?"

I nodded, needing a reason to show up at eight in the morning.

"I'm sure he was out pretty late with Valerie." She gave me a wink. "You may have to go wake him up."

I didn't really want to barge in on Ryan while he was most likely dreaming about Valerie, and truthfully, I wasn't there for him. I shook my head and wandered into the living room. "He can sleep a bit longer," I said. "I'll just enjoy the sun." I sat in Ryan's big bay window all the time, so his mom didn't say anything.

I found my usual spot on the bench and curled up, my gaze focused on the Spanish-style home next door. The one that looked out of place with the rest of the 1950's block-style houses covering the neighborhood. Of course, its inhabitants were different as well, at least one of them. Were the aunt and uncle aliens also? Did they know what he was? Could I have been wrong and just imagined everything? I shook my head. I knew what I'd seen. I knew what he was—sort of.

Everything at the house appeared normal. A green Range Rover in the carport, a welcome mat on the front porch, and at exactly 8:15, an older woman, in knee shorts and a brightly colored button-down shirt, came out to work in the front flower beds. It didn't scream alien invasion.

"Any sighting?" Ryan said, startling me out of spy mode. He walked into the room wearing basketball shorts and pulling a Kanab Cowboys Baseball shirt over his head.

"Sighting?" I asked, thinking for a moment that Ryan knew what–who—had moved in next door.

"Eri?" he said teasingly.

"I don't know. I'm just enjoying the sun."

Ryan picked up a pillow off the recliner near him and threw it at me. "Liar. Admit it; you're stoked he wasn't just some stranger passing through."

Stoked wasn't the word I would have used. Confused, curious, concerned. Those all fit my feelings better. But Ryan wanted to believe me infatuated, and until I knew more about his new neighbors, I'd rather not raise any red flags. Instead of throwing the pillow back in protest, I hugged it and turned back to the window. The woman had gone inside. My watch blinked to 9:20 when I looked down. I'd been absorbed watching her dig up weeds for an hour.

"Man, you have it bad." Ryan sat down on the other end of the bench.

I definitely had something. "Speaking of having it bad," I said, "tell me about the date."

Ryan pursed his lips and sighed, well aware of my attempt to change the subject, but then he went into the full details of his own love life and left mine alone for a moment. I listened, grateful for the change in topic, but my eyes couldn't help wandering out the front window more often than they should have.

"Where are you two going today?" Ryan's mom asked, walking into the room as Ryan completed his play-by-play date coverage.

"Mom, Caty is totally gone over the new neighbor. I don't think I'll get her away from this window anytime soon."

I kicked him, and he feigned pain.

His mom laughed. "Who, Eri? I don't blame you. Did you see those eyes? Oh man, if I was twenty years younger."

"Please, Mom," Ryan groaned, "don't even go there."

"Oh, Ry, calm down. Caty can have him." She winked at me, and the heat rose to my cheeks even though their teasing was normal. "Actually, this works out great. I made brownies to take over, but the hospital just called, and I need to go cover another half shift. Why don't you take them over for me, Caty?"

"I don't know—"

"She'd love to," Ryan said over my embarrassing decline.

I kicked at him again, but he just grinned. "Relax, I'll go with you."

That really wasn't what worried me. But this could be my chance. I wanted to know more about the family next door, and staring out the window would not provide any answers.

At 10 o'clock, I followed Ryan across his yard and up the front porch of the house next door, the plate of brownies clenched in my hands. Just hand him the plate. I could do that much. Hand him the plate and let my fingers brush against his, lingering as long as possible, hoping his home planet would be on his mind again at that moment, or why he'd come here, or anything that would confirm his true self, and possibly even show me why he'd moved in next door to my best friend.

Ryan knocked. Eri opened the door, and I once again lost myself in a sea of green. He smiled, but his arched eyebrows questioned what we were doing on his front step. I thrust the brownies forward. "We brought brownies."

He eyed the plate. "Thanks?"

If I hadn't been so enthralled with his eyes, I might have cared more that the plate practically touched his chest. "Ryan's mom made them." That felt like an important detail to add, as if I'd come for any purpose other than to glimpse inside his mind.

Eri didn't attempt to take the plate. I didn't attempt to pull away. Ryan finally took it and put the chocolate goodness in Eri's hands. "This is Caty. I think you met at Cranston's."

Eri nodded, placing the plate on a small entryway table, then stepping out of the house, a clear indication we were not going to be invited in. Probably because of all the alien technology hidden in there.

"Yes, we met," he said.

"Hi." I really wished I would have spent less time figuring out my memorysight and more time acquiring communication skills.

"Hi." Apparently, he wasn't much of a socializer either. Something we had in common. No, we didn't have anything in common. Not even a home planet.

"So, I didn't get to ask yesterday," Ryan said. "What brings you to Kanab?"

"My uncle is a geologist. He's here doing some surveying. I'm just tagging along."

Sure.

"Well, Kanab isn't much, but we have the best hiking in the world," Ryan said.

Eri nodded. "That's why I'm here." He sounded so honest. Could this be some sort of galactic vacation? Maybe, just like with Valerie, I wouldn't need to touch him to know the truth. But I wanted to touch him—that scared me.

"Well, you're in luck. Caty knows all the best places. She also happens to have an in with the guy over at the Bureau of Land Management, so she can usually get permits for some of the harder-to-go places."

Eri hadn't stopped looking at me, but now his gaze took on a different feel. More of an assessment, but Ryan wasn't lying. Joe took me hiking the day after we moved to Kanab. I never stopped. I probably knew this part of the world better than people actually born here.

"An in?" Eri asked, and his tone made my face heat up.

"I helped the guy out of a bad situation."

"She totally saved him from losing his job," Ryan added. "They accused the guy of theft, and Caty found the real culprit."

I knocked into Ryan just a bit to get him to shut up. Why didn't he just tell Eri exactly how I figured out who the real thief had been? My gesture caused Eri to break eye contact and look back and forth between Ryan and me.

"Wow, so you're a real Perry Mason," he said.

"Who?" Ryan asked.

Joe watched enough TV Land that I knew the reference, but I tried not to smile. Alien boy was a little behind the times.

Eri just shook his head, barely missing a beat at his mistake, and went on. "I actually hoped to start at Coyote Buttes, but I was told I would need a permit."

Of course he would want to go to the absolute hardest place to get a hiking permit in probably the whole United States. "They have a daily lottery. It will be too late for today," I said. I'd never heard of a law-abiding alien. Then again, I'd never heard of a real alien before yesterday.

His smile disappeared, and I suddenly felt like I would do anything to bring it back. Could Ryan be right? Could there be more to my standing here on Eri's front step than just curiosity? Whatever the reason, before I could stop myself, words I hadn't planned on saying came tumbling out. "But we could go to the BLM office and get our names on the list for tomorrow. Getting chosen shouldn't be a problem." I stopped talking. Ryan looked at me wide-eyed, but then grinned in approval. I'd never taken advantage of Park Ranger Clifton's offer before. It never felt right. And now, here I was, ready to cheat the system for a boy. But even worse than that, I was standing on an alien's front porch, offering to take him to a completely isolated destination, and I didn't care.

"Would you mind?" Eri asked.

"No." I responded quicker than I expected and more truthful as well. Why was I so willing to help him? Did it have anything to do with his memory about wanting to go home? Or could it be the fact his smile made me forget everything except for the way he looked at me like I was the most fascinating thing he'd ever set eyes on? Which, coming from someone who had flown across the Milky Way, was enough to melt me in place.

He turned back and yelled into his house, "I'm going out," then pulled the door shut and smiled at me again. I hated to admit it, but the answer to wanting to help him clearly was that smile.

We were halfway across the yard when Ryan made a sudden announcement. "Man, I forgot, I promised my mom I would swing her by something at work. Eri, you don't mind going with Caty, do you?" He gave me a wink. We were going to have to work on his subtlety.

"That would be fine," Eri said just as we reached my car, sounding like an old radio broadcast. He was still finding his tone here on Earth and the thought intrigued me. How did he even speak English this well? Could he speak any other Earth languages? Had he really learned by watching old-time television programs? And then he opened the door for me and waited until I got in before shutting it and coming around to the passenger side. An alien with manners? The longer we were together, the stranger things seemed.

The slight scent of cinnamon and cloves filled the air again in the enclosed space. Ryan waved goodbye, grinning to himself. I pulled away from the curb too fast to avoid Eri seeing Ryan and bit down on my lip to keep myself from commenting on how good Eri smelled.

I slowed down when I noticed him holding onto the grab handle a little too tightly. "Sorry."

He looked at me with those intense eyes. I kept myself from sending anything more than a quick glance in his direction, knowing how lost I got when he looked at me.

"So, where are you from?" I asked, focusing on the road. The question seemed logical until it left my mouth.

He kept looking at me, and I kept my hands at nine and three and my eyes straight. Maybe getting in a car alone with a stranger from another galaxy hadn't been the best of ideas. Joe would have grounded me if he knew I'd gone anywhere with a stranger. But I needed answers. Not that Eri gave me any.

Do you know I know? If I asked the name of your planet, would you tell me? Can you really not read minds?

"Canada," he finally said, turning away from me to look out the window.

Now I took my gaze off the road. Canada? And he said it so naturally as if it were the truth.

"Wow. What's it like there?" *Want to explain how Canada has two moons?*

"Cold."

I snorted. Cold? I waited for him to continue. He didn't.

I wished I could just casually touch him right then, but I knew I most likely had to wait until we got to the BLM to find out the whole truth, so I kept prying out loud. "Well, it's definitely not cold here. Must feel like a different planet to you."

Had that been too much?

"It really is," he said and then started on a Wikipedia-like definition of Canada. He was good—and prepared. He knew exactly what to say when I asked him about his home. No matter what question I threw at him, he had an answer—and he mostly kept to current events. By the time we were about to pull up to the BLM office, I felt as if I'd watched a full documentary, almost to the point that if I touched him just then, I might really see Canada.

I didn't touch him. Instead, I found myself yelling at him.

"Crap. Crap. Crap. Get down." To his credit, he didn't question me and sank down in the passenger seat as if following commands was second nature to him.

I tried to keep my eyes from trailing Joe as he walked out of the office building I'd just been about to pull up to. Of course he would be here. The week of spring break was one of the busiest for Red Rock Hiking Tours, of which Joe was the CEO and founder. I should have taken that into account before I brought not just a boy but a stranger to a place where all of Joe's friends worked.

Luckily, he seemed to be laughing with someone, so I drove by without him looking out to the street. I watched for any reaction from him in the rearview mirror until I turned the corner and pulled into a nearby parking stall, still waiting for a moment, adjusting the mirror to track him as he turned in the opposite direction, past the worn sign faded with heat so it only read "reau of Land Mangemen" and then disappeared from sight. I breathed a sigh of relief, causing Eri to sit up.

"What was that?" he asked.

He'd been crouched for nearly twenty seconds, having no idea what was going on. He seemed scared. Which made sense because he had a secret to hide. A feeling I knew all too well. I could practically feel his heart beating double time. I bet the hair on the back of his neck stood on end just like mine. And I had caused that.

"I'm so sorry. I just." How did I explain to him? "That guy back there. He's my...well, he's like my dad. He and his wife raised me." I wasn't used to talking to people like this. I didn't normally open up about things in my life, but I continued on. "He's pretty cool but extremely protective. I'm not supposed to talk to strangers." It sounded ridiculous. For as down-to-earth casual as Joe could be about almost everything, he was also overprotective to a fault. As my dad's best friend, he took his responsibility for me seriously. I'd gotten used to reporting my every step to him: who I went with, where we were going. But since the answer had always been Ryan, and Kanab wasn't some big, scary town, it had never been an issue. Honestly, I really didn't know what he would do if those answers ever changed, but I couldn't imagine him flipping out to the point where I would force someone to hide. I didn't know why I had done that.

"And I'm a stranger?" Eri asked.

He was more than a stranger. He was a foreign object, one I couldn't share with anyone. His eyes were almost aquamarine, a nebula I wanted to disappear into. Was it that I couldn't share him with anyone or that I didn't want to? I shook the idea from my head.

"I'm not a stranger?" he asked, misinterpreting my action.

"No. I mean, yes, you are." Heat rose to my face. I'd always been awkward around people but never flustered, not like this. What was he doing to me? Did he have some sort of alien spell cast on me?

"Because I'm from Canada?" He drew out the word. I really wished he was from Canada. I would not be sitting here right now if Eri was just from Canada. I would not have even bothered to glance his way a second time—would I have?

I shook my head again. Somehow, I wasn't sure I was with him just because I wanted to find out more about his extraterrestrial heritage. "It doesn't matter where you're from."

"And what about you? Are you afraid of strangers?"

Yes, Eri frightened me—as did the way I couldn't think straight around him. The way I wanted to keep reaching out to touch him. "I usually can tell if I can trust a person or not." Why did I say that to him?

He laughed. "And can you trust me?"

Well, given the fact you have lied to me about everything. No. "The verdict is still out," I said, again completely uncharacteristically of me. Something was going on. Either Eri was doing something to me, or maybe my own abilities were whacking out. Whatever the answer, I knew there was only one way to find out. I put my hand on his.

If I'd had any doubts before, I no longer had them. I floated away from a planet and then a space station as a million stars surrounded me and then sped by. I tried not to gasp in awe at the sight. Eri severed our connection, leaning away from me. His eyes were no longer a playful aqua green but dark like a supervoid. I scooted back also, afraid.

"Who are you?" The tone of his voice lowered to match the darkness in his eyes.

4

☆☆☆

"What do you mean?" I asked. Did he know what just happened? A wave of panic washed over me. It was impossible. No, it wasn't impossible, or he wouldn't be looking at me like that. My emotions ping-ponged back and forth between fear and disbelief. He didn't answer. This had been such a bad mistake. This is why I didn't trust people. Eri wasn't a person. Eri was...

"Caty?" His voice was soft. My heart, which had been beating in quadruple time, slowed. I let out a breath, almost forgetting why I'd been so worried. Everything was fine. I was fine.

"Yes?"

"Where are you from?"

"Virginia, but I moved out here about five years ago with Joe and Claire after my parents died." Strange, I didn't tell people things like that. But I was fine. It wasn't like telling him my secret.

His eyes never left mine. "Where are your parents from?"

Words I never shared came tumbling out. "My mom was from Illinois, and my dad was from Maine. They met in college." I threw the last part in just for context. I mean, he was interested in my family. A cute boy wanted to get to know me. That didn't seem so bad. Except wasn't this something I didn't talk to people about? But although he still looked confused, he relaxed and his smile returned. I liked his smile. I was glad I told him.

Something didn't seem quite right, but not exactly wrong either. A giggle escaped. "Are you using your alien mojo on me?" Oops, should I not have said that? His smile disappeared and I frowned. I guess not.

"It's okay," I said. "I won't tell anyone your secret."

He didn't smile again.

"How do you know what I am?"

"I've seen your whole two-mooned, rainbow-sky world." I put my hand up to my mouth. Oh well. I guess it was too late for secrets. But that was okay. This was okay. We had to talk about this sometime.

"When were you on Rhaev?" He scowled.

"Rhaev? Never been there, just saw it. Right here." I tapped my index finger against my head.

I must have done something right. His eyes softened. Boy, he was so full of emotions. Why couldn't he just be calm like me? So, so, so very calm.

"How?" he asked.

"It's a secret." I put my finger to my lips. A warm giddiness enveloped me. It was a sensation I wasn't used to, but I liked it. I wanted to share everything with Eri.

"Tell me how you know Rhaev."

"I see memories. All it takes is just one touch, and I know what you're thinking. Works on objects too." Why hadn't I told anyone besides Ryan this before? It wasn't nearly as hard as I thought.

"But you're human?"

"Of course I'm human. I'm just special." I laughed again, recalling Ryan's words. I was special; he'd been right.

Eri shook his head, and the confusion and surprise left. "Are you saying you're psychic?"

"Mmm." I shrugged. "Maybe, I can't really see the future, just the past."

"Do you know why I'm here?"

I shook my head. "No, but I know you want to go home." Eri was really easy to talk to.

He nodded once as if agreeing with my assessment. Of course, he should agree. I couldn't be wrong. My memorysight never failed me. I reached out and patted his knee. He tried to move away, but he was too late. The moment I touched him again, everything turned over. My head throbbed, something akin to what I imagine a hangover would feel like. A hangover like I'd been drugged. With my hand still on his knee, I knew I hadn't been drugged because I saw exactly what he'd been doing to me. How he'd been controlling my emotions. How he'd made me calm. How he'd made me share the secret I vowed never to tell anyone.

I pulled my hand away, the rightful fear that should have always been there returned. He reached toward me, and I flinched. He stopped. "What did you see?"

"What did you do to me?" I pulled at the collar of my shirt. The heat in the car scorched my ability to think straight. I had to get out. I grabbed the car handle, but I couldn't open it. I didn't want to open it. No, I did, I just... "Stop." I tried to scream at him, but my voice came out sounding so nice, so calm.

"If I stop, will you not try to run?" He looked at my hand. Of course I would run. I should have kept running the moment I'd seen him at the hardware store. But running now would do me no good. I nodded and let go of the handle, still pressed against the door as far away from him as I could get in the enclosed space.

"I'm an empath. I can control emotions, make people calm, make them feel secure."

"Secure enough to spill all their secrets?" The anger in my voice bubbled over. He definitely wasn't using his calming ability on me now.

"You know my secret."

A hint of guilt traced his voice, but I didn't feel sorry for him. "You didn't know that," I snapped. "I didn't tell you until after you mind-warped me."

"You're not very good at hiding when you see something."

"Why are you here? What do you want from me?"

"From you? I just wanted a hiking permit."

Embarrassment dug into my mind and set up camp. I was so stupid. He wasn't here for me. I'd just been dumb enough to get in the way of his real mission.

"Why are you on Earth?" I tried again.

He looked at me for a long hard minute and said, "To take over your planet, of course." And then he had the nerve to wait while my face paled and my heart stopped before he laughed. "Relax. I have no intentions of harming you—or any Earthling."

My heart started again. As if touching people wasn't something I'd avoided on a daily basis, my first instinct was to slug him in the arm—just like I did to Ryan when he teased me. Except Eri wasn't Ryan, and the minute my fist collided with his arm, his mind pulled me in.

Eri spoke to an older man, both dressed in what appeared to be some sort of uniform. I'd had experiences with memories that were not in English before, but I understood them even while the words being said were foreign to me, so even though they both spoke in a deep, almost sing-song language, the meaning entered my mind as if they were speaking English.

"For all we know, the Tallisians are still there, or more may have gone." The older man's face turned bitter as he spat out the words.

"I'll find the ship," Eri said.

"And if you come across the Tallisians?" the man asked.

"They will be eliminated."

I pulled my fist away. Eri may have been sincere when he said he wasn't here to harm anyone from Earth, but the way he'd said *eliminated*—cold, calculating—left no room for doubt he could.

"What is a Tallisian?" I asked.

His eyes narrowed. "What did you see?"

"You were talking to someone about a ship and Tallisians." I left out the fact I knew he would kill them if he found them.

"You don't need to know."

He was wrong. Now that he wasn't using his calming powers on me, I needed to know everything, or I might lose it. I reached out my hand, and he leaned away from me. Hesitantly I pulled back. "So, what now?" I asked. Where did we go from here? We couldn't just stay sitting in my car in downtown Kanab, acting like nothing had ever happened.

"You know what I am," he said.

"I won't tell anyone." I knew how to keep a secret—well, when no one brainwashed me to spill it—and I'd already kept his.

"What about Ryan? What does he know?"

"I haven't told Ryan. He just thinks you're his neighbor."

Eri eyed me skeptically.

"Look, if Ryan knew you were an alien, there is no way I would be sitting here with you right now." I wanted to kick myself for not telling Ryan for that exact reason. But if I'd told him, who knew what trouble he would have gotten us into. At least now, if something were to happen, only I would be in trouble. I hoped.

"And your family? That guy, Joe. What did you tell him? I assume you have known what I am since we first met."

"Joe and Claire don't even know what I can do. I wouldn't be able to tell them about you without revealing that. I promise, your secret is safe with me...and I hope mine is safe with you?"

Eri looked shocked. "Your family doesn't know what you can do?"

"No."

"Why not?"

I sighed. "You said you're an empath?"

He nodded.

"So, you can mess with," I stopped and took a deep breath, "so you can control people's emotions?"

Another nod. But I could tell he didn't understand my thought process. I didn't understand exactly. How did I explain I didn't tell my family because I was afraid not of them but of myself?

I bit down on my bottom lip. "Is everyone from your…from Rhaev an empath?"

"No."

A car came speeding around the corner, and my first instinct was to duck, but I just turned off my car. Somehow, I knew this conversation would take a while.

"What do they do to you when they find out you're an empath?"

His eyebrow shot up. "Being an empath is an honor."

I scoffed. "Well, being different on Earth isn't really an honor."

"So, no one knows what you can do?" He sounded surprised.

"Ryan does," I admitted.

His eyes narrowed again. "He knows, and your family doesn't?"

"My parents died when I was younger. I'm an only child. I didn't know what I could do until after they died. And I didn't want…" I shut my eyes. "I didn't want…" Why couldn't I finish that sentence?

"You didn't want the only family you had left to abandon you," Eri said.

My eyes shot open, and I gaped at him. "Can you read minds also?"

He smiled, slow, sad. "No. But sometimes emotions are more telling than thoughts."

Now I closed my eyes because I didn't want to look at him. Was it worse that he could read my emotions? I wasn't sure, but it felt wrong—and feeling this way was why I hadn't told Joe and Claire. I didn't want them to feel like I did right now.

"I won't use my ability on you again," he said.

"You're using it right now." How else would he know my thoughts?

"I don't need to be an empath to read your face."

I opened my eyes but kept them focused on the console between us. Once I'd known what he could do, I'd been able to tell when he'd been controlling me. I didn't feel his calmness now, but could I tell if he was just reading my emotions, not manipulating them?

"You're scared of me."

I laughed sardonically. He didn't have to be an empath to know that. Of course I was scared of him, just like people would be scared of me if they knew my secret. I lifted my eyes to him. He was still breathtaking. He didn't look like a killer. He didn't look like someone I should be afraid of. But then again—neither did I.

"Caty?" He seemed hesitant to ask what he wanted to know.

"Yeah?" I really didn't have anything else to hide at this point, so I let him ask away. I had plenty of questions piling up for him as well.

"What do you see when you touch a person?"

"The strongest thought they have."

"So, whatever the person is thinking about?" He seemed to be trying to clarify. Maybe I should have let him believe that, but I shook my head.

"Most of the time, yes, but sometimes what they are thinking isn't always the strongest thought they have. The subconscious mind can hold a lot of deep thoughts."

"I need you to keep my secret," he said.

"I know. I will." How did I convince him? If I couldn't convince him, then what?

He shook his head. "There is only one way you will be able to keep this a secret." He moved his hand closer to me. I lifted my own to block him. I wasn't going down without a fight. But he didn't touch me; he just held his hand out in front of me.

"You need to be able to trust me," he said. "So, you need to see what my strongest thought is."

My eyes widened. "You might not know what the strongest thought you have is." Did he not get I might see any of his deepest darkest imaginings? And what if I did? What if I saw something he didn't want me to see? Something about eliminating people?

"You said earlier you knew I wanted to go home. That wasn't a lie. I don't want to be here. I have to be. Please just try. If you know how I really feel, maybe we will both be able to trust each other with our secrets."

I lifted my hand toward him, hesitating as our eyes met. He

nodded his consent. Our fingers entwined, and his mind became mine.

The lake I'd seen in my first memorysight returned. The water lapped the shore, and I wanted to be there more than anything else in the world. I knew the feeling of homesickness immediately. I'd felt the pain when we'd moved across the country after my parents' deaths, but never this strongly. The memory shifted to a cabin backed by a massive forest so thick it was almost to the point of blackness.

A man emerged from the cabin and made his way toward the lake. He was older, his hair more silver than the black that peeked through at spots. He was comfort. He was family. He was home. I didn't just want to be at that lake. I wanted to be there—with him.

Eri slowly pulled his hand away from mine and the vision faded.

"You must miss him a lot," I said. "Is he your grandfather?"

He looked relieved as he nodded.

"You knew I would see him. How?"

"I hoped. If you knew what I wanted, what my goal was, you would know I don't mean you any harm. You said you see a person's strongest feelings. That is mine. All I want to do is go home."

"Then why don't you?" I didn't feel quite as afraid of him as I had before. I'd felt the desire to go home, but I'd also felt the bond between his grandfather and him—the love. Seeing that made me trust Eri—at least a little bit.

He didn't answer. He just turned and looked out the window.

"What is a Tallisian?" That must have something to do with why he had to be here.

He raked both hands through his hair before answering, but he still didn't look at me. "The Tallisians are my enemy."

"Why?"

"Because they killed my mother."

I didn't need to touch him to know he told the truth or to know his pain as he spoke the words. I wanted more of an explanation, but questions about the death of a parent tend to just tear the wound deeper. "And they are here on Earth—the Tallisians?" That had to be why Eri had come.

"It's possible," he said. "They have been here."

I remembered the first conversation I'd seen in his head. "The ship you're looking for—is it yours or theirs?" Wouldn't he know where his own ship was?

"It is a Tallisian ship. About eighteen years ago, one of our patrol ships followed a Tallisian ship through an uncharted wormhole on the edge of the Rhaevian zone. They searched for them here, but we lost contact with our people."

"You're not the first aliens to come?" I don't know why, but that made things seem better. If aliens had been here for that long and wanted to hurt us, they obviously would have by now.

"No." He sighed and finally turned to me. I'd gone from being infatuated with him to being terrified of him to seeing him now, just a guy who wanted to get back home. Suddenly, he seemed vulnerable. The idea made me almost forget the fact I was in my car having this particular conversation—almost.

"When did you lose contact with them?"

"About five years ago."

"So why are you just coming now?"

"We sent other people. They've been here, searching since then, but only recently did we get a clue. I have to find that ship. That's why I was sent here." He looked frantic as if nothing else could be of greater importance.

"Why is the ship so important? Wouldn't it be better to find the Tallisians?" It wouldn't. As much as I now wanted to believe Earth might not be in danger, I knew Eri finding any Tallisians, if they were even still here, would mean killing them. I should be glad he only talked about looking for a ship.

"The ship is a weapon. It's my number one priority. Everything else is secondary."

"But—"

He put his hand up in the air to stop me. "Look. I'm sure you have questions, but this is not your problem. The less you know about me, the better." His words screamed with finality. I wasn't so ready to let go.

Luckily, I didn't need him to talk to get answers. I reached out my hand to his upheld one, but his glare frightened me enough that I pulled back.

"If you want my silence, then answer my questions." It was bold of me to threaten him, but I still had too many questions to just let him shut me out.

His glare intensified.

I swallowed hard. Maybe that hadn't been such a good idea. "Please?" My tone softened, almost apologetic.

He leaned away, folding his arms as if keeping his hands from my view would stop me. But he talked. "All you need to know is I have to find the ship."

"And you think it's here? In Southern Utah?" I knew we weren't the most advanced planet out there—well, I knew now—but this wasn't 1870. We had satellites. We had all sorts of high-tech equipment. Could a ship really be hidden between the sands and red rock cliffs of this small corner of the world?

"I do."

"You said you found a clue. What did you find?" What had brought this beautiful boy to an obscure town in the middle of a galaxy not his own? If I could just keep him talking, maybe, at some point, this would all make sense to me.

"The ship we're looking for isn't just a regular ship. It's a hybrid—half machine, half living being. For a long time, it was the only one of its kind we knew of. But we recently discovered another one, and now we know the energy signature we're looking for."

"Do you mean the ship is alive?" Given the situation, I don't know why that astounded me, but it did.

"It has living tissue, yes. It can think independently. Perhaps you would think of it as a cyborg or maybe artificial intelligence."

I shook my head. I didn't have time for disbelief, not if I wanted to keep him talking. I just needed to accept the bizarre. "Okay, and now you can track it?"

"We think so. We're going off a cold trail. A signature that is too faint for us to know the exact location. But the ship was here at some point in the last eighteen years. And since we have not been able to find the energy signal anywhere else, we have to assume it's still here."

Apparently, my face didn't hide how weird this all was because he started to laugh, even if his eyes went a more forest green—more serious. "Are you sure *you're* not using some human mojo on me?" he asked. "Because I shouldn't be telling you any of this. We're not supposed to share things with sleeper planets."

"Sleeper planets?"

"Planets that don't know about the existence of other sentient life."

"Oh. Well, no, I don't have any mojo powers—not like you. All I can do is see things."

He looked in my eyes as if he could sense if I lied just from reading them. Maybe he could. Thankfully I passed whatever test he gave me.

"No, I guess you can't. But in the last ten minutes, I've pretty much gone against every rule I've ever been taught, and I really can't mess this up—not by being caught."

"I'm not going to tell anyone." I started to reach out my hand to pat his arm in comfort and then pulled back. All this time, I could have touched people, and they would have never known what I could do to them, but I hadn't wanted to. Now I had this boy I kept wanting to touch, and I couldn't because he knew what I could do. This wasn't going to be easy. I couldn't keep wanting to touch him. I had to pretend he was like anyone else I met on the street—someone to be feared. I laughed to myself, and Eri looked at me questioningly. "Sorry."

"What?"

"It's just weird. I should be afraid of you like I am of most people. In fact, I should be more afraid of you."

"You're not?"

I thought about the things I'd seen in Eri's memories. The way he felt about home, about family. But then I remembered the cold admittance to being willing to eliminate someone. It felt important to place my trust in the stronger of the two memories. "No, I don't think I am."

5

"How many permits did you get? Will it just be the two of you?" Ryan fluttered his eyes at me as he pulled a bag of popcorn from the microwave and tossed it back and forth between his hands. He ripped open the bag and dumped it in the bowl at the center of the counter.

"I only asked for two because I didn't want to abuse the situation." It already felt weird signing up for a lottery ticket I would get. "I put your name down, though, as the other requestor."

Ryan looked at me in surprise, and I explained to him the moment of seeing Joe and not wanting to explain about Eri. I didn't tell him about the conversation in the car. That there was someone else who knew my secret. That his next-door neighbor had never been to Canada or anywhere else on Earth. Basically, I didn't tell him anything. Part of me hated that; the other part felt relief at not having to deal with all the ramifications that would come with telling him.

"Do you really think Joe will care if you go hiking with a guy? He'll be happy you're going out with someone other than me."

"It's Joe," I reminded him. Ryan knew about Joe's overprotective side.

He nodded. "Still, Eri's just a guy. And *you* would be able to tell if there was something strange about him."

"A fact that Joe doesn't know." I grabbed a handful of popcorn and played with a kernel.

"Okay, fine. I'll let you use me like this, but only because I'm so proud of you." He reached across the counter and pinched my cheek. "Look at you all grown up and going on a date."

I ducked out of his grasp and threw the popcorn at him. "It's not a date. I'm actually not going with him. I just helped him get the pass." Eri and I had an understanding. We would not reveal one another's secrets, but that didn't mean we were suddenly BFFs.

I was a means to get what he needed, which when I'd asked why he even cared about getting a permit since he was, after all, not even from this planet, he'd surprised me by saying Rhaevians believed in following the laws of the world they were on. I would go tonight when the permits were announced, and I would give them to him, but I didn't plan on going ship hunting with him. In fact, I didn't plan on doing much else with Eri while he was here. There wasn't a point. As soon as he found the ship, he would be gone.

"You're kidding me, right?" Ryan looked at me like I was the alien.

"I sort of got the feeling he likes to be alone."

"You got the feeling? How? Did you touch him?"

I nodded.

He smiled approvingly. "And?"

"And nothing."

"No. No. No. No. You don't get to say *nothing*. Nobody ever thinks nothing–you said so yourself. Besides, why wouldn't he want a cute girl to take him hiking?"

I blushed at Ryan's compliment. "He's not really looking to form any attachments. He's only here for a short while." I didn't say more.

Ryan frowned. "Are you sure he's the one who doesn't want to get attached?"

I refused to meet his eyes. "He only plans to be here for a short while," I said again. I hated hiding the truth from Ryan.

"So?"

"What do you mean, 'so'? What is the point of getting to know someone who is just going to leave?" I wanted Ryan to answer that question. To give me a reason to see Eri again.

"The point that he isn't staying is exactly why you should go for him. You're too scared of anyone in town finding out about you that you have basically shut off any chance of dating someone from here."

"As if I'd want to." I'd tried to find someone in Kanab I might want to open up to. There just wasn't anyone. As hard as I'd tried not to, I'd seen into more than enough minds from guys at school to know that. "Besides, you know I will never be able to have that kind of relationship. It's one thing not telling Joe and Claire. I don't even have memorysights with them. But how could I keep that from someone I was in a relationship with? I mean, a real relationship?"

Ryan rolled his eyes. "Which is why you should test it out on someone who you won't ever need to tell. I mean, if he's going to leave anyway, why not just think of this as another experiment?"

I looked at him in disbelief. The guy who bugged me way too much about being honest with the people closest to me wanted me to lie? He must have guessed my thoughts because he added, "Don't give me that look. We test things out all the time; this is just another chance to see what you can do. I'm just saying maybe it won't be as hard as you think to be in a relationship—even knowing what you may know. I mean—it subsided for me. Maybe in a few years you won't see anything at all."

"So, I just lie to my potential soulmate for a few years? That would be the start of a healthy relationship." I gave him a thumbs up.

"Do you think Eri is your soulmate?" Ryan asked.

I shook my head furiously. "No, but—"

"But you're obviously attracted to him. What are you afraid of?"

That we're not even the same species. "I think you're forgetting an important fact."

"What?"

"He's not interested in me." Even if I found him attractive, Eri wasn't interested in dinner and a movie. Dating was the last thing on his mind. It should have been the last thing on my mind as well.

"I highly doubt that," Ryan said.

"Why?" I asked, expecting him to give me the same "any guy

would be lucky to date you" speech Claire always gave. I leaned back and grabbed another handful of popcorn, prepping to let him lecture, which would be better than having to continue telling him lies. I doubted either of us would be seeing much of his new neighbor. The house next door concealed alien treasure-hunting headquarters. Still, that didn't mean I wouldn't look over there every chance I got. How could I not be curious? At least this way, Ryan would think I just had a crush.

"First," Ryan said, holding up his finger in answer to me, "because I've seen the way he looks at you."

I laughed and shoved the popcorn into my mouth.

"And second, because why else would he be walking up to my front door right now?"

I rolled my eyes. Until the knock at the door. And then I started choking on the popcorn.

Ryan's reply was to slap me on the back and then go answer the door.

I'd barely regained my ability to breathe properly when he opened it. Eri looked straight past Ryan, and his eyes stopped on me. "Can we talk?" he said, and my stomach began to do somersaults. I'd gotten the impression we'd already said all there was to say to one another.

"Sure." I didn't move.

Ryan opened the door wider and stepped to the side so Eri could come in. "I'll just be in my room." He turned and mouthed, "So into you," as he brushed by me, slightly bumping my shoulder.

I stood there embarrassed until I realized just how dark Eri's eyes had gone. I'd decided the shade of his eyes matched his mood, and they were the kind of dark that meant troubled. Dark like that didn't equal good.

"I'd prefer to talk out here," Eri said, not stepping inside even though Ryan shut his bedroom door loud enough for us to hear.

"Why?" Had something happened? When we'd come back from the BLM, those eyes had been a pale green. Even when Ryan had opened the door, they had been lighter. How had merely seeing me set him off?

"We shouldn't be overheard," he said in a deep whisper. "Unless he already knows everything." His eyes were almost black now. If my eyes could change color, I think they would have been equally as dark. He thought I'd told?

"Really? You really think I said anything?" I whispered back angrily. His eyes lightened slightly, which made me even angrier to the point where I walked straight up to him and glared. "I thought your emotion radar showed you could trust me," I hissed, then glanced toward Ryan's room. His door was still shut, and I could hear his radio.

"Then why was he looking at me like that?" Eri asked, his tone going just as angry as mine.

I stormed past him out the door, pausing only once for him to realize I expected him to follow me. He was right—this was not a conversation to be overheard.

"Well?" he asked when I stopped by the swing set on the side of Ryan's house that had been there since he was six. I turned on Eri, not thinking about the fact I should be embarrassed until the words shot out of my mouth. "He was looking at you like that because he thinks I like you."

He needed to do something about those eyes. They instantly turned a more aquamarine color as a smile played across his lips. "Do you?"

"Not really." I might be attracted to him, but I was ticked off Mr. Emotion Reader naturally assumed I'd broken my promise.

He had the decency to stop smiling, but his eyes didn't change.

"Don't flatter yourself," I said, still irritated.

"What?" he asked, seemingly confused.

"I can totally tell what you're thinking."

"You said you had to touch someone to be able to do that." He took a step back as if maybe just being in arms reach could activate my memorysight.

"It has nothing to do with me." I stepped forward just to see him panic as he stepped back again. His eyes were closer to normal now. Better.

"What do you mean?"

"Your eyes," I said as if he should know what I referred to. He looked bewildered. "They change..." It wasn't really coloring; they were always a shade of green. "The tint."

He looked even more confused. "What are you talking about?"

"Um..." Wait, did he not know his eyes changed colors? Had no one ever noticed that? "Like how they go darker when you're angry. Lighter when you're happy?"

"Apparently you can also read a person without touching them," he said matter-of-factly as his eyes went darker again.

"Oh no," I said. "People's eyes don't change like that. At least not human eyes." I pointed to my own eyes. "See, brown. Just brown, not 101 shades of brown."

He frowned. His eyes turned more hazel. Confused?

"You didn't know your eyes did that?" I asked a little softer. The anger I'd felt before left, but not from anything he did. No, this time my anger left on its own. Possibly because I felt sorry for the confused look Eri held.

"You have never seen anyone else's eyes change?"

I started to shake my head but then stopped, really thinking. "No," I finally said. I really had never seen anyone with eyes like Eri.

"Are you a tetrachromat also?"

I looked at him blankly.

"Can you see colors other people can't see?" He stepped closer to me again, no longer seeming as worried.

"Not that I know of." I knew all my quirks that made me weird. I also knew red was just red and blue was just blue and green was just green—except where Eri's eyes were concerned.

He looked contemplative again. I waited for him to explain whatever he was trying to figure out. He sighed and walked over to one of the swings, sitting down and pushing himself back and forth without his feet ever leaving the ground. "It does put you at an unfair advantage, but maybe that's for the best."

I had no idea what he meant, but I sat on the swing next to him and twisted my own swing around once, twice. "What's for the best? I'm assuming you didn't come over to talk to me because you were worried that I'd betrayed you."

He shook his head. "No. I came over because I want your help."

I stopped twisting. "My help?" What could I do to help him?

"Ryan said you know this area well. You're a hiking guide?"

"Not really. That's what Joe does. But yeah, I do know most of the trails around here." It started with Joe taking me out on the weekends, but once my memorysight had come into play, I learned that out among the sagebrush, juniper trees, and red rock canyons, memories didn't seem to haunt me at every touch—at least not ones that frightened me. The more off the beaten path of the trail, the more I loved exploring.

"I want you to be my guide," he said, and I let my swing untwist itself as I pondered what that actually meant. Time with Eri—perhaps a lot of time. I didn't hate the idea. Which was exactly why I needed to say no.

"I can't," I said slowly.

"Because I'm a stranger?"

"If I help you, then I have to explain who you are to Joe and Claire. And that would lead to a lot of questions. Questions I can't answer without lying to them."

"You already are lying to them," he said. I don't think he meant it to be mean, but it still hurt.

"I don't lie to them. I just haven't told them my secret. That's different. They've never come directly out and asked me if I'm a freak, so no, I haven't lied to them. But if they ask about you, then I have to lie."

Eri thought about that for a moment. "What if you don't tell them about me? Then they can't ask."

"This is Kanab." I laughed.

It was his turn to look blank.

"Everyone knows everyone here. I can't go anywhere with you without someone saying something to them. Remember the BLM?" After our conversation, I'd made Eri stay in the car while I'd gone in by myself.

He looked down at the ground and scuffed the top of his shoe into the dirt trail under his swing. "I don't want to ask you to lie."

I leaned against the chain of my own swing. He didn't want to ask me to, but he would. I knew there was a "but" coming. Did I blame him? What would I do if I were a million miles from home?

"What if *I* answered all their questions?" he said, looking back up at me.

"What do you mean?" Was he offering to do the lying for me so I didn't have to?

"Why don't you introduce me to them? You can say I'm just a guy who moved into town and doesn't know anyone. That's the truth. You don't need to tell them more. I can answer the hard questions."

He looked so hopeful. I sort of couldn't believe he was even willing to work with me. He could just make me do what he wanted. Even if I could tell when he made me calm, I didn't think I could fight if he didn't want me to. What did that make him—a good alien?

"I don't..." But maybe it would work. I mean, I'd have to answer questions about him anyway. The minute they heard Ryan had new neighbors, they would ask me about them. And they would hear. The fact the news hadn't already reached them surprised me. What if I introduced him to them tonight? Ryan could bring him over for a barbecue. He could also invite Valerie. Joe and Claire knew Valerie. They would be happy to see my friend base expanding. I wouldn't have to really lie, and Eri needed my help, and I would get to spend time with him. The last thought was what made me want to accept his offer.

"Caty?" He pulled me from my plan.

"Sorry. If I help you, what would you want me to do?"

"Just guide me and if...if you were to see anything that would be helpful as well." He smiled. I shouldn't let that smile make decisions for me, but I couldn't help it. He was only asking me to help because of what I could do. Was I willing to let myself spend more time with Eri when every minute I spent with him, I found myself wanting to spend another minute more? And also knowing that if he found the ship, he would leave? Not just for another town, not just for a short while. He would leave forever.

It didn't matter. When he looked at me like he was right now, the answer was yes. I'd take the chance. "Okay. Let's try."

6

"A barbecue?" Claire said as she pulled the ingredients for her dark chocolate lava cake out of the cupboards.

"Yeah, I just thought it would be fun." Besides Ryan, I'd never invited anyone to our house.

"And when you say 'a few friends'?"

I could sense her battle between being excited I might break out of my shell and being super confused that I was actually doing it.

"Ryan and Valerie, and Ryan had a new neighbor move in, so we'd probably invite him as well." I didn't bother using Eri's name. No sense in alerting her that I'd already spent half the morning with him—and the better part of the last twenty-four hours thinking of him.

Claire was smarter than that. "A new kid?" She focused now. "And what is this new kid's name?"

"Eri," I admitted, biting my bottom lip.

"And have you met this Eri?" Her voice had the lilt of teasing.

"Yeah."

"Is he nice?"

I nodded. "He seems pretty cool." I mean, aliens could be cool.

"Is he cute?"

I looked away from her as the heat rose to my cheeks.

"I'll take that as a yes." She laughed.

"Claire, please. I don't want Joe to freak out. You know how overprotective he can be."

She stopped laughing but still smiled warmly at me. "You like this boy?"

I shrugged. "I'd like the chance to get to know him." I'd decided playing the crush card may be the best way to introduce Eri. What other reason would I have to spend time with him?

Claire looked at me as if trying to read my thoughts. I tried to look like a girl in love and not like a girl keeping a massive secret from her.

"And you think he's safe?"

There it was—exactly what Joe would say. Strangers are not safe. At least she was asking me for my opinion on the matter and not just telling me no.

"Yeah," I said, and then remembered I shouldn't be as sure as my memorysight allowed me to be. "I mean, as much as anyone I've just met," I added.

Claire nodded. "I'll need you to run to the store for steaks. I think I used the ones in the freezer last week," she said.

"Steak?" Joe said, coming in through the back door.

"Caty wants to have some friends over for a barbecue."

"Friends?"

"Just Ryan and his new girlfriend and such," Claire said. "I'll make steaks and that pasta salad you like. You know the one with the bowtie noodles? I'm already making a lava cake."

At the mention of his favorite dessert, Joe's eyes softened. "I'm not sharing my cake with anyone."

I don't know how she did it, but once again, Claire had worked her magic.

As PLANNED, Ryan, Valerie, and Eri showed up in my backyard at seven o'clock that night. Joe was checking the grill when they came. He frowned when his gaze stopped on Eri. Ryan and I had prepared for that.

"Joe, this is my new neighbor, Eri, and you know Valerie?"

Joe nodded a warm hello at Valerie. He didn't offer such a nod to Eri.

"Where are you from?" he asked instead.

"Canada," Eri said. He stepped forward and held out his hand to shake Joe's. Joe frowned again and held up his charcoal-covered hand —as if that was his excuse for giving Eri the cold shoulder. Claire came to the rescue, setting the pasta salad on the picnic table and wiping her hand on her apron once before taking Eri's still outstretched hand.

"It's nice to meet you Eri," she said, allowing her slight southern accent to shine through—a sure sign Claire would make everything alright. I smiled a thank you in her direction—and gave Joe the stink eye. For which he acted like he had no idea what he'd done. Joe was predictable if nothing else. He didn't hide things from people, so how could I be mad at him?

Claire made every attempt to include Eri in the night's conversation, feeling him out in her own way. Eri answered every one of her questions with perfect ease. His answers sounded less textbook-like this time. He'd obviously been practicing. By the end of the evening, I had one approving nod from Claire and one we'll-see shrug from Joe. I took that as a success.

"So, we'll see you tomorrow?" Valerie said too loudly when they were getting ready to leave, then gave me a hug. "Ryan filled me in on everything," she whispered in my ear. The memorysight her touch provided let me know exactly what he'd told her, which was far from everything, but just the basics of Joe being a worrier. So, I just whispered a quick thanks before pulling away.

I walked the three of them to Ryan's truck to say goodbye. Eri looked at me the way he did, that way that made me wish he wasn't off-limits, that he wasn't temporary.

"I'll see you in the morning," I said, trying to steady my heart. Realizing I wasn't sure about what I'd gotten myself into. Knowing I needed to snap out of whatever my heart was trying to push me toward.

He lifted his hand as if he were going to touch me, and then his gaze went past me, and his hand lowered. "Tomorrow," he said as he got into Ryan's truck.

I turned around to see Joe with his arms crossed, standing on the front porch. My thoughts were conflicted. I'd wanted Eri to touch me. I wanted to see what he was thinking. I wanted to know he wasn't afraid of touching me. And yet, I shouldn't want to touch him for anything more than information. If and when I touched Eri, it could only be to confirm just how much I could trust him. The rest of the time, I needed to keep my hands tucked safely away. For that reason, I couldn't be mad at Joe.

Joe didn't know that. I had to be a typical teenager. I scowled as I brushed past him and stormed into the house. "Real subtle there, Joe," I said.

"What do you really know about that boy?"

"Well, since you interrogated him most of the night, quite a bit," I said, turning toward the stairs.

"Is he really from Canada?"

I was glad I was facing the other way. My face would have betrayed me. Why would Joe even ask that? Why would he think Eri was lying? How could he know that? Everyone else had bought his story just fine. And now, after all Eri had done to keep me from lying, I had to do just that. For a split second, I wondered what Joe would do if I turned around and told him that no, Eri wasn't from Canada. He wasn't even from the Milky Way. I composed my face and turned around, giving Joe my best you-have-got-to-be-kidding-me stare and laughed.

"No, he's not. He's actually a spy, and Canada is just his cover. He's here for a secret meeting of agents from around the world bent on taking over America." It was the plot of the movie Joe and I had watched the previous week. Except the bad guys had met in New York, not Kanab. It also was enough of a lie I didn't have to worry about Joe thinking I was lying.

Joe smiled at me. "Okay, I get it. I'm sorry, you know I just..."

"I know," I said. "But I'm almost eighteen. At some point, you're going to have to trust me."

"I do trust you," he said, the elevated pitch in his voice telling me he was surprised at my accusation. "I just want you to be safe."

"I am safe. I promise you, Eri is not here to hurt me." Until he leaves the planet. I had to keep reminding myself so I wouldn't let myself get hurt.

Joe studied me for a minute and nodded. "If you say so." He sighed. "He seems like a nice kid."

I stepped back and looked at him in shock. He laughed. "Just make sure you're not too nice back."

I gave him my signature eye roll, but a grin followed this one.

7

"I'm not exactly sure what you want me to do," I said as Eri and I made our way along the red dirt trail. I knew he needed my help when I realized that no matter what training he may have, he didn't know how to prepare to spend a full day hiking in the semi-arid Southern Utah landscape. But aside from equipping him with the proper hydration and shade (although he tried to tell me ultraviolet radiation didn't affect his skin and therefore wouldn't burn—unlike mine that had the tendency to burn faster than most people), I wasn't sure what he wanted from my memorysight.

"You see memories when you touch objects, right?"

"Yeah. Sometimes. Objects aren't as constant as people are."

He bent over, picked up a small rock, and tossed it to me. I caught it. "Sorry, nothing." I dropped the stone back off the path.

He picked up another rock—a bigger one—and handed it to me. "This one has been used as a rattlesnake hideout before." I bent over and set the rock back down. "But you don't expect me to touch every stone we see, do you?" I looked out over the rocky path ahead of us and groaned inwardly.

"No, but if you do see anything that might be useful, just tell me. I need to find this ship. I can't go home until I do." His eyes went dark, but not angry dark—sad dark.

"I'll do what I can."

"Thanks."

"But is there anything specific I should keep my eye out for? I mean, what does the ship look like? How big is it? How do you think a ship is hidden anywhere near here?"

"Come here." He gestured for me to come closer to him, setting the backpack I'd given him to use on the ground and unzipping a side pocket.

"Have you ever heard of molecular quantum displacement?" he asked, pulling out an unopened package of trail mix.

I shook my head.

"Think of it like this—put your hands together, palms facing one another, with your fingers slightly spread." I did what he asked. "Good, just like that. Now shift your fingers from side to side, allowing them to intermingle with one another." I merged my fingers together so it looked like one row of ten instead of two rows of five. I looked back at him, not understanding the analogy completely.

"Your hands are occupying pretty much the same space as they were before, are they not?"

I nodded. "Mostly."

"It's the same with the ship. The space between the atomic particles of matter is astronomical when you consider it at their level. If you manipulate matter, you can move it so slightly at a dimensional level that there is now room for two objects to be housed within what appears to be the same space even if it is not quite–or like you said, just mostly the same space."

He held up the package of trail mix and nodded at it before setting it on a nearby boulder. Then he reached in his pocket and took out a small black disc-shaped device. He pointed the device at the rock, and the trail mix fell into the rock, disappearing completely.

"What just happened?" I asked, but I knew the answer. "Are you saying the trail mix is inside the rock now?"

He nodded.

"How is that even possible?"

"Have you ever heard of a boson particle? Or quantum—"

"Actually, let me stop you there." I held up a hand. I hadn't done so great in physics class or really any science class—except geology. It didn't matter to me how Eri had done that. What mattered was that he could. "How about you just make the trail mix come back, and we'll call it good, okay?"

He pointed the disc at the rock again, and the trail mix appeared. "You good?"

It may as well have been magic. But there was no denying I'd seen it happen. "You're saying the ship is hidden somewhere? Like under the sand? Or in a rock?" I looked around at the large sandstone structures that could be seen from where we stood. Was it possible one of them contained a ship? A living ship?

"Exactly," Eri said.

I walked about one hundred feet to my left to the nearest large rock outcropping and put my hand on it. The memory transported me back in time to see a man in a breechcloth, crouching, spear in hand, waiting for some animal. His intense hunger made my own stomach growl. I pulled my hand from the rock. The memorysight didn't surprise me, given our location. I'd seen similar ones in the past, and I expected that if I was going to use my ability to help Eri I would see many more today. Assuming anything that molecularly quantumly displaced itself would be the strongest memory an object held, there was no ship inside this stone.

"Nothing here," I called back to Eri, who had repacked his trail mix and was heading toward me.

"Then we keep going."

"For how long?" This seemed like a futile mission.

"Until we find something."

Yep, it was a futile mission.

"Don't worry." He held up his disc thing for me to see again. "You're not the only one who can look for clues."

"What does it do?" Besides serve as a magic wand?

"Energy readings," he said, offering no further explanation, perhaps because I'd stopped his earlier one. But while I didn't need to be taught the universal truths of quantum physics, there were still several questions I wanted answered.

Eri fell into step next to me, enough to the side that I could sneak glances here and there. I wasn't sneaky enough. But getting caught stealing a glimpse of that crooked smile allowed me to begin asking my questions.

"What?" Eri asked as I quickly looked away from a moment of staring too long.

"I never really pictured aliens looking so...so human."

"Do you think I'm using some light-bending technique to cover the fact I really have tentacles and a third eye?" He laughed.

I shook my head but still remembered my dreams the first night I'd met him. "No. I know this is you—if you were a lizard, I'm pretty sure I would have seen it." I stopped walking and turned to really look at him. "It's just weird that you look like you could be a boy who moved here from Canada."

"Would you have preferred a little green man?" His grin stopped me.

Actually, Eri being a little green man might be a lot easier for me to deal with. "I guess I never thought about it." I turned and moved forward. I shouldn't want to touch him, and yet I so wanted to touch him.

"Sorry, what you see is what you get. We all look the same—every race we've ever encountered. Sure, there are differences: height, coloring, and even a few physical mutations to account for the environment. But it seems to be a law of the universe that higher-intelligent matter manifests itself in this basic form."

"All of it?"

"Well, we obviously have not encountered every species, every race. But for now, this is what we have to go on."

"How many have you met?"

"I don't know. Hundreds." He shrugged.

"Do you think that is all?" Around us, as far as the eye could see, was dirt and rocks and sky. It was as vast a place as I'd ever been—ever imagined. Now I realized just how small my corner of the universe was.

"No. We've only been traveling to the stars for a few hundred years. The farther the planets are, the more unlikely we are to find them any time soon. Our own part of the universe takes up much of our time. But still, we find outliers—like Earth. If you are here, thousands of lightyears from where we are, don't you think there are others?"

"I guess. But if we are so far from there, how did you find us?" I stopped. "Earlier you said something about a wormhole. What exactly does that do?" A slight breeze stirred the air, bringing the smell of cinnamon and clove to me, perhaps just like the wormhole had brought Eri. Did this mean when he left, we wouldn't be as far apart as I imagined?

"Basically, it's like a tunnel, connecting two points of space," Eri said.

"And the one you found? You said it was uncharted, right? What does that mean?"

"Charted wormholes are monitored for stability, and also, so we know who and what is coming through. Going through an uncharted wormhole is a risk."

"But you did it?" I thought about Eri and his desire to be with his grandfather. Was that enough to make him risk anything? What did it mean that it was a risk? I stepped an inch off the path, thinking more about what risk Eri had taken to get here than watching where I walked. The ball of my foot caught a stone, and I stumbled forward.

Eri's hands wrapped around my wrist, and I was in a ship, looking out a window at a darkness that shimmered slightly silver compared to the empty space around it. The ship sailed into the shimmer, and my whole body writhed in intense pain, like being ripped apart, torn, and folded into smaller pieces until it couldn't fold again. And then the pain subsided, and a small rock appeared that I somehow knew as a planet and then another planet came and another, this one with rings, and by the time Jupiter appeared in my sight, my own knowledge knew where I was.

"Are you okay?" Eri asked, his hands still warm on my skin. His grip was firm and steady. I lifted my foot and rolled my ankle a few times. It hurt, but it wasn't sprained.

"Is that what it feels like to go through a wormhole?"

He didn't question, just nodded. "An uncharted one. The stable ones feel more like a quick jolt. We have ways of making sure they won't collapse, that they will yield just the right amount of power to get from one end to another."

"So why would anyone want to go through an uncharted one?" I asked, a shiver tingling down my spine at what I'd felt in his memory.

"It's my job," he said. "Plus, we can't make wormholes, just strengthen them. Anytime one is found, someone has to go through it for the first time."

"How is it your job? How old are you? I mean, you can't be more than a few years older than me. Or do you age differently?" Was Eri really middle-aged on Rhaev?

"In Earth years, I would be almost nineteen."

I was only a couple of months away from being eighteen. Somehow the fact we were compatible in age made me happy. And then made me want to kick myself for thinking that. "How do you speak English so well?" I attempted to get my mind off where it was heading as I pulled myself out of his grasp and stepped more firmly onto the path. No more missteps allowed.

"It was downloaded into my mind," he said as if everyone was doing it. "Although most of the time, interpreter bacteria work just fine."

"Interpreter bacteria?" I cringed.

He laughed, possibly sensing my uncertainty. "They're a special bacterium that colonize in the brain." He reached over as if he were going to touch me again but then pulled his hand back and put it on the left side of his own head, close to the back of his ear. "This area enables comprehension of language, the bacteria aid in that process. They congregate here to interpret what we hear, which is why I still had to learn your language."

"How do you get them in there?"

"Through the ear canal."

My look of disgust seemed to amuse him.

"What is so important about this ship?" Time to not think about bugs crawling around in my brain.

I bent over every once in a while to touch the ground or a rock, more for something to occupy my hands and mind than because I believed I would actually see the ship buried under the red dirt.

Eri wasn't so quick with an answer this time. He just moved forward, a little faster, along the trail. I wanted to be all cool and tell him he didn't need to tell me if he didn't want to, but I couldn't. I needed to know what was so special about this ship that he would come here against his own desires to find it. I needed to know what exactly I was looking for. And I needed to know what Eri would do when he found it—found them.

"You said it's a weapon," I said after a few minutes of silence.

He stopped walking, and I turned to study him, to see if maybe I could read his thoughts just from the troubled look etched across his face. "What does it do?" I found my hand reaching out. If I touched him just then, could I get the answer I wanted? I quickly pulled back. We weren't going to use our abilities on each other. This should have been a no-brainer for me. I didn't touch people if I didn't need to, but with Eri, I couldn't help it. I shoved my hands in the pockets of my shorts and waited.

He sat his backpack down and pulled out the water bottle I'd brought for him. One long sip turned into two, and then he put the bottle back and dusted some of the red sand off the bottom of the pack before putting it back on. He started forward again, and I followed, almost ready to reach out despite our promise. The fact he wouldn't answer made me uneasy.

"It can destroy a planet."

His answer made me more uneasy.

"How do you know that?" I asked, not sure I was ready for the answer.

"Because it has once before."

The pain in his voice made me ache. "You're sure it's this ship? The one you think is here? How does it destroy a planet? Why would it come here? Is Earth—"

He held up his hand, and I stopped. Why did I bug him so much about this? Why did I insist on knowing this information I couldn't unknow? "We don't know why they came here. We do believe it's this ship, though."

"But you're not sure, right? It's just a hunch?"

"It's more than just a hunch that the planet destroyer is here. We found another ship. One that matched the ship that destroyed Sardova. Like I said, these ships are a combination of living tissue and advanced machinery—this new one is the first we've encountered since..." He trailed off.

I closed my eyes, trying to wrap my head around this. "But it's been here all this time? Why? Why would they bring something like that here and then hide it? You said you've been looking all these years. Maybe whoever brought this ship here did it so it can't be found." That could be the case. Earth was safe. Everyone was safe. "Maybe finding the ship is not the right thing to do."

"That is a chance I can't take. As long as that weapon is out there, no one can be truly safe." He twisted around, his face inches from mine. "I need to find the ship."

"And what do you plan to do once you find it?" I didn't move away, but he had to hear how loudly my heart pounded in my chest.

"I will destroy it. I'll make sure it can never be used again. I owe that much to her."

"Her?"

"My mother was on Sardova when it was destroyed." His eyes flashed to a color I'd never seen before. Not the swirling bluish green that revealed homesickness and sadness. And not the same dark green-black of anger. Although this shade was also dark, almost as if green and yellow had meshed and left a spotted trail in their wake. I knew in an instant what this blotted, uneven color meant. It meant pain. I'd known this type of pain. The pain of loss.

"Will you really destroy the ship?"

His head tilted so slowly I wasn't sure if he answered or not. His eyes never left mine, so when he said yes, I trusted the color in them. It was the color of truth.

"Then let's keep looking."

8

Even with all the hiking I'd done in my life, five days straight with a different trail every day and restless nights in bed, thinking of Eri, lying to Claire and Joe about where I went and who I spent my time with, took its toll on me, physically and mentally. The mental part was exasperated as Eri became increasingly more frustrated with our lack of success. I didn't blame him. This all started to seem rather pointless. We'd moved in a circle around Kanab for the past several days, and although I didn't want to tell him, I think we both were coming to the realization the ship wasn't here.

"I'm open to suggestions," he said as we looked at the map spread out over the hood of his Range Rover. He sounded desperate for any clue, any lead.

I pointed to a spot just east of town. "How about here?"

"Why there?"

Because we're exhausted, and it's easy ground to cover. "Less populated, less touristy," I said, thinking that would go over better.

He nodded, folding the map. I had to remind myself not to reach out and help him, to avoid the casual brush, the comfort of touch I wanted to share with him. For the past several days, I'd acted exactly like a hiking guide should act. Show an interest in your client. Not a hard thing to do when I wanted to know everything I could about Eri. We talked a lot about space and technology and his grandfather. I'd learned to avoid asking anything about the Tallisians, even though I found that the most intriguing subject.

I'd kept my hands to myself. Except now. Now, seeing the resignation in his eyes, hearing the frustration in his voice, I just couldn't take it anymore. I wanted to tell him everything would be okay. I wanted to tell him we were close to finding something. Neither of those I believed. I reached out and patted his back, not surprised that the strongest memory on his mind was of him reporting his failed attempts to the others, his supposed aunt and uncle.

"We won't give up," I said, offering the one truth I could promise even though exhaustion enveloped me. Even though our quest went nowhere, if Eri wanted to continue searching for a needle in a haystack, I would help him.

He looked at my hand as I pulled away, and a rush of regret swept over me. I shouldn't have touched him. "Sorry, I didn't mean to... I wasn't trying to—"

"It's okay. I understand."

It made me feel better, but not much because he didn't understand. He couldn't understand how hard it was to not be able to do anything to help him—least of all, offer something as simple as a comforting touch. How could I have been so thoughtless? When I slid into the passenger seat, I made sure to sit on my hands.

"You don't have to do that," he said, starting the Rover. He nodded down to my imprisoned appendages.

"Yeah, I do." I should not have touched him before. Keeping my fingers trapped ensured that wouldn't happen again. At least he didn't know this was the first time I'd ever had a problem wanting to touch someone. That *he* was the only one I wanted to touch.

"You really have no way of controlling when you see something?" he asked.

I shook my head. "No."

"But you seem so relaxed with Ryan—you touch him."

His eyes didn't leave the road. Did he sound jealous? Me and my wishful thinking.

"I don't get memorysights with Ryan anymore."

"Why not?" He looked over, but just as quickly, his eyes went back to the highway.

"We think my memories diminish the more I know a person. I've never had one with Joe or Claire."

"Never? How is that possible?" He still didn't look my way, but he frowned, causing a crease in his forehead.

"I've known them my whole life. They have no secrets from me." I knew Joe and Claire better than anyone. What could I see in their memories that they hadn't already shared with me?

"You know my secret, and you still see things," he said. I wished that were enough, that knowing Eri's alien status gave me free access to touch him. I pushed my hands farther under my thighs.

"We've known each other for a week. I think it takes a little longer than that." I laughed at our absurd situation. No matter how alien the desert landscape we were driving into looked, it still wasn't as strange as the boy sitting next to me.

"Then maybe we need to get to know each other more."

I wasn't sure what that meant or why he couldn't bring himself to just look over at me so I could see what shade his eyes were and try to figure out his thoughts, but I definitely wasn't expecting him to reach over and pull my hand out. "I'm okay with this," he said as he laced his fingers in mine. I wasn't sure if this meant something different on Rhaev. I didn't have time to ask because his memories took over.

More thoughts of life with his grandfather flooded my mind. This time they were in the cabin, I could still see the lake from the window, but a sheet of ice covered the blue-green water. In the center of the room, a fireplace glowed. A younger version of Eri sat on one of the couches surrounding it, with a tablet device on his lap. He swiped over the top, and a woman appeared, not on the screen itself but projected like a 3D image. She had the same sandy brown hair and green eyes as Eri. She held a newborn baby.

"Tell me about my mom," he said. A man walking into the room sat down next to him. I recognized his grandfather from my previous memorysight.

"She loved you," he said, putting his arm around Eri. "But being an only child herself, she'd never been around kids. When she found out you were coming, I think she read everything ever written about how to be a parent. And then she told your dad that none of it sounded right. The only thing she knew was if you could be raised here, in this house, surrounded by the people who loved you, everything else would be okay."

Eri looked up at his grandfather. "That is why Dad lets me come here for school break." He said the words as if he'd memorized them.

Eri let go of my hand and returned his to the steering wheel. I didn't say anything for a moment, trying to process things. He must have been young when his mother died. In the memory, he could have only been seven or eight. Had he meant to show me this? Why? How?

"Are you going to tell me what you saw?" he asked and finally glanced over.

"What do you think I saw?" Was it possible that somehow, he could make me see what he wanted me to? The thought had occurred to me before, but I'd dismissed it. This time I wasn't so quick to push it away. If Eri could make me see the memories he wanted me to see, could he fabricate those memories as well? Ryan had tried to manipulate his memories when we first started our experiments. He'd never been able to. But Ryan wasn't an empath. I already knew Eri could change my emotions if he wanted to. Could he change my memorysights as well?

"I was thinking about my mom, but I don't know what you saw."

I leaned back against the seat and the door and tried to assess him. Was he telling the truth? I didn't have a lot of experience with touching him on my own terms. I thought back to the time he'd made me tell him about my memorysight, the drunk, out-of-body feeling I'd had. I was certain he wasn't doing that now. But I also was uncertain about a lot of things. I reached out and touched his arm, and this time, I didn't feel as guilty. He'd been right that day at the BLM; I needed to be able to trust him, and right now, I could only do that if I used my memorysight.

This memory took on a different location and age. He would have been a teenager—maybe fourteen or fifteen. He was definitely at school. He sat in a group of desks that circled around a central point. The teacher in the middle appeared to be another holograph.

"Can anyone tell me the significance of the Prytate Contract?" the projected image asked. Eri tightened his hand around the octagonal writing device he was holding, and I felt like the edges were digging into my own skin. Across from him sat a girl with long straight blonde hair and deep chocolate-colored eyes. At the question, she looked at Eri, and the pain in her eyes reflected the pain in his. The other kids in the room looked anywhere but at Eri or this girl.

"It was the treaty made with the Tallisian Empire after the Sardova incident," Eri said finally.

"Correct," the holographic image said. "The Prytate Contract took place on—"

Eri pulled his arm away from me.

"Sorry," I said. The heated rush of apology couldn't overlap the lingering pain from the vision. I remembered Eri speaking about Sardova, the planet that the Tallisian ship we were looking for had destroyed. The planet his mother died on.

"It's okay. Was it about my mother again?"

His words produced the same tightening pain in my chest I'd felt when the police officer had come to our door and told me my parents' car had gone over the side of a ravine. That their bodies had been burned past the point of me ever being able to see them again. I knew his pain, and I hated that I'd brought it forward.

"Yes." I slid my hand under my leg once more. My touch hadn't just been invasive. It had caused pain. Both to Eri and to me.

"Please don't." He nodded at my hands. I pulled them out but kept them in a ball on my lap. "I'm sorry," he said.

"For what?" Why was he apologizing to me?

"You told me you feel the emotions of the memory you see. It hurts you to see about my mom. I didn't mean—"

"Eri, you don't have to apologize for sharing with me. I'm fine."

"I'm an empath; I can sense your pain. I don't want to hurt you." I saw his fingers tighten on the steering wheel.

"You didn't hurt me. The pain you're sensing is your own. What I feel right now is sadness that you had to go through that. That you lost your mom. I understand that."

"Because of your parents," he said.

I nodded even though I knew it wasn't a question.

"You know, I meant it when I said I wanted to get to know you better. But not if it is too hard for you...if you don't want to see...if..." He took a deep breath. "My thoughts are not always happy. If you don't want to see them, you don't have to. I just want you to know you're safe with me."

I looked out the window. A small dirt devil raced across the sandy desert floor. In the past several days I'd spent with Eri, the question of my own safety had almost faded. My physical safety wasn't why I worried about being here with him; I worried for the safety of my heart. I lifted my right hand, the safer option, the one farther away from him.

"This," I said, looking at my fingers as I curled them into a fist, "has nothing to do with me fearing you." Quite the opposite, actually. I feared myself and what allowing me to become too comfortable around Eri would mean.

"You've just avoided touching things your whole life?"

"Not my whole life, just since my memorysight appeared." I used to be affectionate—back when my parents were still alive. Giving Dad enormous hugs. Falling asleep on Mom's lap. Now only Ryan didn't make me shy away. Even with Joe and Claire, I still worried anytime I touched them that this time I would see something. I worried that no matter how close we were, somehow my not telling them what I could do would drive a wedge between us, and this time, they would really have something to fear by being close to me—even if they didn't know. "Now I just find avoiding people easier than having to see into their heads."

"That must be hard."

I hated the pity in his voice, but I nodded in agreement. It was hard. Especially right now when I wondered what it would feel like to have Eri's arms around me.

I shook my head. "Pull off here." I pointed to a dirt road that veered to the right of the highway. We drove another mile in silence until we came to a parking area with only one other car. I pointed to some red rocks a few miles off in the distance.

"How about that? Would you hide your spaceship there?" I joked, trying to dissipate the sadness our previous conversation had taken on.

Following my cue, Eri laughed. "It's as good of a place as any." He put the car in park and leaned forward, placing his chin on his hands that were crossed over the steering wheel, looking over the vast expanse of desert that sprawled out around us. The brilliant landscape took on a dark feel as, once again, the impossible task ahead of us loomed in my sight. A wicked self-gratifying thought crossed my mind. If we never found the ship, did that mean Eri would stay? For how long? A month? A year? It didn't matter; eventually, he would leave. That was all I had to remind myself. I opened the door and jumped out of the car. I needed to go back to being a tour guide.

The other car in the lot belonged to a family with three small children. The dad worked on getting the baby in a hiking backpack while the mom applied sunscreen on the noses of the other two children. The hike ahead was easy for me but ambitious for such a family.

"Hold still, Garrett!" The mother demanded of the oldest child, who looked to be about six or seven.

"No," the boy protested loudly.

"You need to wear sunscreen," the mother said, squeezing more into her hand.

"No!" The boy jumped off the back bumper of the car and ran away, straight into my legs. I caught him to keep him from falling over and knew in an instant the reason for his escape. The sunscreen his mom was applying stung his skin. His memory that jumped into my mind even as I steadied him was one of pain—enough to make my own eyes start to water.

"Are you okay?" I asked as his mom ran to me, apologizing profusely.

"Sorry," he mumbled.

I opened the front zipper of my bag and pulled out the organic sunscreen Claire had been making for me and my fair skin for years now.

"Here." I handed the bottle to his mom. "This stuff works wonders. Guaranteed sting-free." Her look went from apology to gratitude to confusion (because how did I know that) to skepticism as she had the good sense to balk at a stranger handing her a generic tube of something, but her features softened as I squeezed a small amount into my hand and applied it to my own face.

The mother smiled and applied a small drop to the boy's nose. When he didn't scream, she rubbed the cream over his cheeks and forehead.

"Thank you. He usually hates everything I use."

"I have sensitive skin too, so I make this, but if you can find a natural brand that uses carrot seed oil, you might be able to avoid the sting."

The family thanked me once more as I turned and found Eri waiting for me by the back of the Range Rover.

"Ready?" I asked. He smiled as we started past the trailhead sign. I couldn't help but be aware his eyes stayed on me more than the path as we walked.

"What?" I finally asked.

"You know, for someone who likes to avoid people, you sure seem to help a lot of them."

I frowned. "What do you mean? That kid? That was nothing."

"Not to him, it wasn't. You knew exactly what he needed."

I didn't say anything. Thinking of my memorysight as something other than a curse didn't come easily to me.

"Your memory showed that he hated the sunblock his mother was using, right?"

"Yeah."

"You use your ability for good a lot."

"No, I don't." I didn't use my ability at all—not intentionally.

"What about that family at the river trail yesterday? Or that couple at the gas station?" He cited examples from the past two days. The mother of the family had slipped on a part of the river walk and was trying to figure out how to keep her kids dry when she couldn't stay dry herself, so I showed her how to wrap their spare clothes to ensure they didn't get soaked. The couple had simply taken a wrong turn and were having their first fight as newlyweds. I showed them how to get back to where they wanted to go. Neither case was that big of a deal—both times, however, I knew what they needed based on what their minds had shown me, not their words.

"My dad always said you should help people when you can."

"You should," Eri said. "But not everyone does."

When Ryan gave me the lecture on using my powers for good, I always got annoyed. When Eri said basically the same thing, I blushed. But it might have been the way he looked at me when he spoke. The aquamarine in his eyes. The way the left side of his mouth turned up just higher than the right side. I moved down the trail faster to take my mind off those lips.

Eri followed and grabbed one of the straps of my backpack, slowing my progress and making me face him at the same time. I found myself close to him. Too close. I stepped back to put some distance between us because all I could do was smell his cinnamon and clove scent. I wanted to reach out and grab him.

He stepped forward, closing the gap once more.

"Don't be afraid of me." His eyes transfixed me.

"I'm not," I said.

"Then don't be afraid to touch me."

"I can't."

"Why not?" How was it possible for him to get closer? Still, he managed.

"We shouldn't use our abilities on each other." I swallowed. Why did he smell so good? I stepped back. Behind me, I felt the prickly stems of a juniper tree. I didn't have anywhere else to go.

"I won't use mine on you," he said.

"And I won't use mine on you." Even though I really, really wanted to.

"But you can." He stepped forward. I had to look up even as he looked down.

"Why?" What was going on in his head? Why would he let me use my ability on him? Was he feeling the same attraction I was?

"Because you are nothing like what I expected." His eyes turned into the sea on a sunny day. My head felt dizzy. My hand went toward him, but the movement threw me off balance, and I stepped back—right into the tree, and right into the exact memorysight I'd been searching for all week.

"What?" Eri asked, our moment lost as he searched the startled expression that washed over my face.

"Here." I spun around, looking at the tree. Feeling the branches again, even though I knew they wouldn't give off another memory. Still, I knew what I'd seen. What I'd felt. "There is something here."

I looked around, making sure we were alone.

"Something not from Earth."

9

"Where?" Eri asked, and I pointed to the tree. He dropped to his knees and looked up at me. "Here? How far down?" He pulled one handful of dirt away from beneath the tree.

"No, not under," I said, "in." Because of course the hooded figure that had placed whatever they were hiding here had done so in the same way Eri had made the trail mix disappear into the rock on our first hike.

He understood my meaning without question and pulled the small disc device out from the pocket of his backpack. I'd seen him use the device plenty over the past days as a scanner of sorts. He used it that way at first, sizing the tree up and down for a moment before turning the dial on top to the left. Even though I'd seen it done before, it still felt like magic when an object the size of a whiteboard marker floated out from the tree.

Eri grabbed it before it fell to the ground. I shook my head. "I will never get used to that," I said. He gave me a courtesy laugh but focused on the once-hidden object.

"What is it?" I asked.

He shook his head. "It's definitely Tallisian." He held the object out, pointing to a row of strange markings, which I assumed were Tallisian, but meant nothing to me. "Probably a compression bolt."

I'd never seen a compression bolt, but it couldn't be anything spectacular based on his tone. Still, someone had hidden it—in a tree. "Why would they do that?"

Eri looked up in question.

"If it is just a compression...bolt thing, why would they hide it?" I spun around and looked at our surroundings. Red dirt and juniper trees gave way to sloping paths and mesa tops. The nearest rock wall stood about a mile from where we were. "Do you think...could the ship be here, maybe?"

Eri turned the scanner and inspected the vicinity. "I'm not picking up anything else. You?"

I walked around, touching a rock here, another tree there. No other memories, at least none that contained alien artifacts. After about fifteen minutes of Eri scanning and me touching every outcropping in sight, I shook my head.

"Maybe this is just the start of the trail. Maybe we need to keep going?" I tilted my head in the direction of the nearest mesa. Eri looked at the object again and handed it to me to see if I got anything, but no memory appeared.

As we made our way back up the trail, he had me go over what I'd seen at the juniper tree. No matter how hard I tried, I only remembered a hooded figure on a moonless night stopping at the tree and hiding the part there. I'd seen no face, no distinguishing marks or characteristics.

"I'm sorry." It was a useless feeling. Had I not been so startled earlier, I would have held onto the tree longer, tried to see more.

"Don't be sorry. If you hadn't been here, we might not even have had this." He nodded toward the bolt.

"Not that it means anything."

"Actually, it means a lot. It means we're on the right path. They were here." The renewed energy in his voice lifted my spirits a little.

"So now what?"

"Now let's go see what is out there." He pointed to the mesa, his face and whole appearance taking on a more energetic feel.

I followed him down the path, but he suddenly turned, stopping me. Once again, I found myself in his orbit. His eyes were like a sunbeam shining on a field of emeralds. "Thank you."

I swallowed, startled at our proximity and the heat coursing through my body. "Of course." I said it like it was no big deal, but I stepped away, not allowing myself to be near him. Not allowing myself even the thought of touching him, even if he acted okay if I did. How could he be okay with that? How could anyone? Even with Ryan in the beginning, it had always been on his terms. I understood that.

Still, Eri grabbed my wrist and once again let me see in his mind. This time I saw me—and the feelings were of relief, of gratitude. A blush spread across my cheeks.

"It isn't easy to get here—to Earth," he said. "Even though the wormhole significantly decreases the time, it's taxing."

I shuddered as I recalled the memorysight of his journey here and the pain it inflicted. "I know." Although I didn't know why he told me this.

His eyes grew more intense, and he nodded. "I know you do. You understand me in a way I don't think anyone else could...anyone else ever has. I know you hate your ability, but I don't. I spent my entire journey here imagining what it would be like. Wondering how I was going to accomplish this task on some unadvanced rock." He looked at me and a small smirk of apology played on his lips. "No offense."

"None taken." I couldn't be mad at him. Something in his atmosphere made every molecule in my body ignite.

"When I met you, I was certain I'd blown my cover. My mission had failed before it even began. How could I trust someone from Earth with my secret?"

"I really won't tell," I interrupted.

"I know that. And I don't know which fates are blessing me. But I believe I met you for a reason—and I'm glad it is you. Thank you, Catelyn."

My full name on his lips took me by surprise. I'd told him my real name once—second day, hiking through a river canyon trail. I'd also told him how no one called me that—no one except my dad, and me when I was talking to myself. I never knew how hearing it, in his deep, slightly accented voice could affect me so greatly.

He let go of me but ran his fingers down the length of my arm. "Thank you," he said again. His memorysight let me know I no longer had to stay a step behind or sit on my hands. I had his trust. Right here, right now with Eri, I could just be me.

"I hate Trig," Ryan said, sinking into the desk in front of mine and turning around. "Can't we go back to spring break?"

I agreed with him more than I could say. Not that I hated Trig, but spring break being over meant long days at school—away from Eri. It had been several days since we'd found the Tallisian artifact. We'd looked everywhere within a twenty-mile radius of that tree over the next few days with no luck. By the time school started, I'd gone back to thinking the mission was futile.

It wasn't until I'd sat through my first day of seven and a half hours of classroom misery that I wanted to bolt from the school and get back to looking—futile or not. At least looking meant I'd be with Eri. Now I just shuffled through my school days, each one a reminder that he was looking for clues that would allow him to leave, and all I could do was learn to solve for X.

"You going to see Eri tonight?" Ryan leaned over and whispered.

"He's gone," I said, and I had to wonder how much more those words would hurt when they were permanent.

The look of shock on Ryan's face gave me some glimmer of what it might feel like. "Not gone, gone." I clarified. "He's helping his uncle with something. He'll be back." At least he'd said he would be back. But that had been three days ago.

"And things are going good?" Ryan said. "Memorysight wise?" Ryan's whisper wasn't that soft, and I glared at him.

"No one heard or cares," he said, but lowered his voice.

"Things are fine."

"Touch-touch fine or kiss-kiss fine?"

Valerie slid into the desk next to Ryan and turned in my direction.

"Did Eri kiss you?" she asked excitedly. Apparently, she also had Ryan's volume control issue. A few kids at nearby desks looked over, and my blush flared warmer.

"No," I said in a harsh whisper. "We're just friends." Having Eri's permission to not stifle my hands didn't mean I followed my every whim and touched him whenever I wanted. In fact, it sort of had the opposite effect. While I no longer worried about a casual brush or taking his hand to make it up a particularly steep incline, I guarded any touch beyond that to the extreme. I can't say if my new caution came from worrying if my hand lingered any longer on his than necessary, I might find myself never wanting to let go, or because each foray into his mind made me want to see more. I'd learned so much about him with just a simple touch here or there. I'd learned his likes and dislikes, his life before coming to Earth, and his dreams about the future. Each glimpse in his mind gave me another reason to not want him to leave—the exact reason why I had to keep them few and far between.

Thankfully, Mr. Carston walked in and handed out that day's quiz before Ryan and Valerie could do more than give me smirky looks that said they didn't believe the "just friends" plea. I allowed them their smirks by spending the rest of the class period imagining how they would react if they knew why Eri and I could only be friends.

I finished the day having kept the number of times I checked my cell phone under the million mark—I think. Monday night, after we'd produced nothing again, Eri texted me saying Mathis–his fake uncle–had found something in his search, and Eri would be going with him for the next few days.

I would have offered to help, except I couldn't justify missing school to Joe and Claire. Also, despite finding the first clue that Tallisians had been here, I hadn't found anything else, and I knew Eri had not told his companions about me—at least not more than as a tour guide he used as a cover. He'd made it clear it would be best if they never knew more than that. I had to wonder how much less scary they were than the murderous Tallisians. But then again, they had never destroyed an entire planet—at least not that I knew of. At least not that I'd seen in Eri's memories.

Still, maybe if they knew about me, I could help Eri more out in the open. I shook that thought from my head. Eri had his reasons to keep me from them, just as I had my reasons to lie to Joe about how much time I was spending alone with Eri. It all kind of sucked. Ryan took advantage of my occupied time to spend all his extra time with Valerie. When Friday night rolled around, not only did I miss a boy I should not have been missing, but I also missed my best friend.

This is what my future holds. I'd known I would be lonely when Ryan left for college, but I hadn't really understood what loneliness felt like until I'd met Eri and realized being in an actual relationship might be possible for me—if I could find someone with a secret of their own—someone who could relate to me. Unfortunately, the one person I found who fit that description lived on another planet. I didn't imagine I'd have a steady stream of alien suitors for me to pick from. And really, I didn't want one. I wanted Eri. Not alien Eri. Not I-have-a-secret-of-my-own Eri. Just Eri, the boy whose memories were like a mirror into my own soul. The boy who understood my heartache because he'd experienced his own, who could acknowledge my secret ability because to him, it was almost commonplace, the boy whose smile made my knees weak just thinking of it.

I'd dozed off when the text came through.

Can I see you?

I tapped the light on my nightstand and caught sight of the clock. It was past midnight. I couldn't very well drive over to him without Joe and Claire hearing me.

Come to your window.

I rolled over on the bed and stared at the window across the room. Could he really be there? My hand went to my hair falling out of the braid in messy bed curls. Crap. Did I want him to see me just now? I pulled the elastic from the end of the braid and ran my fingers through my curls a few times before pulling my hair back into a ponytail. Standing, I glanced at the mirror by the closet. Not great, but better than bedhead.

I tiptoed across the room, an unnecessary gesture because even if Joe and Claire heard me, they would think I was going to the bathroom or getting a glass of water. They'd have no clue a cute alien waited outside my window.

And yes, he was there. Right where the edge of the yard hit the weeded field of the empty lot behind ours. He wore jeans and a black T-shirt, so I could barely make him out except for his silhouette, but still, when he looked up at me, I knew he had that smile on his face.

He gestured for me to come down to him. I turned and inspected the door behind me. I'd never snuck out before because I'd never needed to. Joe wasn't a tyrant. If I planned on going to Ryan's or on a late-night taco run, he'd just ask for me to bring him something back. But if I got caught sneaking out to see Eri—a boy who Joe seemed to be accepting even if somewhat grudgingly, would that small acceptance melt away?

I looked back at Eri. He waved me down again. It wasn't like I wasn't going to go. I didn't know why my nerves were on edge—like I was committing some sort of a forbidden act. I was just a teenage girl sneaking out to meet a guy—one I could barely even touch. It all was perfectly safe.

10

"Hey," I said, finally breathing normally for the first time since I opened my bedroom door and glanced down the hall to Joe and Claire's room.

"Hey," Eri replied, and I was stricken at just how much I'd missed him the last few days. He stood with his hands in his front pockets, his shoulders slouched forward slightly. It was my stance—the stance that said I won't touch you, I don't want to see into your mind. I'd stood that way for years. I wondered if his stance meant the same—I won't touch you. Or if it could possibly mean what mine had changed to over these last few days: I really want to touch you, but I know better.

"How did the search go?" *Please say you're not leaving.* I put my own hands in the pockets of my shorts and mimicked his position, rocking back and forth on the balls of my feet.

"Good. Mathis isn't quite as enjoyable to be around as you are, though." He looked at me under his eyelashes, only the light of the full moon and the neighbor's backyard deck allowed me to see his face with that grin that caused the right side of his mouth to pull up just a bit higher than the left. It was still too dark to see what color his eyes reflected—which was for the best because his words already made my heart skip a beat. What would I have done if I'd seen the aquamarine tint that had been apparent the more time we spent together? The tint that made me wonder if Eri ever thought any of the things I did—even though his mind had never confirmed it.

The darkness also kept him from seeing the heat flash through my body. I didn't know how to respond, so I just continued the conversation as if he'd never caused my heart to palpitate. "Did you find anything?" I shouldn't have been disappointed when he pulled out a silver oval-shaped object, which looked like it had similar symbols as the bolt we'd found in the tree. The surface shimmered, even in the darkness, and made the object look like perhaps it wasn't quite solid.

"What is it?"

"On its own? Nothing spectacular. But mixed with a hydrogen compress and a few other parts, it has the correct properties to begin the chemical reaction needed to create an explosion, possibly one that could..." He looked away from the object and up to the night sky.

"Destroy an entire planet?" I finished for him.

He nodded. "Here, alone like this, it barely even contains a trace of radiation, but I still hate having to ask..." His eyes met mine now.

I held out my hand. Of course, he wanted me to see, besides crazy alien etchings and traces of radiation, if the object held any other clues. I braced myself for the worst. If this had really been part of a device that had blown up a planet, that had killed Eri's mom, who knew what it might show me.

Wherever the memory was, it was dark. The dark of a cave that wouldn't even allow you to see your hand in front of your face. People spoke—at least two voices, though I couldn't make out who they belonged to. They seemed to be arguing, but their voices were muffled just enough that I only picked up a word here and there.

As the supposed argument continued, the place lit up. Not much, but enough I could verify that yes, there were two of them. One wore a jacket with an upside-down triangle with a circle that overlapped the edges. The argument continued, growing until it became physical, and then in the midst of flying punches, a flash of light so bright I thought I would go blind exploded across the wall in front of them. No, not a wall, a window. A shockwave pushed across the space with enough force to knock me over, even here, with the time and distance of the event far behind us.

I fell, but I didn't hit the ground. Two strong arms wrapped around me. No memorysight took over as those hands grabbed me—nothing could be stronger than what I'd just experienced. Nothing could take the place of the destruction of a world. I looked up into Eri's eyes, filled with concern.

"Catelyn, are you okay?"

Instead of pulling myself away, I sank into him, my head resting against his chest, my eyes closed as if that would be enough to erase what I'd just seen. But memories were like pictures in my mind, and it didn't matter how tight I closed my eyes, they would remain.

"Catelyn?" he said, softer this time, less frantic, but his hands loosened on my back, and he took my shoulders, pulling me away enough to look at my face. One hand brushed a strand of hair from my eyes; the other hand held me steady.

"I'm fine," I said, realizing there was little to no distance between us. I tried to step away, but his grip tightened, and he pulled me to him again.

"I shouldn't have asked you to do that." His hand stroked the back of my head. His breath stayed warm on my ear and neck. "I'm so sorry."

By now, I'd come to my senses enough to realize I no longer held the object. I looked to the ground a few feet away where it lay in the grass. I tried to reach for it, but he stopped me again.

"Don't touch it." His voice gave away his worry.

I shook my head. "I won't see anything again." I tried to go to it once more, but my words must not have given him enough comfort. "What if I broke it?"

"Who cares?" He seemed genuinely unconcerned about a clue that could get him home. He put his hand to my cheek again, stroking my jawline. "Are you okay?"

I nodded. I was more than okay. In his arms, as long as he didn't break contact with me, no new

memories came from him, and nothing could keep me from staying right there.

"I saw that planet, Sardova. I watched it get destroyed." His body went rigid, but he didn't let go of me. He held tighter as if now I kept him upright and not the other way around. I wasn't sure if he was ready to hear what I had to say next, but I took a step back and pulled his face to look at mine. I wound my fingers through his, not daring to break this touch.

"Where did you find that?" I nodded my head in the direction of the fallen object.

"About fifty miles north of here."

"Don't you think that's strange?"

"What? That they are playing with us? Leading us on a wild chase that is going nowhere?" He didn't direct the anger in his voice at me, but he still lifted my hand and brushed the back of my knuckles with his lips before apologizing. "I'm sorry."

His gesture stilled me but also gave me more determination. I always held back—what I thought, what I felt, who I was—because I couldn't risk someone getting close to me. But Eri had already crossed that line, and as stupid as I kept telling myself it was to let him, I wasn't willing to stop him, and I was done trying to stop myself. I wasn't going to hide thoughts and feelings from Eri.

"Before...before the explosion..."

"Yes?"

"There were two men. I didn't see them. It was dark—and I couldn't hear what they were saying. The sounds were muffled like the object had been in the room but covered. But they were fighting. At least, I think they were. I think one of them tried to stop the other. And now here, on Earth, with these parts spread with no apparent rhyme or reason, I don't think it's a wild chase. I think these things were hidden on purpose." I didn't have any proof, but the moment I said it, I felt I was right.

Eri would take much more convincing to believe that. He shook his head.

"Why? Why is that not possible?" I asked.

"You don't know them. They take what they want. And if they

can't have it—they destroy. What happened on Sardova was not an accident. They deliberately planned its destruction—even to the point where the people were warned something might happen. Only the fight they prepared for was not the one that came."

With his hands still in mine, I felt the shudder run through his body.

"What did they want?" The feeling I had wavered.

"On Sardova? A girl." He looked up to the night sky and swallowed.

"Why did they want her?" How do you destroy an entire world over one person?

"Because of the things she could do. Most people who have abilities are like us. One or two things, some more powerful than others. The Tallisians like to improve upon powers—their own and others. This girl had a power they wanted, and if they couldn't have it, no one could. My mother went there to protect the girl."

"I'm sorry," I said. Who did that? How did a civilization become like that? "What is wrong with them?" I mumbled to myself, but Eri answered.

"They weren't always like that." He turned away from me, so we now stood side by side with just our hands clasped, and he pointed up to the sky with his free hand.

"There are worlds out there without numbers. Of those, the oldest we know of are Tallis and Rhaev. We were the first two civilizations to find one another, and together we explored the stars. At first, a new world was studied before our presence was made known. Some were far too primitive to understand people from another planet. They agreed those should be left alone to continue to grow on their own. But some worlds were like Earth—just on the brink of discovering the truths the universe holds." He took a deep breath before he continued.

"The Rhaevian Council believed that even these worlds should be left alone as well. That giving people knowledge before they discover for themselves could be damaging. They claimed the only contact that should be made would be with people who had the ability to travel on their own, past their solar system. The Tallisians didn't agree. They claimed it was their duty to help the younger races to grow and learn. In return, the other races would help to make them stronger. The Rhaevian Council worried that technology, put too soon in the hands of less civilized species, could lead to destruction."

"I'm sorry I couldn't see more to tell you."

His hand tightened on mine. "This is enough. Thank you for giving me the strength to go on. Catelyn, I—"

His words were cut off by the kitchen light. It was bright enough to warn that someone had come downstairs. I pulled on Eri, and we both fell to our stomachs on the grass.

"Crap," I said as the back door opened, and Joe came out. Eri held a finger from his free hand to his lips, and I remained silent. There was no way Joe hadn't seen us. That he wasn't coming toward us right now. That I wasn't going to get the lecture of a lifetime.

But he hadn't, and he wasn't, and there would be no lecture. Instead of coming back to us, he headed to his shed in the opposite corner of the yard. I held my breath until the door shut, and then I allowed myself to prop up on my elbows. Eri followed suit.

"What is he doing?" Eri asked.

I shrugged. "No idea. Maybe he can't sleep." I had no idea what Joe did at—I looked at my watch—1:30 in the morning out in his shed. Actually, I never had any idea what Joe did in his shed. His mancave remained strictly off-limits, which was fine by me as I wanted to avoid being hauled into one of Joe's home improvement projects that always came after he'd spent some time in his shed.

"I don't think he saw us," Eri said, and he sounded relieved, just like a teenage boy who had snuck out with his girlfriend would sound. I smiled. If we were normal—either of us—if things were different, maybe that is what this could have been.

"What?" Eri asked.

"Nothing." No way would we still be lying here in the grass, my hand still grasped in Eri's, if Joe had seen us. No way would my heart be pounding in anticipation of what would happen next, lying this close to Eri, close enough to smell the cinnamon and clove aroma natural to him, to feel the heat that radiated from him like a blue star.

Maybe I glanced at our hands. Maybe Eri realized how close we were. But whatever spell we were under crashed.

He sat up, letting go of my hand even quicker. Then he put a distance between us that was unwelcomed. "I should go."

I knew if we touched again, I would have a memorysight. There would be no more free touches—unless maybe they were accompanied by horrific ones like I'd originally seen when he'd handed me the object. It could take years before the ability faded, just like it had with Ryan. Eri and I didn't have years. If I came into contact with him again, I would see in his mind. And if I got any closer to him, I wouldn't want him to go. The look in his eyes told me I could not touch him again. That made me mad, which was ridiculous. I shouldn't be wanting Eri any more than he appeared to want me. I shouldn't be wanting him at all. I reminded myself of this for the millionth time and then glanced around looking for the object, anything to not meet his eyes.

I picked up the orb, hesitant only for a moment that perhaps another memory really would come. When I stood and handed it to him I made sure we didn't touch in the transfer.

"Catelyn—"

"You should go." I reminded him. With our moment past, I no longer had the desire to stay out here. I felt cold—something I hadn't realized when I'd first snuck out barefoot and jacketless. But maybe the awkwardness of the situation made it cold. "Make sure Joe doesn't see you," I warned and then tiptoed across the lawn in record speed, pausing only to turn back to the shed when I got to the kitchen door to make sure Joe was still in there. I didn't look at Eri again.

11

I couldn't tell Ryan everything about the night before. No exploding planets or strange alien voices that, even now, I couldn't quite shake from my head as I sat on the edge of my best friend's bed while he worked on his bicep curls on the weight bench across the room. But I could tell him the worst part.

"So, you were holding hands," he grunted, setting the weights on the rack next to the bench, and leaned forward, "and Joe came out, and then Eri freaked?"

I nodded, hating remembering the look in Eri's eyes that clearly told me that would never happen again—the hand-holding, not the freaking out.

"Caty, he almost got caught by his girlfriend's—"

"I'm not his girlfriend."

Ryan scoffed. "The point is, he probably just felt awkward."

If he were a normal human boy, I might have allowed myself to believe that. But Eri hadn't pulled away last night because he felt awkward. He'd pulled away because we shouldn't have been that close in the first place. We both knew it, but just because I knew didn't mean I liked it. In fact, I found myself torn between being humiliated—how could I face him again—and heartbroken—how could I survive not facing him again?

"I don't know if I can do this anymore," I said.

"You really like him, don't you?" Ryan came over and grabbed a towel off the dresser next to me.

I nodded in defeat. Yes, I really liked him. In terms of weeks, I barely knew him. In terms of memories, I'd already seen a lifetime of his. I didn't just want to see his memories anymore; I wanted to make memories with him, but being a memory of Eri's is all I would ever be able to be.

"That's not a bad thing," Ryan said, obviously noting the anguish on my face.

Yes, it was a bad thing.

"What if I invite him to Lake Powell?"

I looked up from the pillow my chin sank into as I hugged it tightly. I'd forgotten about the senior trip to Lake Powell, which was the first in a series of events that started after spring break and went in full force until graduation. Graduation was only six weeks away. It was so close—that moment where we were supposed to leave behind our old lives and embark on new adventures. Except my adventure was here now, and who knew if he would even still be on the planet in six weeks.

"There, it's done." Ryan put his phone on the dresser. I hadn't even seen him texting anything, being so lost in my own head, but a second later, his phone buzzed, and he picked up, smiling before showing me Eri's reply.

Will Catelyn be there?

"Try telling me the guy doesn't like you now."

"He didn't say yes. Maybe he's making sure he won't have to see me." I was good at self-pity when I wanted to be.

Ryan threw his sweaty towel at me and typed a response. I picked up the towel with two fingers, made a gagging noise, and tossed it back at him.

His phone buzzed again. Ryan turned the screen to me.

I'll come.

My insides flipped a little.

"You could at least smile," Ryan said.

I did. And then I told myself I shouldn't be smiling. I shouldn't be having any emotions over this simple little comment at all. And yet the idea that Eri wanted to see me again made me dizzy and giddy at the same time.

Lake Powell is a vast expanse of blue-green water in a world of fire-colored rock and sand. Stretching out for 186 miles through Southern Utah and Northern Arizona, it is a galaxy all its own. A hidden cosmos that burns like the sun and sparkles like the stars and is nothing short of miraculous.

Eri had said he would meet us at the designated campground, so I spent most of the two-hour drive sitting in the backseat of Ryan's truck, pretending to be asleep so he and Valerie didn't feel like they had to keep me involved in their conversation. Besides, I had to plan conversations of my own.

It had been six days since the night he'd come to my house. He'd sent texts. He'd told me he was ship hunting with Mathis. He'd asked advice on trails and roads and a handful of tips he could have just looked up online. I'd told him that on the third day. He didn't ask anything on day four, which I kicked myself about, but last night he'd sent one text.

I'll see you tomorrow.

It was tomorrow, and all I could do was think about those words. He'd see me and what? Ask a million more questions on how to get to certain canyons and what the best medication for blisters was? I couldn't believe that. Why bother leaving his search to ask that? Or maybe, given the location, he'd just continue his search. I'd told him about Lake Powell. I'd told him about it being my favorite place on Earth, that the two pictures in my bedroom were a star chart and a photograph of Lake Powell, both of which had hung in my dad's study. I'd mentioned to Eri it might be a place to look on one of our hikes.

But maybe, just maybe, *I'll see you tomorrow* meant that despite knowing he shouldn't, he wanted to see me.

When we got to Lake Powell and Eri was nowhere in sight, I gave up hope of him coming just for me. By the time we got our tents set up and a game of flag football was in full swing with most of the senior class participating, I was certain *I'll see you tomorrow* was a lie.

Ryan didn't try to beckon me to play. My not wanting to be socially active was normal. I knew, however, that there was something definitely wrong with me when I began entertaining the idea of joining in simply because seeing everyone else's memories would at least keep me from thinking about Eri and his. I stood and inched my way closer to the action. I even almost picked up the ball when it landed near me.

Eri beat me to it.

"Hi," he said, not watching as he perfectly arched the ball across the beach straight to Ryan.

"Hi," I said, focusing on the game instead of allowing myself to get lost in his eyes. I wanted to turn to him. Wanted to say something. I didn't know what to say. We watched the game, but not really. Apparently, awkward silence was a universal thing.

He snuck as many furtive glances at me as I did at him. Which is why neither of us noticed the football flying in our direction until it was almost too late. Luckily Eri's reflexes were faster than the ball, and, with one quick motion, I was in his arms, his hand pulling my head to his chest as he spun to make the ball hit his back and not me.

I wanted to ask him if he was okay. But the memory I was caught up in wouldn't allow me to do anything. Most of the things I'd seen in Eri's mind were about Rhaev. That was pretty much always the constant in his head. But right now, something else held a stronger power over his subconscious.

Me.

And I knew he felt the same.

He let go of me almost as quickly as he had the last time we'd seen each other.

"I'm sorry," he said, turning away.

I wanted to reach out and turn him back. I wanted the courage to stop wanting things and actually do them. But how did I tell him that every thought I'd just seen in his mind had been running through my head for the past week as well?

The next time the ball headed in our direction, we stepped away, avoiding any touch at all, but Eri finally spoke.

"Is there someplace we can go talk?"

I motioned toward some camp chairs set up nearer to the tents than the game.

"Someplace a little less crowded?" he said when five of the eight chairs became occupied as we made our way in that direction.

I turned the opposite way, and Eri followed. The place I had in mind was a little bit of a hike but would offer privacy. "Do you mind walking? There is a great view up there." I pointed to an outcropping of rocks. "It was one of my dad's favorite places."

Eri nodded, and I grabbed a nearby flashlight from the beach as we picked our way from the shoreline to the rocky canyon ahead.

"You told me your dad liked this lake," he said. I hated going back to making small talk, but at least we were talking, so I played along.

"Yeah. When we first moved, Joe brought me here to camp. I hadn't done much camping before that, and I hadn't been super thrilled about sleeping in a tent. But I knew the minute we came around the curve and the lake appeared for the first time that this place was special. The fact that my dad loved it as well just made it more so."

"You were close to him." It was halfway between a comment and a question. I took it as the latter as a way to keep the conversation going.

"Yeah. I have my mom's hair," I said, pulling on a dark curl, "but everyone always said I was my dad's twin. From the time I was little, I wanted to go wherever he went, do whatever he did. I wanted to be just like him."

"And are you?" Eri asked as we ascended a small canyon trail.

"I don't think I'll ever be as brilliant as he was. He knew everything—at least to my eleven-year-old self, he seemed to." A small laugh escaped me. I had a hard time talking about my parents, even the good things. But it felt nice to talk about them without pain. Was I relaxed because Eri made me calm with his ability or because with him, I really was? "But I try to be as good as he was."

"Good?"

"My dad did everything for anybody. If there was a need, he went the extra mile to fix it. I hope someday I can be like that."

"I think you've succeeded." The sincerity in his voice made me stop in my tracks. He stopped just short of me, the heat of his breath tickling the back of my neck, but I didn't turn around.

"I think my memorysight keeps me from getting close enough to people to really help them."

"I think your memorysight allows you to help people in ways no one else can."

Now I turned. I had to look up to meet his eyes. I didn't have to touch him to know his earlier thoughts about me were still on his mind. They were on my mind too.

"You know my thoughts," he said, looking into my eyes.

I nodded because I didn't dare speak.

"I shouldn't be thinking about those things."

"Neither should I, but sometimes our hearts don't always get the memo." It was the only way I could find to confess that he wasn't alone in this. Even though the night already felt warm, the heat radiating from him as we both stood there, neither one moving away, made me warmer.

"I'm going to leave. Maybe next week, maybe in a month, I don't know, but when the time comes, I have to leave. This...whatever these feelings are that I'm having, they're not fair. I can't act on them and then just leave." The apology in his words attempted to outweigh the want in his voice. Everything he'd said was the truth, and a dark cover appeared around my heart, like a black hole, sucking all the light away from the heat of the moment. Except black holes were once stars that had shone so brightly, so hotly that they'd exploded. If my time with Eri was going to end as a black hole, I wanted any time I had now to be a supernova.

"I'd rather have memories than regrets," I said.

It was the only answer he needed. His mouth was on mine, his arms wrapping around my waist, pulling me to him. My hands found their way around his neck, my fingers tangling in the waves of his hair. I tasted his scent, felt his desire. It was as if we both knew if we were going to do this, there was no taking our time. As his fingers pressed into my back, as mine pulled his head closer to me, the memorysight occurred.

But it wasn't a memory.

I saw myself with Eri now, tomorrow, for days, for a lifetime. We grew old together. Discovered an entire life filled with each other. Things I knew could never happen were right there—gray hair, wrinkled skin, still as enamored with each other as we were at this moment here, now. I'd seen people's wants and desires before, but I'd never seen the future.

This seemed like the future.

Our future.

One that couldn't happen.

When we finally had to pull away from one another or risk hyperventilation, his arms only loosened enough that he could look at my face. "What was that?" he asked.

Although I knew it couldn't be, I also knew exactly what he was asking. "What did you see?"

Word for word, scene for scene, every touch, every kiss, every moment I'd just experienced, Eri repeated back to me as if he'd memorized it all as if he'd lived it all—just as I had. "You saw my memorysight," I said, not understanding how that was even possible.

"That wasn't a memory." His hand came up and caressed the side of my face, pushing back a strand of hair.

"I know." I'd just had an entire lifetime with him. The arms holding me felt familiar in a way that was measured by decades, not days.

"Has that ever happened before?"

I shook my head. And then I stepped backward, out of his reach, breaking all contact.

Eri frowned.

"I just need to see something." With contact broken, a new memorysight would take place the moment I touched him again, hopefully one that would offer some explanation of what had just happened. Ryan was the only other person I'd ever kissed, so I had zero experience with this, and I hadn't seen anything like this with Ryan.

I hesitated before I reached out to Eri, wondering what I would see now. My fingers curled around his hand—and nothing.

I didn't see anything.

I pulled my hand away and tried again, this time bringing my fingers around his arm. Still nothing. I was scared and elated all at once. How could this be happening? It couldn't have been the kiss. I'd still seen Ryan's memories for more than a year after we'd kissed.

"What are you seeing?" He looked worried.

I moved closer. "I just need to try one more thing." I reached up and pulled his head down to me. If one kiss had changed everything, would another one put it all back? When our lips met this time, there was no memorysight or futuresight or anysight. The moment was just the two of us. His hands did not hesitate to pull me closer. His lips explored mine, soft and then more intense. And every brush, every point of contact, everything happened here and now, and I experienced it all, not being transported away into someone else's thoughts. This was happening to me, and I was allowed to enjoy each caress.

I kissed him again and again. I didn't know what was going on. I didn't care. I just knew I didn't want this moment to end. I didn't know if earlier I'd seen the truth or a wish. The hope that somehow this future could happen was too much for me to trust. But right now, everything was normal. I was just a girl. He was just a boy.

We finally parted, just enough that I could see the hint of a grin on his lips. "Anything else you need to try?" he asked and laughed as I looked away, embarrassed. He pulled my chin back to him. "What did you see?" he asked for a second time.

"Nothing."

"You're not going to tell me?" He frowned.

"I didn't see anything." I smiled and pulled away from him, then placed my hand against his chest. "Nothing. No past. No future. We're just here. Just normal."

"How is that possible? You said it would take years not to see my memories." He sounded curious, but his eyes turned the aquamarine color that told me he was happy.

"I don't know. Maybe it works differently because you're not from here." I shrugged. It was as logical an explanation as anything.

Eri contemplated this, but then that smile returned, and he drew me closer again. "So, nothing? You don't get anything when we touch?"

I took a deep breath. Just because I didn't see anything didn't mean I didn't feel anything. I felt a lot of things right then, and none of them were being overrun with my usual memorysights. "I don't *see* anything if that's what you're asking."

His smile grew bigger. "So, is this okay?" He kissed me again, but just the softest brush of his lips to my forehead.

I nodded. "And this?" Another kiss, this one closer to my ear.

I nodded again. "And this?" He continued to trail kisses down the side of my cheek and across my jawline until his lips found mine again.

"What just happened, those things," he said, pulling away, but keeping his forehead touching mine, "is that possible?"

"I don't know." It was becoming my common answer. Everything I knew about my memorysight had been flipped upside down.

"But your other memories, they have never shown you lies?"

"No."

A small grin settled on his face. "Then it's possible?"

I didn't know how, but that wasn't what Eri was asking. "Would you want it to be?"

He didn't answer right away. He just looked at me—and even if I couldn't see his thoughts anymore, I knew what he felt just from looking into his eyes. I felt it also. A hope that it could be true. "Yes," he said. "If there is any way for that future to be true, I would want it."

He kissed me again.

12

It was dark when we made our way back to the camp, this time hand in hand. After a while, I'd come to my senses enough to see if my memorysight was gone altogether. It wasn't. Objects still showed me their past. Only Eri had fallen into the safe-to-touch category.

"This place is amazing," he said as we walked along the shoreline. The moon reflected on the gently lapping water. "It's different from the lake by my house."

I nodded, remembering his lake—his home.

"It reminds me a bit of one of the moons of Bezos."

"How many worlds have you been to?" I asked.

"A lot. My dad is military, so I always visit him on whatever Allegiant world he is on when I'm on break from school before I go to the lake."

"Allegiant world?"

"When we make contact with a world, it is usually more of a diplomatic meeting than..." He paused, searching for his words.

"Than just showing up and hanging out with the small-town locals?" I guessed.

Eri's hand tightened around mine. "I happen to think that meeting one certain small-town local has made this first contact very worthwhile."

I was glad for the dark so he couldn't see my grin. "So, what will happen with Earth? Now that you have been here, will we become an Allegiant planet?"

"That depends."

"On?"

"On if the Tallisians make the first contact. Rhaev won't. Your planet isn't ready for us."

"Because we don't have the technology yet?" I asked, remembering our previous conversation.

"That, and also because of you."

I stopped walking and turned toward him. "What do you mean?"

"Not all worlds we have encountered have people with gifts like yours or mine. But of the ones that do, the worlds that honor those gifts are more likely to accept the fact they are not alone in the universe. Worlds willing to not only look beyond differences but honor them. They are ready. The fact that you have to hide what you can do—this amazing gift of yours—means Earth isn't ready yet."

I'd never thought of my memorysight as an amazing gift. Eri was right. On Earth, what I could do was considered different—and we were more afraid of being different than anything. I looked down the beach to where Ryan's bright yellow windbreaker shone in the light of one of the few fires set up around the campsite. Although this wasn't considered an official school-sanctioned activity, most of the senior class was there. All normal. At least what I considered normal. I'd bumped into enough of them through the years to know most of the secrets at Kanab High, and only mine entailed secret abilities. I laughed.

Eri arched an eyebrow in question.

I motioned my head toward the group we were returning to. "It's just that you're right. Ever since my memorysight appeared, I've hidden my true self from everyone—except Ryan. All I've wanted was to return to normal so I wouldn't be singled out as different. Now you're telling me there are other worlds where what I do would give me a place of honor and not a cage in a science lab. It's a lot to take in."

Eri smiled. "More than aliens?"

I laughed again. "For me, actually, yeah. Normal has been my desire for so long that nothing else can trump it, I guess."

He pulled me close to him. Kissing my head, just at the temple, he bent over enough to whisper in my ear. "You are extraordinary. And not just because of your memorysight. I've been here long enough to observe not everyone stops to help strangers or cares about people like you do. I don't know why anyone would want to be *normal* if they could be like you. But if normal is what you want, then I'll give you normal."

I tilted my head, curious about his meaning.

A sudden calmness came over me. He was using his ability. I knew, and I didn't stop him. "Tonight, you are going to enjoy just being like everyone else." He looked into my eyes as if waiting for permission to continue calming me. I nodded my consent and let him lead me back toward the group. Instead of allowing me to go off to the side like I was prone to do, he pulled me to a spot of sand next to the campfire where Ryan and Valerie sat.

They grinned when we settled next to them. Ryan introduced the others around the fire to Eri, and he greeted each of them before putting his arm around me and pulling me close to his side. This got a few gapes, but they didn't last for long. Eri's calmness reached out not just to me but to everyone else in the circle, and soon, the stares were gone, and all that was left was a group of kids laughing and talking about their plans for the summer. I was included in that group, just a normal girl, snuggled nicely next to the guy she liked. It was everything I'd dreamed of—and Eri had given it to me.

THE REST of the weekend proceeded like Friday night. I became part of the group. Eri kept me close enough to him that I didn't have to touch anyone else, except for Ryan or Valerie. Since the only memorysights Valerie gave off included her happiness of no longer having to consider me "competition" for Ryan and how hot he looked without a shirt (gross), it wasn't all bad. Any time I felt anxious, Eri sent a wave of calmness, allowing me to let go and just enjoy myself.

We swam, hiked, played volleyball, and made s'mores. Eri joined Ryan in teasing me about my chocolate addiction, but Valerie took my side and said chocolate was an essential element of a girl's diet and if they were going to make fun of me, then we weren't going to share, and proceeded to take the bag away from them, which led to a game of keep away. By the time Sunday morning arrived and we'd packed our stuff, I'd had the best weekend of my life.

"Thank you for this," I said to Eri as we rolled up one of the tents and stuffed it in a bag. "I know you could have spent the last few days searching. Thank you for spending them with me."

His hand brushed over mine, more so than just to get the last of the tent pushed into the bag. "I wish it wasn't over."

I stood, brushing the sand off my knees, and looked up at the sky. The sun was still in the east, showing we had some time before we had to leave. The campsite was packed up, some people had left, more enjoyed a last dip in the lake or one more game of football. I took Eri's hand and pulled him away from the group. "There's one more place I want to show you."

He linked his fingers through mine as I led him down the shoreline.

We walked for a few minutes, following the lake as it rounded a corner and led us to a hidden cove away from the others. Here, the shore stopped and became only a rocky base of a cliff. I had to let go of Eri as we maneuvered our way carefully across the rocks until the cliff wall rounded once more and a small beach began, just big enough for maybe one campsite. Even though I considered it my private beach, it wasn't secretive enough that no one else knew about it. Half of the time when I came here, a boat claimed the spot. No one occupied it today.

"What is this place?" Eri asked.

"We call it Star Home. I should have brought you here at night. It has the best view of the sky. I'm sure other people have their own name for it, but that's the one my dad chose. Joe brings me out here when there is a meteor shower so we can watch."

Eri ran his fingers across the red cliff that was tattered with hundreds of little pockmarks in the sandstone, making the stone look like a honeycomb. "It's remarkable."

"I like coming to places I know my dad once visited. It really does make me feel like I'm home." I followed him, trailing my hand along the cliff face as well. "And look here." I ran across the sand and pulled myself up on a few rocks until I was about ten feet higher than Eri. "There is a..." I stopped as my fingers brushed along a certain piece of wall that had been weathered down almost to look like a UFO. A piece of wall I could have possibly touched before but had never shown me anything now told me a secret. I sensed the molecular displacement, just as I had the tree.

"What is it?" Eri asked, climbing on the rock next to me.

"Here. This area of the wall—its..." I looked at him and frowned. Why here? Why had they hidden something here of all places? "There's something in the cliff."

Eri reached into the cargo pocket of his shorts and pulled out his device that would allow him to open the rock wall.

"You're always prepared," I said, trying to joke because I knew whatever hid in the wall would be a clue that could lead Eri closer to leaving.

He shrugged. "Training." He pointed the device to the wall, and the sandstone disappeared just enough for me to reach in and grab a wooden box.

I knew before the memory had time to form that the box was Tallisian. I hadn't counted on finally seeing the hooded face that had hidden this object. That had hidden the one in the tree. A face I had etched in my memory forever.

My dad.

I dropped the box.

"Catelyn?" Eri lunged for the box and caught it before it crashed on the rocks below. My knees went weak, and I grabbed onto the wall behind me, too afraid to touch Eri.

My dad hid the objects. Did that mean... Could it be possible...

"Catelyn?" Eri said again, his free hand coming to my shoulder and steadying me. "What is it? What did you see?"

"He destroyed an entire planet." My voice shook, and the words burned my throat. It didn't even matter that I'd just discovered my dad could possibly be an alien. All that mattered was if he was the Tallisian Eri had come for, then he'd taken the lives of an entire planet.

"Who did?"

I looked up into Eri's eyes. Had my dad killed his mom? I looked away, shame filling every corner of me.

"Catelyn, it's okay." Eri pulled me into his embrace. I sunk my head against his chest as the tears poured from my eyes. It could never be okay.

"He killed them. And then he hid." A sob heaved from my chest.

"Who? Did you see the Tallisian?"

I couldn't tell him. How could I say what I'd seen? I shook my head. A lie. I finally had someone I had no secrets from, and now I had to lie—again. But my life appeared to be one big lie, so why not? "How could anyone do anything like that?"

I wanted Eri to answer. I wanted him to give me an excuse why. But he couldn't. He couldn't excuse what the Tallisians had done. "It was an entire planet!" I sobbed.

"It's okay. I'm sorry you had to see that. I'm so...so sorry." He stroked the back of my head. I wanted to keep crying, anything to not look at him. But I didn't want him to feel guilty. I was the guilty one.

"No. It's fine. I'm sorry." I pulled away and wiped my eyes against my arm. Eri should not be comforting me. If he knew the truth, he would hate me. He *should* hate me. Even if I was wrong. Even if my dad wasn't Tallisian, at the very least, he knew about them. He'd helped them hide their things. I had to get home, I had to talk to Joe. Joe would know. Joe would tell me the truth. He would have an explanation of what my dad had been doing.

My knees tried to give way again. Eri moved back just enough to tilt my chin and force me to look in his eyes. I hated the concern in them.

"You have nothing to be sorry about. I don't care if you didn't see more. I wish you wouldn't have had to see that much."

He thought I apologized for dropping the box and ending the memorysight too soon. I wish the apology I needed to give him could be that easy. "Eri?" I sniffled and looked away again.

"Yes?"

"Can we go back? I don't feel so well." In fact, I felt worse than I ever had. No flu, no stomach bug, had ever destroyed me in the way this moment had.

"Of course." He helped me down the rocks and across the rocky trail. He never let go of my hand, even while he held the box in his other hand. He should have let go. He shouldn't have to worry about me—about the daughter of the man who may have killed his mother.

We got back to camp with few words, but every touch, every worried glance was devastating. I needed to get away from Eri as much as he tried to get closer to me. Ryan and Valerie were saying goodbye to a carful of people when we got back. I saw the extra seat in the back as an opportunity, not a punishment. Even though I'd brush against Brady Taylor at every bump in the road, that could never be as bad as staying here.

"Do you have room for one more?" I asked as we approached. Everyone in the car looked surprised, but none more so than Ryan and Eri. Both of whom I was lying to now.

"Sure," said the girl who was driving, one of Valerie's cheer friends.

"I can take you home," Eri said.

I turned to see the storm in his eyes, and then my gaze fell to the box in his hand. I leaned forward, kissed him on the cheek, and whispered, "You need to stay here and keep searching. I'm fine. I just don't feel well." I would never feel okay again.

The storm didn't pass, but I could tell he knew he needed to search some more—even if the last thing I wanted him to find was evidence of the truth. He nodded reluctantly as I slid into the seat next to Brady. So many things I didn't want to see entered my mind as our arms touched. Which of the three girls he'd hooked up with in the last week he planned to call or if he should maybe take a stab at me. I wanted to smack the player's grin off his face, but I couldn't stay with Eri when only lies could escape my mouth. I had to get home and talk to Joe; only then could I really sort anything out.

I smiled at Brady the best I could since I'd have to be sitting by him for the next two hours. I didn't say anything more to anyone as we pulled away. I tried avoiding Eri's worried look. I saw Ryan's look of utter confusion. I leaned my head against the window and closed my eyes. I'd have to come up with another lie, but right now, I didn't want to think about anything.

13

Joe had a stargazing tour, so Claire came to my room that night. I'd barricaded myself in there the moment I'd gotten home. At first, I feigned exhaustion. It gave me a good four hours of alone time. After an intense stage of disbelief, I moved to anger. I screamed into my pillow and yanked my dad's pictures off my wall, then hung them back up before I could smash them to the floor. Next, I tried to be logical. There had to be a reason my dad had hidden that box. He wasn't an alien. He always tried to help people. His goodness had been his downfall. He'd been tricked into helping them. Logic led me to tears. If Dad was Tallisian that meant I was... I couldn't even think of the idea. Instead, I cried until exhaustion and sleep came.

My dreams haunted me. Sardova exploding. My dad watching it happen. Eri finding out what I'd seen. My own world shattered.

By the time Claire knocked to check on me, I'd worked myself to numbness. There was nothing more I could decipher while I was curled in a ball on my bed. So I let her in.

"You feel okay?" she asked.

"No." I felt nothing—and everything.

"You don't look so hot." She put her hand to my forehead and frowned. "Do you want me to make you some chocolate chip cookies?"

This elicited a laugh. Most people got offered chicken soup when they were sick. Claire pushed chocolate. Not that I minded. Her cookies always made me feel better. But the empty hole inside of me could not be fixed by any amount of chocolate. I grabbed her arm before she could leave.

"Joe and my dad were friends from school, right?" I asked.

She looked concerned because of course I knew the answer—or at least what I'd always been told. "Yeah, friends forever," she said.

"In Maine."

She nodded once, but had she stalled? Hesitated?

"And then they moved to Virginia together for college."

She nodded again. But this nod changed her features from concern to sadness.

"Oh, honey. Are you worrying that Ryan is going off to school? You know you can always go with him—or anywhere. We've saved for your schooling. Your dad wanted you to have an education."

I bet. Anything to make me seem human. Claire looked at me like the only care I could have in the world was Ryan going off to college. Would she do that if I wasn't just a regular human girl? Maybe Claire didn't know anything. Maybe they lied to her, too.

"I don't want to go to college," I said. I didn't want to do anything my dad would have wanted me to do. Even as I thought about it, I regretted it. He was good. I'd never seen him be anything but good and kind and charitable. Someone like that didn't destroy planets. Then I remembered last week's memorysight. One of the men hadn't wanted the destruction to happen. The voice had seemed familiar—my dad? Had he tried to stop what happened? Why couldn't I have a memorysight with Claire or Joe? Getting answers would be so much easier. But maybe there was something else I could touch.

"Actually, can I have some cookies?" I asked.

Claire smiled sadly but nodded. She straightened the picture of Lake Powell as she left the room. "Caty, everything will work out okay."

I nodded like I believed her. I really wanted to believe her, but just then, I didn't know how anything could be okay. I counted to ten after I heard her opening cupboards downstairs before I tiptoed to the edge of the stairs. I made sure I heard the measuring cups clanking and then turned and went to their room. I touched everything I could think of, hating that I was violating their privacy with each drawer I opened and rummaged through. To hear their clothes talk—Joe and Claire were as normal as apple pie. By the time I'd made it all the way through the closet, the first timer beeped. Claire would come up with hot cookies in a few minutes, and I hadn't learned anything I didn't already know about them. No secrets were hidden in this room.

I barely got back to my bed when I heard her coming up the stairs. Had I hit a dead end? Nowhere else in the house could have hidden secrets. Their bedroom was the only place I rarely ventured into. Even Joe's office, with all the books and different model cars, had my fingerprints all over the place. No more memorysights to find there. The only other place in the house I rarely went to was the crawl space above my closet. The answers I sought couldn't be hidden among Christmas decorations and spider webs.

I realized where I had to look next the moment Claire walked in the door with a plate full of still-warm cookies and a glass of chocolate milk. It was all I could do not to look out the window at Joe's shed while I took the tray and thanked her. She studied me for a moment, long enough to realize I just wanted to be alone. She left with just a quick pat on my arm.

I abandoned the tray on my desk the minute she shut the door. Bolting to the window, I tried to plan my next move. I needed to get into Joe's shed, but it was locked with a passcode. I'd never thought anything of it before. We had a lock on the garage, too, and it was just a safety measure. But now, the lock seemed like a keep-out measure. Joe's shed was the only place on our property I'd never been—never even been allowed to be. I had to get in there.

After my mood the day before, Claire and Joe only gave me a moment's hesitation when I announced the next morning I didn't feel well and planned on staying home from school. A worried glance passed between them, but I pushed aside their offers to stay home. I waited a good half hour after hearing both their cars pull away before I slipped out of bed, put on shoes, and headed straight for the backyard.

I hadn't even bothered changing out of the shorts and tank top I'd slept in. I stood before the door to Joe's shed and stared down at the passcode box as if my pleading glare would be enough to open the lock. It wasn't. I contemplated long and hard before I tried my birthday, knowing if it mimicked the garage door, it would lock out after three wrong attempts. The only way to reset it would be for Joe to call the security company.

It wasn't my birthday.

It wasn't Joe and Claire's anniversary.

I debated back and forth between Joe's birthday—the code to the garage—and Claire's birthday, even though I knew the chances of it being anything that reasonable were slim. I'd settled on Claire's birthday when another day hit me. I typed in the day my parents died without thinking further. The lock turned from red to green, and the latch clicked. I pulled up the handle and entered Joe's shed for the first time in my life.

I'd seen bits and pieces of the inside when I'd tried to peek as Joe entered or left—and true to what I'd seen, hammers and saws and screwdrivers covered the immediately visible area. Sawdust and metal shavings littered the floor, making me glad I'd at least had the sense to slip on my tennis shoes before coming out here. I turned to the area toward the back-right side that had always been blocked from my view. That was where normal stopped. Objects made of smooth metal, sleek and silver, with strange carvings on them, objects that were pure science fiction, cluttered the back shelf. Objects like the one Eri had brought over last week.

I placed one hand near the workbench, ready to catch myself if anything shocking appeared in my memorysight, and then I picked up the closest of the silver orbs. It was cold and smooth but warmed to the touch as I held it. Both Joe and my dad were in the memory that came.

"You know you'll have to tell her eventually," Joe said, shifting the metallic stone back and forth between his hands.

"She hasn't displayed any abilities. Maybe we won't need to tell her at all."

"Aden, she has the right to know what she is. Where she came from."

"She has the right to grow up normal. Just a regular kid. She doesn't need this burden."

"And what happens if someone from Rhaev comes? Or someone from Tallis? What then?"

"Joseth, it's been ten years. No one is coming. Catelyn never needs to know about any of it."

"And Trilla? She's hidden away. What happens to her when we die? Who will take care of her?"

My dad sighed. He took the object from Joe and ran his fingers along the black carved runes. "Fine. We will tell her, but later. Let her get through high school. Let her live a normal existence until that point. Then we will take her to Trilla. We will explain everything. But until then, Catelyn deserves the chance to just be like anyone else on this planet. She doesn't need to know about Tallis or the war or...any of it."

A noise sounded outside the memory, and I let go of the object.

"Catelyn?"

I didn't turn. I couldn't look at Joe. Even when he came up behind me, I kept my eyes closed. I wasn't surprised. I'd already come to this conclusion. Joe and my dad were from Tallis. I assumed my mom was as well. I was still uncertain about Claire, but there was no room for doubt on one thing. I was not from Earth. Shock overtook me, leaving a sudden lack of any feeling in my body.

"You're supposed to be on a hike," I said, remembering his schedule. I'd checked that morning. My words sounded too calm, not like when Eri calmed me, but like I had complete control of myself. I didn't.

"They got food poisoning and had to cancel." He sighed. "Did you see a memory?"

So not only had he lied to me about who he was, who I was, he'd never bothered to let me know about my memorysight? Never asked me how I managed to cope with this strange, awful power?

"How long have you known I can see memories?" I looked at the object on the workbench in front of me. He hadn't known when that conversation had taken place.

"For a few years. Caty, I'm—"

"Why didn't you tell me?" Tears welled up in my eyes, and I squeezed them shut to stop the pain from spilling out.

"I wanted to. Claire wanted to, but you were doing fine just keeping your secret—and you had Ryan. You were trying so hard to be normal, we just—"

"But I'm not normal." I whirled around and faced him. "I'm not even human."

He tried to grab me, an apology in his eyes I refused to accept. I stepped out of his reach.

"Is Claire..." What word did I even use?

"Claire is from Earth," Joe said.

"Does she know that you're, that we're..."

"Yes. She knew before we got married."

I don't know if I expected that to be a relief, but it wasn't. It made me madder. "You told a human you were not from here, but you couldn't even tell me? One of your own kind?" Rage, hot and painful, coursed through me. My parents, Joe, even Claire had lied to me my entire life.

"Caty, it's not—"

"No. I don't want to hear anymore." I fled past him to the door and then stopped.

"Caty, you need to listen—"

"I need to listen? You sure didn't care if I knew the truth before now. I don't need to listen to anything you have to say."

I stormed out of the shed and slammed the door on Joe. Then I started running. I ran until I couldn't breathe. I ran until my head and lungs felt like they were going to explode. I ran even after I knew Joe wasn't following me. I ran until I couldn't think anymore because I didn't want to think. I ran until I reached the last place I should have been running to.

I ran straight into the arms of a boy I could never be with.

14

I don't know if he'd seen me or if fate played a role, but Eri opened the door before I had time to ring the bell. He stepped onto the front porch, shutting the door behind him before taking my hand and pulling me around the corner of the house and away from the prying eyes of his "uncle" who stood at the front window.

He wrapped me into his arms the minute we were alone. "What's wrong?"

A wave of calmness spread through me, stopping the rage, stopping the physical nausea of overexertion, but no amount of calmness stopped the pain in my heart.

What should I say? How did I tell him? I couldn't. "I'm sorry, I just had a fight with Joe and..." And what? I buried my head in his chest and stayed silent.

"Do you want to talk?" he asked, stroking my hair.

I looked up into his eyes and shook my head. "No." I didn't want to talk about anything. I wanted to make everything go away. I wanted to pretend I was anything but what I really was—a member of the race that had killed his mom. A member of a race he hated.

Eri ran his thumb across my cheek, catching a stray tear. I thought all the concern on his face was for me until I caught him glancing to the side of the house. I stepped out of his arms. Even here, now, without meaning to, I'd hurt him.

"I shouldn't be here. We shouldn't be together." If his uncle walked around the corner just then, what would happen?

"It's okay," Eri said, taking my hand.

I pulled away. "But it's not. I'm jeopardizing your whole mission just by being here." A mission to find and eliminate my family.

"*You* are not jeopardizing my mission. I just can't be what they want me to be." He reached again for my hand, and I kept mine in his this time. "I'm not living up to my potential," he said as if quoting someone else's words.

"You've done nothing but search for the ship since you got here. How can they think that?"

"I'm supposed to be doing more than searching for the ship." He traced small circles across the top of my hand with his thumb. The feeling sent chills through me—both of desire and regret. "I'm supposed to be seeking out Tallisians—seeing if they are still here."

A cold dread shot through my body. Eri's eyes clouded over in a storm of deep green. He frowned, and I worried I'd been caught. But his response didn't agree with that conclusion. "I'm not sure I can do what would be expected of me if I ever found them."

He didn't know.

"What would be expected of you?"

He looked down at the ground, but his hand tightened around mine. "I'm supposed to eliminate them." He sighed. "I hate them. I don't know how not to; it's all I've ever known."

I couldn't see in his mind now, for which I was grateful. I didn't want to see any more of the hate he felt for my kind.

"But I kind of hope I won't have to kill them," he went on.

"What do you mean?"

"Before we lost contact with our people here, they sent a message saying they eliminated the threat."

Everything started to spin.

"Of course, there was no response from them after that, so who knows, but perhaps there are not as many Tallisians left here as there might have been. Maybe I won't have to be put in that situation."

My chest ached like a knife had been shoved into it. I couldn't breathe. I couldn't move. My dad had been that threat. Had Eri's people caused my parents' accident? Had they killed my parents?

His other arm came up and pulled me to him. "Catelyn, I'm sorry. I know that sounded awful. I promise I wouldn't harm them, not if I didn't have to."

I let him hold me because if he let go, I would fall over. My whole body had gone stone cold and limp. What was I supposed to do? Were we "even" now? My dad killed his mom, and his people killed my parents? Did that negate everything? Did it make things that much worse? And what did he mean by not if he didn't have to? If he knew who I was, who Joe was, would he have to do something?

"I have to go."

"Catelyn," he pulled away. "I'm sorry. I'm sorry you have to see this side of me."

"I just need to think." He had to keep believing my behavior was just shock—which was partially true, but not in the way he thought. I looked into his eyes. I could never see Eri again. Whatever I'd seen when we'd kissed at Lake Powell must have been wishful thinking. Since I'd never had a vision, that was easy to believe, especially knowing what I knew now. This would be my last moment with him. I kissed him, a goodbye kiss as much as an apology kiss as much as a selfish desire kiss. It would never happen again, so I made sure to make the kiss long and hard and fervent. Maybe he understood because he returned it just as fiercely as I offered.

"I'm sorry," I said, pulling away at the moment I knew I had to, or I might just surrender my life to him there and then. I didn't wait for him to respond. I bolted down the side of the house and toward home, running even harder and faster than I had run to get there.

Joe and Claire were both waiting for me when I rushed through the door, breathless.

"Is everything okay?" Claire asked. She pulled me into her arms before I collapsed. I went to bury my head in her shoulder, to allow myself to cry, but before the tears came, a memory took over.

Claire telling Joe they should just tell me. Joe saying he was certain Ryan knew. That I was okay. That they had time.

I pulled out of her embrace. A memorysight? How was this

possible? The only thing that was different was I knew what I was. But I hadn't had one with Eri. I hadn't had one with Ryan when he'd said goodbye at the lake. Why here? Why now?

"Caty, what is going on?" Joe asked.

I looked at him, my pain replaced with anger. It didn't matter what I'd just seen. They'd lied to me.

"What is going on? I'm an alien! You're an alien!" I stepped farther away from Claire. "You both lied to me. Everyone has lied to me!"

My tears started again. Because even with all the lies, I'd had enough time on my run home to know exactly what I had to do. I could be mad at Joe and Claire all I wanted, but it didn't change the fact that the Rhaevians were here, and they wanted Tallisians dead. They wanted Joe and me dead, and that wasn't going to happen. I had to tell them everything. I had to tell them about Eri.

I took a deep breath to gain control of all the emotions surrounding me. "What is wrong is that I don't know if it is worse that you never told me I was an alien—" another deep breath, this one burning through my chest, "or that I fell in love with one."

The color drained from Joe's face. Claire gasped and grabbed the back of the couch to steady herself. "How could you..." she said.

"How could I?" I knew she hadn't meant it like that, but even knowing what I had to do, what had to happen, I was angry. I wanted to make them hurt like I hurt. "Because no one ever told me there was such a thing as good aliens and bad aliens. And that, oh yeah, I am one of them." I didn't add that the worst part was that I didn't know which alien faction I belonged to—the good or the bad—but based on my memorysight, I could guess.

"We need to get out of here," Joe said, regaining his composure. "Both of you. Go grab whatever you need—only what you can carry. We have to leave. Now." He turned to go.

"Wait, what?" I knew leaving would be an option, but we had time. I couldn't just pick up and leave. I was supposed to graduate and turn eighteen and go to parties. I needed time to say my goodbyes. I needed time to talk to Ryan. "Eri doesn't know what I am. None of them do. He thinks I'm psychic—I *thought* I was psychic."

Joe turned toward me. "I'm sorry, Caty. I'm sorry we never told you. I'm sorry this is happening, but I don't have time to explain. These people—they killed your parents. They will kill us. We have two choices—fight or run, and the last time I fought... I can't become that person again." He looked at Claire and then back at me. "Now go."

Claire jumped to action, running to the kitchen possibly to grab our seventy-two-hour kits. I stood there, watching them both flee. I felt things in slow motion, but Claire and Joe were in hyper-speed. I'd never seen either of them with that much fear in their expressions. Eri wasn't a killer. He wouldn't kill me. He wouldn't do that. Even if he knew, he wouldn't tell the others. Everything was going to be okay.

Claire and Joe just needed a minute to calm down. I didn't even run to my room. I just walked slowly, taking each step one at a time. I wanted to call Ryan, but until I knew what I would say to him, it was probably better I didn't. Right now, I just had to go to my room. Joe and Claire would realize we were not in panic mode—we would never even need to hit panic mode. I just had to give them space. We all needed space.

I sat on my bed, and my head fell against the pillows. Space and time. This would all clear over. Except I heard Claire downstairs. From the sound of cupboards opening and closing, I guessed she was still packing in the kitchen.

I jumped from my bed, realizing something my overworked, tired mind hadn't. They may not have told me the truth. But they were still Claire and Joe. Normal Joe would have given me time to work through my feelings, which would be followed by a long talk when I was ready. Normal Claire would be standing by the door, waiting for me to let her in so she could hug me and tell me everything would be all right. Instead, they both went straight to preparing for our departure. I now processed a different fear. One for my life.

And then the crash sounded.

15

Claire screamed, and I ran to my door. My first instinct was to rush down and see what happened. Help her. But she screamed once more before her voice was silenced. One word was all she got out. "Run."

I opened the window, ripping out the screen. Someone came up the stairs. I didn't have time to run away. I'd run as much as my body was going to let me in one day. My muscles ached in protest from the last two sprints I'd gone on. I needed to hide. Under the bed was too obvious. The closet was a better choice but still not great. My gaze moved up to the entry of the crawlspace. It was spiders or whoever silenced Claire.

We usually used a stepladder to get to the crawlspace—a luxury I didn't have and couldn't use without detection. I managed to squeeze into the corner of the closet and use two large Tupperware boxes of out-of-season clothes as my step without moving them. I pulled myself up on the top shelf, trying to be as quiet as possible. It wasn't sturdy, but it held my weight with only a slight creak. The trap door, molded as it was against the ceiling, barely budged when I pushed on it.

A door shut somewhere close by. My room was the last on the right. If they went room by room, there were only two or three more, depending on which side they favored. I stretched and leaned over enough to push the ceiling door open. A spring latch on the other side helped it slide up without too much noise. Inching over, I pulled myself into the crawlspace and lowered the door.

Heat attacked me, sweltering and intense. Cobwebs clung to the wooden beams above my head. In one corner were the boxes with all the Christmas decorations. In the other corner were the things we'd saved after cleaning my old house in Virginia. Some were memories. Most of the boxes contained clothing and bedding meant to go to charity, but somehow none of us had the desire to part with it no matter how much we didn't need the items, and they ended up here in the attic.

I walked over to a bag that held the quilt my parents had on their bed. I'd already seen the love—the moment my mother had placed the last stitch. There were no more memorysights for the blanket to offer, but I remembered their love now, even just looking at it. I sat down on the bag, pulling my knees close to my chest and wrapping my arms around them. Another door opened. It closed almost just as fast—the bathroom. Nowhere to hide in there. My room was next.

Sound was strangely amplified up here. Each step sounded as if they were close enough to reach out and grab me. Tears tried to fight their way out. Something had happened to Claire, something bad. And that meant something had happened to Joe first because had he heard her scream and been able to come after her, nothing would have stopped him.

The intruder tried my room. The lock jostled back and forth, but the door remained closed. I moved slowly, putting my head near the floor to hear better. They kicked the door. Another kick. This one sounded like wood splinted with the force. A third kick finished the job.

A rough screechy grate, like nails on a chalkboard—a sound from horror movies—came as the intruder pushed the door open. I held my breath. They were in my room. Would they see the open window and assume I'd jumped out? We were on the second story, but I could have easily hung over the side and dropped. Would they search the closet, look up and wonder about the trapdoor?

They scuffled away from the closet, each step dragged noisily. Something fell to the floor. It sounded like the window screen. Only one pair of footsteps echoed through the ceiling. I looked around to find something I could use as a weapon. Could I surprise him and get a good blow to the head before he had a chance to react?

A set of wooden candy canes by the Christmas decorations were the only thing that stood out. They adorned the walkway to the house each year from the day after Thanksgiving until the day after New Year's. They'd fared well through more than a few freak blizzards. I wondered how one would handle in a fight.

Below, my clothes were pushed aside—first one way and then the other. They'd made their way back to the closet.

"I have them in the van," a deep voice said.

A woman's voice answered in a language I knew was Rhaevish from my memorysights. Eri's fake aunt.

"Let's go," the man said. "Eri will find her. She trusts him." The words echoed in my mind. That would have to be Mathis—the fake uncle. Nausea built in me. I knew the Rhaevians had come for us the minute Claire screamed, but I couldn't believe Eri was part of this. He couldn't be.

I debated using the candy canes one last time. I could take them—maybe. But then again, based on looks alone, Joe and Claire could have taken them. They either had weapons, or they were a lot stronger than they looked. After all, it would have been the supposed Mrs. Smith who kicked in my door. The one time I'd seen her out in the garden, she'd looked like someone's grandmother.

Loud footsteps raced down the stairs, then another door slammed. I didn't move. I had no way of knowing when the van pulled away, but I assumed after several minutes that they had left. And still, I stayed where I was, lying flat on the ground, my ear pressed against the crack by the trap door.

They'd taken Claire and Joe. They were gone. Eri would be coming back for me. He knew they were here, that they were after us. When had he figured it out? How had I given us away? When had he changed his mind about coming after Tallisians?

I needed to come up with a plan. I tried to think of anything Eri said that would give me some idea about where they would take Joe and Claire. I tried to recall even the smallest memories of the times we hadn't been together. The times he'd gone off on his own. Where had he gone?

I pulled my phone from my back pocket and checked the time. If I had any hope of tracking them down, time was of the essence. I lifted the door and lowered myself to the ground.

Looking around my room reminded me once more of the mess my life had become. The door was broken in, coming off the hinge. The picture of Lake Powell that hung above my desk had been smashed to the floor; glass shards were shattered around the room. The blankets of my bed were tossed up. I pulled them back down, a habit of always having a tidy bed. I glanced around, seeing if there was anything I might need. Nothing jumped out at me, but then again, how was I supposed to know what to take, where to go, what to do? I needed help. I pulled my phone back out and dialed the only person I could still trust—Ryan. A door opened somewhere downstairs before I pressed the green phone button. I froze. They were back.

"Catelyn?" Eri's voice called. The third stair creaked. There wasn't time to get back into the crawl space. The wind blew the curtains of the open window. I could try to jump, but he'd see me running away and catch me. This time the most obvious spot seemed like the only choice. I dove under the bed, barely managing to squeeze between the springs and the floor. Lying on my stomach, facing the door, I saw his feet when he walked into the room.

"Catelyn?" he said again. He walked toward me, and I pulled myself in tightly, each muscle tensing. I held my breath, but my heart pounded.

His feet stopped by the bed. I closed my eyes. Then I heard him move away. He went over to the frame, broken on the ground, and picked it up. I had a better view of him from this angle. He looked the same as he had earlier.

Except the gun in his hand. The gun was very much not like my Eri and very much like the Rhaevian that had been sent to kill me.

"Catelyn," he called a third time. "We need to talk. I have to believe you didn't know."

I closed my eyes to fight back the anger. If he thought I didn't know, why had he immediately turned on me? I couldn't stand the idea of facing him, but he was the only way to ensure Claire and Joe were safe. I slid out from under the bed, the side opposite of him, enough to keep our distance—although bullets didn't care where in the room I stood. He sighed. Maybe he was glad I was safe or maybe he was glad he could take me as a prisoner. Either way I didn't think he would shoot me.

"I didn't know," I said, not looking at him but at his gun. He lowered it. "Not until today."

He nodded. His face was torn in conflict.

"What are you going to do to us?"

"We—"

"Eri?" A voice rang out from downstairs. Mathis.

A startled look crossed his face as he glanced toward the door, then back at me. "You need to hide," he said in a rushed whisper.

I couldn't hide. I had to go with him. I had to be with Joe and Claire. I shook my head, even as I heard Mathis creeping up the stairs.

"Catelyn, please." His calmness rushed over me. I wanted to fight, but I couldn't. "Just stay here." He held his finger to his mouth. I nodded like we were playing a game, even though this time I fully understood what he was doing to me. I still couldn't fight against his control of my emotions. I sat down on the bed, that drunk mind-fog feeling coming over me.

"She's not here," he said, leaving the room.

What a joker. I was here, and I should be following him, shouldn't I? No, he'd told me to stay. Confusion swirled in my mind—his calmness won out.

"Karin has the other two secured. We need to find her," Mathis said in the hall.

"The girl is no harm. She doesn't even know what she is," Eri said, and maybe he used his calming ability on Mathis as well because the man didn't come closer. He didn't look in the room and see me, sitting on the bed, waiting for Eri to tell me what to do. He started back down the stairs. Third one creaked.

Eri turned back, and our eyes met. I tried to speak. He shook his head.

I couldn't do anything but look up at him. "I'm sorry." He mouthed and turned to leave. I didn't follow him. I couldn't, but that was okay, everything was okay. Everything was...

I jumped up the moment the downstairs door shut. Eri's calmness cut off from me. I ran down the stairs and flung the door open, but his Range Rover was already turning the corner of the street. I rushed back into the house and grabbed the keys to Claire's car.

Two hours later, I sat in front of Ryan's house. I'd driven through town and taken 89 out of Kanab both ways. I would never find them. They were off my radar before I'd even put the car in drive. Why had he left me behind? Did Eri think I would be okay trading Claire and Joe for my own life? I had to save them. I needed clues. And I needed help. Keeping secrets when I was the only one involved was one thing. Now that Joe and Claire were... I couldn't put too much thought into what was happening to them. I just had to find them. I needed the only person I could trust. I needed Ryan.

16

"What's going on?" Ryan asked as he opened the door. Based on his tone, I must have appeared a mess. I glanced over at Eri's. The house looked like the empty husk of a burnt-out star—dark and forlorn. Ryan followed my gaze, his mouth set firmly in a scowl. Ryan's red truck was the only vehicle in his carport. Hopefully, his mom worked the late shift.

"Let's go inside," I said.

The door had barely shut when I began my story—a secret agent spy novel wrapped around aliens and intergalactic wars. The events of the last day didn't even sound possible as I related everything. Ryan tried to act as if he believed every word I said, but his doubt was visible in his furrowed eyebrows and pursed mouth. I was just about to tell him about my parents and how their death was not an accident when he finally stopped me.

"Where are Joe and Claire? What do they say about this?"

I swallowed. Tears stung my eyes. "They took them."

"What do you mean? Took them where?"

"I don't know. I don't know anything. I only know Joe and Claire are in danger." I fell onto his couch and put my head in my hands.

"Do you really think Eri will hurt them?" Ryan placed a hand on my shoulder.

I shook my head. "Eri? I don't know. His people? Ryan, they killed my parents. What other intentions do they have for taking Joe and Claire?"

"Whoa. Wait. I thought your parents died in a car accident."

Ryan paced the room. He took this a lot better than I had—but his voice still held a lot of questions.

"So did I." I waited for something more—for the next onslaught of questions. He stopped in front of me.

"What do we do?" If there had been time, maybe Ryan would have had a my-best-friend-is-an-alien freak-out moment and attempted to convince me to do all sorts of crazy experiments just to test my abilities. But there wasn't time—and he loved Joe and Claire as much as I did.

"We need to figure out where they are," I said.

"How do we do that?"

"We break into his house." The only place that might offer a clue waited right next door. I needed a memorysight to lead us to them. Breaking in was also against the law, dangerous, and might very well prove to be a trap.

"Let's go." Ryan started for the door without hesitation. He seemed possessed to action with no thought of what we might have to do. A twinge of guilt for dragging him into this played inside me.

"Ryan, maybe it would be better—"

He turned back to me. "Caty, we're in this together. We'll get them back."

I nodded. I couldn't think of an alternative option.

Outside, the sky was dark. A storm had finally come in to quell the heatwave that had been holding on the last few days. Lightning brightened portions of the sky to the west, and a heavy breeze carried a dry layer of red dirt that stung my skin as we walked over to Eri's.

We didn't even bother with the front door, making our way to the courtyard between the garage and the house. Ryan jumped over the small fence, and I followed. Ryan wasn't the rebellious type. I wondered how far he would go with this before questioning me. He picked up a semi-large stone from the rock garden and threw it at the sliding glass door. A crash of thunder shook the air.

Being a little more careful, he kicked aside shards of glass before reaching through and undoing the latch. He turned and looked at me as if he just now realized the act of vandalism he'd committed. "You're sure about this?" It was a little too late for that, even if I wasn't, but I nodded and walked in.

I flipped on the kitchen light. Nothing was on the counter, not a roll of paper towels, not a cookie jar or kitchen appliance. There wasn't even a towel hung over the stove or a sponge in the sink. The living room was pretty much the same. Furnished, but not lived in. The bedrooms gave away that someone had actually resided here, but not by a lot. The beds were all made neatly, and there were some clothes in the closets, but not a full wardrobe.

Vague memories lingered throughout the house. Mrs. Smith cutting bread on the kitchen counter, Eri thumbing through a book in the living room, Mr. Smith throwing down the remote control in disgust over something he'd seen on the television. I touched every surface. So many memories—none of them gave me anything—except the start of a headache.

In the room that held Eri's clothes, I found a piece of paper in the garbage can. I pulled it out and uncrumpled it. With my memorysight, I saw him, hunched over the paper, eyes in concentration as he wrote something and then crossed it out almost violently. His hand came to his head, his fingers running through his hair, and he groaned.

Now I looked at the paper, curious about what I'd seen. What had caused him such frustration? My name bordered the top. Under that were facts about me. Things I'd told him, observations he must have made on his own. "Bites her bottom lip when nervous." "Sings along to the radio." There was the one he'd crossed out with severe scratch marks. I held the paper up to the light to try to make out what he'd written, wondering why it was in English–had he left this here for me?

A noise outside the room took my attention to the doorway. "Ryan?" I called. He didn't answer. The hairs on my arm stood on end as I shoved the paper into my pocket. "Ryan?" I called again. I stepped toward the door, wishing Eri had something in his room I could use as a weapon. I doubted the king-sized pillows on the bed would do me any good.

It started to rain. Not a light splatter, but a violent rush of raindrops slamming against the roof and ground. "Caty?" Ryan yelled. "I think I found something." I started out the door, turning off the light as I went. I couldn't help but still think of the list, what Eri had made it for, what he'd crossed out.

Ryan stood completely still in the living room. I couldn't place the expression on his face except to say there was none. He stared at me like he'd fallen into a void. Like his body was there, but nothing was inside.

I looked over my shoulder, where he seemed to be staring–right at a woman who had a gun pointed at my head.

She spoke in a language I didn't understand, but her tone sounded every bit as sinister as she appeared. She wore a tight black pantsuit that showed every curve of her body. Her hair was short and spiky straight.

"Soria," a deep voice from behind me said. Someone else was with us, but nothing could turn my focus away from the gun pointed at me. "She is Tallisian." Whoever spoke used English with a heavy accent, and he sounded surprised.

The woman stepped closer to me, her gun lowering slightly. She looked me over with fierce intensity. I returned the scrutiny. The arch of her brow line, her nose, her lips, the brown eyes staring back at me —everything was vaguely familiar, like looking into a mirror and seeing myself in fifteen or twenty years. Her reaction mimicked mine, only in reverse.

"Aden," she said reverently.

My father's name. This woman knew my father, and from the way she spoke his name, it was clear she cared for him.

"Aden was my father," I said. Our eyes never left each other, so even as she fought all emotion, she couldn't hide the tears forming in her eyes, though she kept them from spilling. She bit her bottom lip, just like I'd done my whole life, but she quickly stopped. She spat out another string of words I didn't understand before switching to address me.

"Was?" she asked.

"My parents were killed." I'd always said died. Now I knew the truth.

"When?"

"Six years ago."

"How?"

Depending on who this woman was, my answer could have a variety of different meanings. But she cared about him. I knew she cared. I gave the only answer I could. "The Rhaevians."

A grim scowl settled on her face. "And Joseth?" she asked. "Is he dead as well?"

This woman knew Joe as well. She must be Tallisian. Relief washed over me. I wasn't alone. My quest to find Joe and Claire no longer seemed like a futile mission.

"They took him and Claire," I said. "Who are you? How do you know my dad?"

She remained silent for far longer than I think either of us was comfortable with. I heard Ryan and the guy behind me breathing. The clock ticked loudly on the wall, but I couldn't take my eyes off this woman—Soria, I assumed.

"He was my brother," she said.

Everything stopped. The pounding of my heart, the sound of the falling rain. Maybe even the spinning of the world. A complete state of shock took over. Once upon a time, I'd made up a whole pretend family—an aunt and uncle, grandparents, a bunch of cousins, on occasion, a sibling or two. It seemed the thing an only child of two only children would do. But my dad wasn't an only child. Why wouldn't he have told me about a sister? Why was he here on Earth playing at being human when he had family out there?

I stepped forward. I had an aunt. Should I hug her? She still had a gun in her hand. Maybe not. How was I supposed to greet this sudden relation? She stepped away from me.

"Brand, does she have the touch?" she asked. She knew about my memorysight; hope sprang in me. Would I finally have answers?

"She does not."

I turned to look at the mystery voice. A guy, probably about my age but much taller—6'4" or 6'5", at least—stood next to Ryan. Like Soria, he wore all black, and the clothing matched his hair—so dark it seemed to have streaks of indigo—and his eyes.

What did he mean I didn't have the touch? How would he know? And if he did, why would he lie to her?

I opened my mouth, ready to correct him. I stopped when I caught a glimpse of Ryan. Something was seriously wrong. Ryan hadn't changed the expression I'd seen him with when I first walked in. I'd gone through about a hundred emotions in the last few minutes. He had to have had one or two himself after hearing Soria's story, but he didn't smile or frown or furrow his eyebrows—he stood robotically still.

"What's wrong with him?" I asked. The boy looked at Soria like he was above speaking to me and bid her to do so for him.

"Brand is a Darkothian," she said. When I didn't respond, she elaborated. "Right now, he has seized control of the Earthling's mind."

I looked back and forth between the three of them, not able to mask my shock. My gaze settled on Brand. He didn't move a muscle even as I gave him my best smoldering glare.

"Well, stop it," I said.

Brand looked at Soria, and I realized he wasn't above speaking to me—it's that he wasn't allowed. He sought permission from her. My aunt was the one in charge. Good.

"Please get him out of Ryan's head." I addressed her this time. Her mere presence required respect—or fear.

"It's best he knows nothing of this," she said.

"But he already knows everything. He can help us find Joe and Claire."

"How?" she asked. "How can he do anything? He's an Earthling. What does he have to offer us to make a difference?"

That stopped me cold. What Ryan had to offer was peace of mind—for me. I didn't know if I could enter this new life suddenly flung before me without him. But that was selfish. Was I willing to risk Ryan's life to ease my own anxiety?

"What do you plan on doing with him?" I asked. I wasn't so sure letting this tall, dark stranger play in his mind was a whole lot better than just letting him come with us.

"Brand will take care of him. He won't remember anything about you or us."

"He won't remember me?" That was a stab to the heart. And scary too. How could Soria sound so calm about what this Brand guy could do?

She smiled. "No, he'll remember you, just not that you are Tallisian. It wouldn't do to erase you completely, might draw too many questions from others who know you. Brand," she turned to the boy, "why not send..." she paused and looked at me expectantly.

"Catelyn." It was Brand who said my name, my full name. He would not have seen that in Ryan's head. Which meant he'd been in mine.

Soria nodded. "Send Catelyn, Joseth, and this Claire," there was a touch of bitterness in her voice, "woman on an excursion of some sort."

Brand's gaze went straight to Ryan.

"Is that safe?" I asked Soria. If I understood correctly, he went in Ryan's head and not only erased his memories but gave him new ones.

"Your friend will be fine," she said.

"And us?" He'd obviously found my name; had he messed my mind up without my knowing?

Her brief moment of laughter seemed like a new emotion, as if she didn't do it often. "Brand won't hurt you. He is on our side." That didn't make me feel much safer.

Color and feeling came back into Ryan's face. The stone statue cracked, and my friend smiled at me, just like he'd done a million times before. But it wasn't the same. He might not know what Brand had done to him, but I did.

"Well, I guess I should get home," Ryan said. He spoke like he was finishing a conversation we'd already had. "Have fun in Toronto."

Toronto? Really? What was with aliens and Canada? I guess it wasn't politically correct to think of them as aliens considering my own heritage, but he could have sent us somewhere a little more exotic.

I smiled at Ryan—a forced smile. Would he even notice? What else had Brand changed while tiptoeing through Ryan's thoughts?

"I will," I said, and then I hugged him. I held onto him like I was never going to see him again—because who knew now? I sure didn't. Would my aunt and this mind controller hurt me or help me? I didn't know. I had to take the risk. If Soria had told the truth, at least Ryan would be safe. I hugged him tighter. He laughed and hugged me back.

"Geez, Caty, you're only going to be gone for the weekend," he said. That didn't sound bad. Like a small trip. I hoped that was all we needed—one weekend—but what would happen if I didn't come back because, at this point, I couldn't imagine a scenario where life returned to its normally scheduled program.

"I know; it just seems like so much longer." I finally let go. "I'll miss you." I barely choked the words out. *I love you. You're the best friend anyone could ever have. Take care of yourself. I'll never forget you.* If I said any of those things, would Brand just go back in and remove them?

"I'll miss you too. Tell Joe and Claire bye for me, and be safe." For a second, he looked at me as if he understood everything going on, as if he wasn't being mind-controlled, as if he were my Ryan. But that look faded quickly enough. He opened the front door.

We were all so focused on Ryan that it took a second to register that someone blocked his path to leave. Eri stood in the doorway, rain dripping from him. Immediately, I wanted to run to him, to hug him and tell him everything would be all right. I hated myself for even thinking that.

He'd let them take Joe and Claire. He had a gun pointed straight at me. But then he didn't really point the gun straight at me; he pointed it just beyond, at Soria. At my aunt.

"Get down," he said. Ryan obeyed him instantly—too quickly. Brand still controlled him. Eri's look at me in that second sent a flood of longing through me. I loved him. He'd saved me. No, he took Joe and Claire. I couldn't let him take the only family I had left. My sudden anger knocked me a little senseless because my next move put me right in between his gun and my aunt.

17

The confusion on Eri's face only lasted for a microsecond before it was replaced with the same void I'd seen in Ryan's eyes. The gun lowered and slipped out of his fingers, hitting the floor with a reverberating clang. Brand moved behind him and shut the door.

"You know him?" Soria asked.

"Yes." With Brand in the room, I couldn't lie to her. "He's Rhaevian." It felt traitorous telling her, but my honesty really didn't matter. Anything I chose not to say, she could learn from Brand. But he didn't add anything more, and although I didn't know why he'd lied to her about my memorysight, I could only hope he'd lie to her about Eri as well. If he heard my silent plea, he didn't acknowledge it.

"Brand, find where they have taken Joseth," Soria said.

He turned to Eri, leaving poor Ryan in a dazed state again. Brand seemed to search intently through Eri's mind. What did he see? Everything? Me wrapped in Eri's arms? Brand's eyes went back to nothingness, except for a brief quick questioning glance in my direction. My cheeks burned, but thankfully Soria focused her attention on Eri and not me.

"He doesn't know where they are," Brand said.

That didn't make sense. Eri had been with them. How could he not know? Soria pulled out what looked like a long steel whip from the side of her belt. It uncoiled and hung quivering in the air, just in front of Eri. "Release him," she said and then flicked her wrist.

Just as Eri seemed to come back to himself, her whip slashed across his arm. I gasped involuntarily as the steel cut into his flesh and lingered there for the briefest of moments. I wished I could be as spaced out as Ryan, who stared at the wall ahead of him, not watching the scene unfold. But I never wanted to be under Brand's control like that. A drop of Eri's blood fell to the floor, and he moaned and shuddered, his knees shaking. There seemed to be more pain than a single slash should have caused. I felt pain just watching him.

He was sent to kill you. Someone spoke to me, but no lips moved. I looked at Brand, but my eyes immediately went back to my aunt. Brand had taken control.

Stay still. I couldn't move my head to shoot a glare at him, so I thought one, along with a lot of other hateful thoughts about getting out of my mind. He didn't reply, but he didn't leave, either. This time I felt it as he wound his way through my mind. The feeling made me nauseous, but I hoped I would at least still be aware of what was happening, not become a mindless zombie like Ryan appeared to be.

"Why are you here?" Soria asked Eri. Instead of answering her, his gaze found mine. I wasn't the only one who noticed something in that look. Soria's head snapped in my direction.

"Catelyn?" she said, and my name sounded like it held her curiosity and disgust at the same time.

I hated him for that look. For the way his gaze piercing into me revealed my follies to my aunt. I hated that he still looked like he wanted me. I hated that I still wanted him so badly I could taste him, feel his touch on my skin. But he took my family, and right now, Joe and Claire were the most important thing. Nothing else mattered but getting them back safely.

"He manipulated me, used me," I said. I'd never thought of helping Eri as being used. I also didn't think he'd pretended to have feelings for me. But we hurt the ones we love. And Eri's betrayal cut deep within me.

His look never changed. "I didn't—" Soria stopped his words with her whip across his already bloody arm. Another gash tore the fabric on the sleeve completely away, revealing the tattoo I'd only seen when we'd been at the lake. Soria grabbed his arm. Her eyes widened with surprise at the series of rune-like symbols around his bicep.

"Brand," she snapped. Eri's eyes glazed over immediately.

I didn't ask her what the symbols meant. I knew they represented his military ranking.

"He's not just Rhaevian," she said. "He's from a high family as well." A small button on the handle of the whip retracted it, and she put the weapon on her belt before taking hold of her gun again. She was going to kill Eri. If I could have moved, I might have reached out and tried to stop her. I froze, not knowing if my own fear or Brand kept me still.

She won't kill him. He spoke into my mind again. He must have been listening to my thoughts. He knew I loved the enemy, but he still didn't say anything. What would his silence cost me?

Thankfully, he was right. Soria didn't shoot. She turned the gun around and smashed the butt into the back of Eri's head. He fell to the ground. With Brand controlling him, he didn't even have a chance to fight back.

"What now?" I asked, trying to keep my eyes off Eri's crumpled body, refusing to look for any sign of movement. Refusing to let the concern that coursed through my body show. Trying to pretend like none of this fazed me.

"We will find Joseth, retrieve your father's ship, and return to Tallis," she said, talking as if we had known each other our whole lives, and this had been her plan from the moment she'd woken this morning. She stopped and looked me up and down. "You have not had much training, have you?"

My blank stare caused her to sigh. "That is disappointing. Well, we can add training you to the list."

It was as if she were getting ready to go to the store. Milk, eggs, and, oh yeah, train Catelyn. I didn't even know what she meant by training me. Maybe she wanted to help me learn to use my ability, but no, Brand had told her I didn't have—what had she called it—"the touch." She had another form of training in mind. She stepped over

Eri like she hadn't just bashed his head, with only a trace of disgust on her face, and I wasn't sure I wanted the type of training she had to offer.

"Where is Trilla?" she asked, her toe poking into Eri's ribs to see if he reacted, but she addressed her question to me.

I'd heard that name somewhere. In a memorysight. "The ship?"

She nodded once, looking at me expectantly.

"No one knows but Joe." I knew what that ship could do. Even if I had a clue where it was—which several weeks of searching didn't provide me—I didn't know if I wanted to turn anything so deadly over to Soria, family ties or not.

"He never told you?" She eyed me, both shocked and dismayed.

"He was trying to protect me. I didn't even know about the ship until the Rhaevians started looking for it. I don't know why my dad came to Earth." I had to appear useful, but I also needed answers to my questions. Questions I should have asked Joe from the start. Questions that now only Soria could possibly answer. These questions terrified me.

"I also don't know why your father came here," she said. Silence followed until a far-off look filled her eyes. "I was sixteen when Aden and Joseth left Tallis. I was at school, training to be a fleet commander, just like my older brother. He was twenty-three and," she paused, "brilliant. He was the youngest fleet commander ever. Your father was a genius. The things he understood about quantum physics, wormhole technology, were amazing. He was amazing. He designed a ship named Trilla for our grandmother. This wasn't just any ship. Behind closed doors, people boasted it would end the war.

"Joseth was his best friend. What Aden did with his mind, Joseth did with his hands. Joseth built Aden's ship for him." She stopped and took a deep breath.

Soria seemed good at covering her thoughts; she was what you might call *composed*. The few times I'd seen her struggle with any emotion at all, she gained her neutrality right back. But each time she spoke of Joe, a brief tremor captured her voice.

"There was a demonstration the day they left. I was the only one in my class with the clearance to attend as I was Aden's sister. We stood on the observation deck of the Clarion—the command ship in Aden's fleet—admirals, members of the Tallisian High Council, even the President had come.

"It was impressive. The ship did more than what it had been designed to do. It could end the war for good."

She smiled as if remembering fondly what had happened. But I knew what the ship had done. I'd seen that moment. She pictured a world being destroyed and reveled in the thought. My stomach lurched, but I held myself still.

"The ship was beautiful, a work of art." She smiled lovingly at the memory.

The ship was a monster. A killer.

"What happened then?" I knew my father's invention had destroyed a planet. I needed to know what he'd done next. I needed to know if my father was as uncaring as his sister appeared to be.

"They disappeared," she said.

"Disappeared?"

"One minute we were basking in the marvel—the next, Trilla was gone. Everyone assumed they were dead. That the power it had taken to tear apart a planet had destroyed them. I refused to believe they were dead.

"I have thought of them every day for eighteen years. Everything I have done has been because of them. And then I came here only to find Aden dead. But not in the way everyone thought." Her words held anger. The kick she gave Eri's semi-lifeless form held more.

"Why did you come here? How did you find Earth?" I asked. Were more Tallisians coming? Was this the invasion Eri had told me about?

"My crew and I were on a mission near Rhaevian space when one of their ships entered an uncharted wormhole. We followed them here."

Was that Eri's ship? Had he led her here? Brand was still inside my head, poking at thoughts. I wanted to yell at him, but he wouldn't let me. The room began to heat up. A trickle of sweat dripped down my neck, and I found myself pulling unconsciously at the strap of my shirt for air. An uncomfortable weight laced with years of lies and newfound truths suffocated me, causing each breath to be heavy, labored.

I was aware of Eri's nearness. It took a lot to keep from looking down at him. *Careful.* Brand's warning echoed in my mind. I needed to say something, do something to cover up what I really felt. Brand put words in my mouth.

"How are we going to find Joe and Claire? Ryan and I came here looking for clues, but we didn't find anything."

If Brand had told the truth, if Eri really didn't know where they took Joe and Claire, then we had nothing to go on.

"We came to see if we could find the missing Rhaevians. We suspected there were at least three left, judging from what Brand found out from the others. We need to find this one's accomplices." Another kick.

I hadn't thought about more being here than the three I knew of. Eri hadn't mentioned much about his mission or who he'd come with besides that he needed to find the ship and that his "aunt and uncle" shouldn't know about me. All his memories had been focused on Rhaev. "What others?"

"They had a base camp, about an hour and a half from here. We gained control of it. That is how we found out to come here."

"You took control of their base? Then the ones you captured, can they tell us where Joe and Claire are?" It couldn't be that easy.

"I'm afraid," she said, "that we were not able to take survivors."

Soria didn't sound upset about the fact they were all dead. I had to keep reminding myself they were at war and people were dying.

"If there are no clues here, then we must go back to the base and see if anything was found there," she went on. "Then I will go and begin the search."

"You mean *we* will go." Joe and Claire were my responsibility. If

I'd trusted them in the first place, the Rhaevians would never have found us. This was all on me.

"What skills did your father and Joseth teach you?"

None. I felt small. "They kind of wanted me to blend in like a real...Earthling." The word sounded bizarre coming from my lips. I might not be from Earth, but it was all I'd ever known. "We didn't talk much about Tallis or the war." Like ever. I tried to keep from glancing at Brand. He'd played in my mind. He knew the truths I didn't say. He remained silent.

"I will go. You will stay at the base," she said more forcefully.

"You can't expect me to sit around while Joe and Claire are in danger." I sounded more like a pouty teenager than the strong fighter I knew she wanted, but I couldn't help it. I would do anything to get Joe and Claire back.

"Catelyn, I have no intention of having you sit around. I'm not sure the motivation behind not training you. I will question Joseth about that when I find him. For now, you have missed years of learning, and I intend for you to start immediately. You will not come because you are weak. But you will learn, and because of the blood that runs in you, I have no doubt you will learn fast, and you will be ready when we need you."

What Soria meant by training me would have made me sick if I already didn't feel nauseous. I tried to stand up straighter. I wasn't that weak. So yeah, maybe I couldn't knock someone out with the butt of a gun or mind-warp control them, but I had an ability that could prove helpful. I could do my fair share to find Joe and Claire. I could use my memorysight.

No. Brand spoke to my mind. I wanted to ignore him, but my head grew cloudy. I went to say something, words lingering on the tip of my tongue. My mouth closed. I tried to speak again. I couldn't fight whatever Brand silently commanded of me.

"Is there a problem?" Soria asked.

Hadn't I wanted to tell her something? My mouth was really dry, and a headache consumed me. I rubbed at the ache that beat in the middle of my forehead. My hands still shook noticeably. And strangely, in addition to being thirsty, I was ravenous. I could use a chocolate bar big time.

I'd always been a little hypoglycemic, although Ryan joked I was "chocoglycemic." I couldn't remember the last time I'd eaten. Not today.

I tried to muffle my audible breathing, but it came too fast, like I'd run a marathon and had to gasp for each breath. Was I having an anxiety attack? No, I didn't feel anxious, just sick, very sick.

"Catelyn, when was the last time you had some sephrum?" Soria asked, her look changing from a stern one to more concern.

Her words made no sense; she might as well have gone back to the language she'd used when I first came into the room.

"Chocolate," Brand said. "When was the last time you had chocolate?" What did that matter? Something strange was happening to me, and he wanted to talk about candy?

I started to sway, and Brand reached out his hand to steady me. A memorysight took over, spotty, just like my real vision seemed to be. Brand was somewhere, and he felt something, but I couldn't tell what. I tried to grasp at the memorysight. I tried to grasp onto Brand. I wasn't successful on either account. My world went black.

18

The cold, damp room smelled strongly of sulfur and sweat. A tall stranger stood over me with an empty syringe in his hand. There was no question where whatever had been in the syringe now resided. My left arm throbbed, but at least my head didn't hurt anymore. I blinked a few times to adjust my eyes to the bright fluorescent light that filled the room and bring Brand into better focus. I remembered him now, my aunt's tall, brooding, mind-invading sidekick.

My mouth tasted like desert sand, but I managed to speak. "What's that?"

"Something to help you feel better," he said. "Is it working?"

I shook my head. In addition to the throb in my arm, I still felt nauseous. I sat up, looking for someplace to be sick, and ended up vomiting all over his shoes. Remarkably, when I stopped retching, I did feel better. Even the pain in my arm stopped.

Brand called to a man standing by the doorway to clean up the mess, and then, just as if I hadn't thrown up all over him, he slipped off his shoes, stepped around the puddle, and picked me up. Shocked, I held on as he carried me from one cot to another on the other side of the room. I didn't have a memorysight, more like déjà vu. His touch felt—familiar.

"It appears you did not need as large a dose," he said in his monotone, inexpressive way.

"It's fine. Sorry about your shoes." He didn't respond, and I remembered he wasn't one for talking much. I remembered a lot of things. Joe and Claire were missing. Eri had come back for me. Soria had knocked him out. The Tallisians had taken over the Rhaev base, where I assumed we must be. And Brand had walked through the passageways of my mind. "What happened to me?" Had he done this?

"You ran low on sephrum."

I waited for him to expand. "And that is?" I prodded.

"Sephrum is a compound Tallisians need to survive. The closest thing this planet seems to have is found in chocolate."

Chocolate? I needed chocolate to survive? The corners of my mouth twitched, and I couldn't suppress a small giggle. "I always knew chocolate was a health food." I laughed. Brand looked at me with questioning concern. I laughed harder. Tears poured from my eyes. I held my side as a stitch settled in. And then I wasn't laughing anymore. The tears in my eyes were a pent-up well of emotions, which chose that moment to seize control.

We weren't alone in the room; others came in and out, doing whatever it was someone did after they killed everyone on a base and took over. They all wore black jackets with the upside-down triangle and circle like I'd seen in the memory of my dad before he'd blown up a planet. I cried more. People looked at me, but no matter how hard I tried to stop, the sobs kept coming in big hiccupping gasps. And then, instantly, they stopped. Brand was back in my mind.

"You're in my head," I said, feeling all sorts of anger he wasn't allowing me to express. He must have only been controlling my outward emotions because inside my mind, I screamed all sorts of profanities at him.

He looked mildly surprised. "Yes."

"Soria said you were safe." My tone accused him of just the opposite. Safe, in my book, meant I didn't have to worry about him stealing my thoughts. I hated knowing someone was in my head. I hated the violating feeling that rolled through me. And yet, each time he'd been in my mind, he'd helped me.

He'd kept Soria from shooting me. He'd kept me from losing

control when Eri appeared. Even now, he'd stopped me from making a scene. How could I argue against what he was doing when his actions always benefited me? What about the other things he'd done while he'd roamed the hills of my mind? He'd kept me from telling my aunt about what I could do. Had that been helpful?

"Why did you lie to Soria? Why did you tell her I don't have the touch?" I asked.

"You don't," he said.

"Yes, I do." He could read minds. How had he missed my memorysight?

"What you can do is not the touch," he said. And then, if possible, he lowered his voice even more. "And it is not Tallisian."

A chill ran through me. "What do you mean?" If I wasn't Tallisian, then what was I? And who was Soria? I had to be Tallisian. There was too much family resemblance for me not to be. Soria *was* my father's sister. "My mother," I said, the certainty dawning on me. My mother wasn't Tallisian.

Brand nodded. "That is information you should keep to yourself."

"Why? What was she?" She couldn't be human, I guessed, or I wouldn't have my memorysight. I pictured my mother. She was the most beautiful woman in the world—and kind and perfect. But the way Brand looked at me, the sudden clenching in my stomach, I knew my mother didn't come from Tallis, and that was bad.

"I know nothing of your mother, but it is best to let Soria assume she was of this world."

Somehow, I knew I had to believe him, even if I didn't want to. It felt like betraying the only family I had by not being honest with Soria. I should trust her. I wanted to trust her. I wanted so badly to trust someone. But I didn't. Not Soria, not Eri, not Joe. I had no one I could trust.

"You can trust me," Brand said.

I scoffed. Trust the guy who could mess with my mind? I should trust him least of all. Except I sort of did trust him. I shouldn't have; I didn't even know what he was: tall, dark, and handsome if I wanted to be stereotypical. A weapon if I wanted to be factual. Still, something about him was safe. But for all I knew, he'd put that thought in my mind. I didn't feel safe with my own aunt; why should I feel safe with her lackey?

"What would happen if they found out?" I asked. I wanted to ask what would happen if *my aunt* found out. Family or not, there may be a good reason my dad flew across the universe and left her behind. I recalled her smiling as she talked about what the ship had done. Then I thought of the memorysight I'd had of the planet being vaporized. No, I couldn't let her know anything about me—at least nothing she viewed as a weakness. There were so many things I needed to figure out. Most importantly, where Claire and Joe were. But slightly less vital included who I was, who my parents were, and, if I was going to be stuck here, who my aunt was.

Brand didn't answer. He'd gone rigid. I looked behind me to see Soria enter the room. Brand wasn't the only one who came to attention. Did I need to stand or salute or something?

"Catelyn," she said. "You are up." She came over, genuinely cheerful, but she didn't touch me. I couldn't help but notice the long black gloves she wore. I shivered. I could never wear gloves; my hands would combust from the pain. I'd tried gloves once, wanting to be memorysight free, thinking if I didn't have actual skin-to-skin contact with people, everything would be normal. I was wrong.

She looked at the floor and noticed Brand's shoeless feet. By the look on her face, I figured he'd broken some regulation.

"I threw up on him," I said, feeling as if I should take the blame. I pointed over to the man cleaning Brand's shoes. He didn't look happy.

"Brand, you are excused," she said. "Go get cleaned up. We leave in an hour."

Brand left without looking at me, but he'd already struck a nerve. I looked at my aunt and wasn't sure I wanted to be left alone with her.

"Where are you going?"

"We have a lead," she said. "There were several sets of coordinates on one of the terminals. Perhaps one will lead to another meeting point. We will start with those."

"And me?"

"You will start your training."

I nodded. I didn't really have much choice. This game needed to play out. For one thing, I had no idea where I was. For another, I got the feeling I couldn't just ask to be sent back home. I was stuck here to be trained—whatever that meant.

APPARENTLY, being the niece of the person in charge doesn't imply royal treatment. Soria called a man to lead me to my room. He looked at me oddly, then nodded to my aunt and turned abruptly, without a word. I had to increase my speed to keep up with him. He wasn't the only one to acknowledge my presence with a fleeting glare. I counted at least ten others in addition to Soria and Brand. Each of them gave me an equal look of disgust. Besides Brand, who looked like a depressed but beautiful Greek God, the others all had a quality similar to me, my dad, and, now that I thought about it, to Joe—higher cheekbones, fuller upper lips, a more heart-shaped face.

On the bright side, he took me to a room of my own. We were in an old mine, which I hoped was safer than it looked—or smelled. But there were doors and lights and more paths than they would have used for mining. He waved his hand several times over a small blue orb on a table and left me with a pile of clothes, all black, and a gesture to get changed. He fled as quickly as possible with his appointed task finished. No "nice to meet you" or "enjoy your stay." Maybe he hadn't had English downloaded into his brain. The door, on some type of electronic slider, shut soundlessly behind him. I surveyed my new home.

There was a cot in the corner with a square pillow and gray blanket. The small blue orb sat on a table next to the cot. A chair in the other corner held the clothing he'd left. Not much, but the room had a door, which shut, and, at the moment, that was all I needed.

I sat down on the edge of the bed and cupped my head in my hands. I didn't have a headache—not one that was physically apparent anyway—but it felt like an overload of information might burst out of my temporal lobe at any moment. I wasn't sure what time it was or how long I'd been out. Everything had happened so fast. My whole life had been a lie. And now I was expected to be trained to become—what? Some type of warrior? For who? People I only knew horrific things about.

I placed my hands on either side of me, gripping the cot in frustration, my head too full to remember why I didn't touch things. A memorysight sparked clearly. None other than Mathis, Eri's fake uncle, had occupied the room sometime before me. He sat on the bed, much like I did, but in his hands, he held a small picture—a child with golden curls smiled up through the frame. Since my memorysight came from the bed and not the man, I couldn't actually feel his emotions, but I saw them in his eyes. A hatred he did not direct at the child in the picture.

I stood, shaking my hands unconsciously as if trying to wipe something off them. Why did that hatred feel directed toward me? I looked wearily at the cot. The memory forced me to ask a question I'd been trying to avoid. War was bad for both sides, but was there an actual good side in this war? And if there was—was I on it?

I remembered Eri's face when he'd told me about the war. About the things the Tallisians did. Had he told me the truth—or just what he'd grown up believing? I knew what I'd seen in his memories. I'd never doubted my memorysight before, but since meeting Eri, I doubted it more and more. And there was also the fact I'd known my parents and Joe and Claire my whole life. They may not have told me about my heritage—or theirs—but it would have been pretty hard to act out every fake thought, every fake feeling, for eighteen years. They were all truly good people, and they were Tallisian—at least my dad and Joe were. I wasn't sure where my mom came from or if I'd ever know the truth.

I was broken.

I walked over to the pile of clothes left for me and stripped off my own shorts and top. The clothing was simple, a short-sleeved crew neck shirt and fitted but comfortable pants. The material felt like a mixture of cotton and Lycra, and the minute I slipped into it, my body temperature regulated, calming the shivering cold I'd begun to feel. I looked at the long gloves with two small blue circles around the top and left them on the chair. I couldn't bring myself to put them on.

The shoes were tight so I pulled my own sneakers back on instead. I was tying the laces when the knock came. Scrunching my eyes closed, I willed myself to get it together.

Brand stood on the other side. Relief at seeing him still here flooded through me. I didn't understand the emotion. I couldn't trust him. I'd trusted Eri, and that had turned out disastrous.

Brand looked at me but didn't say anything. When you can read people's minds, you don't need to ask what they're thinking. He motioned to the gloves. "Put those on."

"Why?"

"Everyone wears the gloves."

"You don't."

"You need to wear the gloves," he said wearily as he looked down the corridor both ways. Why would someone with his ability ever be nervous of anyone or anything? Not that I'd seen him interact with a lot of people, but I'd seen him nervous before—around Soria. There had to be some reason he followed her, though I couldn't guess why. Maybe I made him nervous because of our family connection. Even though logic screamed he wasn't safe, my intuition wanted to side with him. Not sure which to believe, I decided to see just where I stood with Brand.

I left the gloves untouched. "I don't want to."

"The gloves show rank and honor. Tallisians wear them as a sign of respect." He stopped and looked at me, that cold, deep stare that went straight through me.

"I don't like gloves. They make my hands itch." I tried being truthful.

"All the more reason for you to wear them. You don't want to stand out. Put them on."

And now I knew why I needed to put the gloves on. For the same reason I went along with Brand, not letting anyone speculate on the other half of my heritage. The looks I'd gotten from pretty much everyone told me the people here didn't trust me. I had to be all-Tallisian to them if I wanted to fit in. I planned on listening to Brand, but the opportunity to test him remained.

"Make me," I said, looking up at him. He was almost a full head taller than me. I wondered if he had violent tendencies. Maybe pushing his buttons to see what made him tick wasn't such a good idea. But I had to know. From now on, I had to question every person I ever met because it was the only way of knowing who or what they truly were. I could have touched him. If I reached for him now, I might be able to see a memorysight, but after I'd just given him every reason to slap me upside the head and force me to put the gloves on, I decided not to press my luck.

Brand looked at me, those dark eyes pulling me in. Thankfully, he turned out not to be a hitter. Another fact about controlling people's minds—it's a lot easier than resorting to physical violence. "Put your gloves on," he said again.

This time I obeyed. I had no choice.

I DIDN'T HAVE to worry about having a language downloaded into my mind. I got a shiny tube of interpreter bacteria pumped into my ear canal. It hurt like—like bugs crawling in your brain should hurt.

"Why this and not just downloading the language?" I asked Soria as I rubbed my ear, wishing the wet-willy feeling would go away. There had to be a less disgusting way.

"Not all spoken languages are as easy to download as English." She switched from English to the more Slavic-sounding language she'd spoken earlier. I heard the words I shouldn't know, but this time my mind registered their meaning immediately.

"Wow," I said. As much as I still hated the idea that some type of bacteria had just camped out in my brain, it was kind of cool. I wanted to hear her speak more, but I didn't know what to say. There was something I wanted to ask, something I needed to know—well I needed to know everything, but this was something more. Something important—something to do with Eri, but I couldn't remember what.

"What did you do with the Rhaevian?" The word didn't sound normal coming from me. I wanted to say his name. No—I hated saying his name out loud. I felt relieved I wouldn't have to deal with him ever again—didn't I? Should I have been sad? I noticed Brand staring at me—he sure did that a lot. But no, I wasn't sad about Eri.

Part of my mind fought through reminding me that I did want Eri. Brand was stronger. My emotions did exactly what he wanted me to do.

"We got what we could out of him; unfortunately for him, that wasn't much."

Panic rose through me. Had she killed Eri because he didn't tell her what she wanted? What about his status? Why did she even bother bringing him with us? Or maybe she'd left him dead at his house. My head screamed all sorts of things at me, but as I tried to formulate what Eri's fate may have been, images of Ryan started to take over.

"What happened to Ryan?" I asked, still thinking I should feel something about Eri but not being able to.

"Brand took him home. He sufficiently wiped that last little scene from his mind," Soria said. "He's fine."

My eyes locked with Brand's, and immediately, I turned away

and bowed my head in slight inclination toward Soria—not my own doing. "Thank you." Not my own words.

Her eyes lit up. Once again, I'd done something right—because of Brand. I hated feeling like a puppet in his show. Every time he went into my mind, he seemed to help me, but I couldn't stop mentally adding to his running toll. What would he expect from me in return? I glanced at him out of the corner of my eye and then felt foolish. He still watched me, but of course he wasn't controlling my mind. Soria would never let him do that. What was I thinking?

"We may be gone for a few days," Soria said, and my attention went back to her. "Adamos will begin your training."

I noticed a man standing by us for the first time. He was tall, with dark hair starting to gray, but he didn't look old. He looked big. Not as tall as Brand, but more like a brick wall. He smiled when our eyes met, which I hadn't expected, but this wasn't a pleased-to-make-your-acquaintance smile. It was more like a prepare-to-be-obliterated smile. I couldn't bring myself to smile back.

Listen to him. There was Brand in my head again. Even when he spoke in my mind, his voice held a definite inflection. He wasn't telling me to listen to Adamos because he would train me well. He was telling me to listen to him or else. Looking at the tank of a man in front of me, I had no shortage of imagination on what *or else* meant.

19

I followed Adamos from the main room we'd been in, through a long, brightly lit corridor, past my room, into another space that bordered on enormous. It was bigger than any room I'd ever been in, bigger than I imagined a concert hall or professional sports stadium. If there was an opposite reaction to claustrophobia, that is what I felt when I stepped into the room.

I could see to the other side only because of the faint lights at the far end, though I couldn't make out much more. My gaze followed the wall nearest me, up and up and up. Blue lights, like the one in my room, lined the wall to a certain height and then faded into nothing, not a top, not a ceiling, just blackness.

"What is this place?" I asked.

"The space room," Adamos said.

"Space room?"

"For people who are born off-world." Even though he spoke in what I assumed was Tallisian, his intent was clear. He spoke down to me like I was a child, making me feel small. He didn't elaborate on what he meant as if I should have a clue. I didn't push. Brand said to listen to Adamos, so I decided to keep all my questions to myself for the time being, especially the one that kept pushing into my thoughts. Why did my aunt pick him to train me? Was he the best? Was he the only one available? Or did choosing him open some insight into the type of person she really was? Maybe his harsh tank exterior was just a façade—maybe not.

Wasting no time with small talk, Adamos moved to the wall near the doorway. He grabbed two long sticks, which looked like broom handles.

"Your staff," Adamos said, throwing the stick at my feet.

I bent to pick up the staff, and he dealt a blow against my spine. I fell to the ground, the air expelling from my body.

"Never take your eyes off your opponent."

I trained my eyes on him. Was he insane? He circled around me. Would he strike again before I regained my breath? The first gasp of air stung, but soon the relief spread through my body. I moved to my feet, clutching the staff in both hands. He swung again. This time I moved my staff up to protect my body. It would have done the job if the sheer force of his strike hadn't made me stumble backward. The moment I staggered, he swung again, right below my knees, knocking me off my feet.

I looked up at the blackness above me. Where were all the stars? My thoughts floated away, replaced by pain. If there had been any stars, they would have been spinning for sure. I'd kept my breath, but my head took the brunt of the fall. If the floor hadn't been semi-padded, my skull would have most likely cracked open.

"Keep your feet planted firmly on the ground. Do not give your opponent leeway." My vision blurred and, for a few seconds, there appeared to be two of him standing above me. Four cruel eyes glared down on me. I waited until he came into focus before trying to move. He kicked my ribcage, and I rolled to the side, scrambling to get away from him. Each kick came so quickly, I never had a chance for a memorysight to form, but I felt anger and hatred pouring from him all the same.

"You must learn to react quickly. You would be dead by now."

So much pain ran through me that it just now sunk in—these were my lessons. Had Brand advised me to listen because he knew of this training method? He could have given me a bit more warning. I rose on my hands and knees, following lesson one and not taking my eyes off Adamos. Each move sent a sharp burst of pain across my ribs. He kicked me again, right in the stomach. Blood dripped from my mouth. No matter how badly my aunt wanted me trained, this couldn't be what she intended. This wasn't training. This was torture.

"Why are you doing this?" I could barely speak.

"You are weak. I was told to make you strong." His words filled the air with bitter disgust.

His leg came again, and I rolled past his kick toward my staff, and then it was in my hands, but the pain was too much, and I couldn't stand. He kicked me in the chin. My teeth sliced into my tongue, my mouth filling with blood. I rolled to my stomach, trying to spit out the bloody saliva to keep from choking.

"Get up," Adamos said.

I couldn't. I hoped his next strike would knock me out. Could you still feel pain if you were unconscious? Where was Soria? Why wasn't she stopping this? She wouldn't. No one would. No one except the boy who could speak to my mind. I'd said a lot of things to him in silence. He'd not acknowledged any of them. It was ridiculous to even try, but I had no choice.

Brand. Brand. Brand. I tried to listen, but... I coughed up more blood. This was pointless.

What's wrong? Brand's voice rang through my head.

I had to be delirious, imagining Brand was responding to me. He was with Soria. They'd probably left by now. How long had I been beaten senseless? Enough to hear voices.

Catelyn? I heard him again, but I didn't answer. My mind was playing tricks on me. I hadn't really called him—and even if I had been able to, it wasn't like someone here would care about me. I'd seen the way they'd all looked at me. I couldn't trust anyone here.

I was alone.

The blackness took me in first. Adamos still yelled at me to get up. He kicked me again. Pain came, but I detached myself from it. His voice seemed farther away and then nothing.

I GASPED Eri's name when I woke. I'd been dreaming, wanting him to be there and wrap me in his arms. I sat up and noted that nothing hurt. My hand went to my chin, feeling for my jaw to be dislocated, feeling for some trace of pain, but there was none. It had been a dream. My hopes rose. I blinked several times and looked around. I was still in the space room, and my gloves were covered in blood. Eyes stared into mine, but not Eri's eyes. I began to sink again.

"You should forget him," Brand said.

"How?" Couldn't the mind reader understand I would if I could? He didn't answer. "What happened?" I asked that a lot.

"You had your first training."

"Where is Adamos?"

"Soria is speaking with him. He went too far," Brand said. *Even for her tastes.*

I looked up sharply. "What does that mean?" I asked.

Brand seemed angry. He didn't answer me. It was time to use my memorysight to get some answers. I reached out to him. He stepped back—glowering.

"I need answers," I said.

"You need to keep your head down and follow orders."

"Your orders?" I asked. Maybe he wasn't trying to help me. Maybe he only saw me as someone lower than him on the command chain.

"Catelyn," Soria said, walking into the room. "I see you are better."

I nodded. I expected her to tell me Adamos had been punished, that she was sorry for what happened to me. She didn't.

"I hoped you would be able to adapt more quickly to Adamos's style. But not to worry, Brand will be your new trainer. At least that way, I can be sure nothing is damaged internally." She didn't seem to feel bad that Adamos had beaten me. I had the strange feeling she believed my lack of being able to defend against him was my own fault.

"You do need to exert yourself." Her disappointment rippled all around me. Did she really think I hadn't tried?

"I'll try harder." My voice. Brand's words.

"I know you will," she said, smiling.

She turned to Brand. She held something in her hand, and her finger rubbed it almost absentmindedly. "I can count on you to make sure she learns the things she needs to."

He bowed his head, but his eyes never left her hand even as she walked out of the room.

I didn't say anything to Brand for a long time. Even though we were alone, I moved closer to him so I could whisper. I didn't want to get either of us in trouble, but I had several things to say to him. "Stay out of my head."

"I'm not in your head."

I'd felt him when he was in there, even if I was sure he'd been in my mind more than I could remember. I didn't feel him just now. "Not now," I said. "But you have been. I know when you are in here." I tapped my finger next to my temple.

"That is not possible." He seemed intrigued. A slight breeze blew across my brain.

"Get out," I said.

He complied quickly. "We should start your training." He went back to his robotic gaze.

"Why don't we start with some answers?"

"Not now."

"Yes, now."

"I could make you forget you even have questions to ask."

I glared at him. If I did what he wanted, he wouldn't force me? I hated to tell him it was pretty much the same thing. But without him in my head, at least I would know I was myself.

"When?" I asked.

"You'll know."

"Will you at least tell me why I'm not hurt?" It would have taken days to heal from the thrashing Adamos had given me.

"I healed you. Pick up your staff." He pointed to my weapon and made it clear he wouldn't discuss anything but training with me at the moment.

I glared for a minute longer. Just do what he says, I told myself, and then you'll get your answers. Remembering my earlier fight clearly enough to hold fast to those lessons, my gaze never left him. I stood just far enough away that if he swung, he would most likely miss me. I waited for him to say something, to make a move. After about five minutes of staring each other down, I broke.

"What do you want me to do?" I asked.

"You're nervous."

"Yes." *Wow, you're so perceptive.* The look he gave me said he'd heard me, but how? I hadn't felt him in my head. Another question to add to the list: What exactly could Brand do?

"You should never let your opponent know what you are feeling —hate, anger, nervousness, these are all things that can be used against you. They are weaknesses that give your opponent the upper hand," he said. "To win, you must give nothing away."

"You must win all the time." The sarcasm dripped from my voice. Brand showed his emotions less than anyone I'd ever met. Even the few times I'd seen his face change, I could only guess at his thoughts. Maybe that was the purpose, a mind game of hiding your emotions until your opponent slipped up.

Brand stiffened. "No, not always," he said. And there it was, his moment of weakness, an anger barely visible in his voice, but there. I used it. I swung my pole at him. It hit him in the arm hard enough to hurt my own hands but not enough to even make him flinch.

Brand answered back, his own pole angling down and hitting just below my knee, knocking me off my feet and onto my back. It was a familiar scenario and hurt plenty, but I wasn't about to let him go all Adamos on me. Instantly I was back on my feet.

I held the staff in front of me, and we circled each other. This slower method of fighting was much more effective. I followed Brand's movements and mimicked his footwork. He struck at me, and I parried his blow.

"Good," he said. "Try keeping your feet planted firmly on the ground when you strike. It will give you better balance."

I nodded and struck again, doing as he instructed. He barely stopped my blow, and not because he gave me the upper hand. I smiled. Brand needed to teach Adamos how to be a trainer. I got off a few more decent jabs before losing my concentration. I'd turned from blocking a strike to see Adamos standing in the doorway. Brand struck again, and his staff crashed down on my head.

The intensity of the blow made me drop my staff. One hand flew up to my head in time to feel a trickle of blood seep through my hair. Adamos smiled as he walked away. Brand came to my side. One of his hands steadied me, the other cradled the back of my head. I don't know if I felt him go into my head; an intense pounding made me unsure of anything. He seemed to be looking inside of me, but this time there wasn't blankness in his eyes. The pain left, as well as any memorysight I might have had at his touch.

"I'm sorry," he said, dropping his hands. I wasn't sure if his apology was for knocking me out or for going into my head. It didn't matter. I knew how I'd been healed earlier.

"You made the pain go away."

He nodded.

"How?" He'd barely even touched me.

"The mind is a powerful thing. So many of our physical ailments come from our thoughts, from the way our mind responds to pain. I just convinced your mind it was healed. Your body responded the way it believed it should."

"When you go into someone's mind, what exactly do you see?"

"Everything."

"Everything?" I couldn't fathom that.

"I see all your memories, all your thoughts, everything you think and feel—I see," Brand said.

"You're kidding, right?" How could a person even process that?

"You can't alter a person's thoughts if you don't know them," he stated as if he had no qualms about what he did to people—what he'd done to Ryan, to Eri, to me.

"You do know that is completely wrong? I mean, healing a person is one thing, but changing their thoughts is another. Why would you do something like that?" His power disturbed me so intensely, and yet deep down, I couldn't hate him. He'd kept Ryan safe. He'd kept me safe. But I knew Soria did not have Brand using his ability to keep people safe.

"There is a war going on. This planet, these people, they know nothing. You have lived here in this little corner of space, free from all harm. You lost your parents, but you didn't have to watch them slaughtered before your eyes, you didn't have to see your sister ripped from your dead mother's arms and watch as they took her away. You didn't have to spend years in a prison camp with a brother who eventually died from the awful conditions. I do what I do to survive. You have no right to judge me."

The pain in his face showed. I'd finally gotten a strong and definitely readable emotion from Brand, and it hurt me as much as it hurt him. I didn't want to invoke any more pain, but there was one thing I had to know. I swallowed hard.

Never in my memories with Eri had I seen the cruelty Brand just described. But standing here, seeing Brand break before me, his pain was not made up. All Eri had shown me was how awful the Tallisians were, never what his own people were capable of. He hadn't told me his people were just as bad as mine. "The Rhaevians did that?" What else had Eri lied to me about?

Brand didn't answer. He tried to control his anger. He obviously wasn't used to sharing this. Why had he? "Your aunt instructed me to train you. We should begin again." The conversation was finished, but he had increased my willingness to learn. I needed to learn to defend myself against them—all of them.

"What do we do now?" I asked. I'd been tired before. Now I

found myself revived and ready. I didn't care if I got hurt. I didn't care if Brand went into my head. All that mattered was learning to fight, learning how to protect myself, how to protect others. For too long, I'd wrapped myself in a bubble, not wanting to see more than necessary. I'd closed my eyes to hide behind my own fears of inadequacy. I didn't want to have to deal with things beyond my control. What I needed now was to take control, to be a stronger person. No more weakness. Never again would I allow myself to be lied to.

"You've fought well, but we need to make you strong," Brand said, going back to his emotionless manner. I nodded. I wanted to be strong.

For the rest of the day, I ran. I did sit-ups. I did push-ups. I attempted pull-ups. I did every strenuous physical exercise Brand could think of until my legs felt like gelatin and my arms tingled with a throbbing pain as if they'd been pounded with a meat mallet.

Brand did everything right alongside me—hardly breaking a sweat while every possible ounce of liquid in my body poured out of me—and when I finally collapsed on the ground after a set of triangle pushups, he stopped his own set and came to sit by me. It hurt to lie on my stomach. I groaned and rolled over to my back. That hurt too.

"You're insane," I said. It even hurt to talk. "Okay, I'm ready for you to work your magic." I didn't think I could handle the pain anymore.

"No," he answered.

In my mind, I gave him a mental lashing. Out loud, I just groaned some more.

"It's for your own good," he said. "When I make pain go away, your body forgets how it is supposed to feel, and it won't strengthen. Striking you before was a mistake, but this is part of your training. In order to be strong, you must go through this."

"But you healed me after Adamos's training," I said.

"I wouldn't consider anything that man did as training."

"But this is?" I didn't mean to compare him to Adamos. Brand had been more than fair to me. I was just sore, and the key to undoing that was two steps away, refusing to help. It was like holding the bottle of Ibuprofen in your hand and not being able to get the childproof cap off. I wanted relief, and I was mad at him for not giving me any.

Brand walked out of the room, leaving me lying on the floor. I hated him. I knew why he left, but still. The cold, hard floor dug into every ache, even with the mat-like material under me. I hurt when I touched anything, but Brand was right. This would make me stronger. And when it did, no one would be able to hurt me again.

My training had begun.

20

Adamos greeted me when I woke up. He stood above me, smugly smiling down. I hated waking to strange faces. The only face I wanted to wake to could only happen in my dreams now. I wanted to close my eyes and go back to those dreams. I didn't hurt in them, and everything was fine.

My life was no longer a dream.

"Hello, Catelyn," Adamos said.

I shuddered. I assumed he hadn't gotten in much trouble for what he'd done, not by the way Soria spoke of my training. That meant I better tread carefully with him.

Every inch of my body hurt. The irritation the gloves caused in my hands spread up my arms, and I wanted to claw my own skin off to be free from them. Right now, though, I just wanted to be free from Adamos. Not taking my eyes off him, I rose to my feet. I wouldn't soon forget that lesson. I stood, locked in a showdown with his hellish gaze.

"Can I help you?" I asked.

"How is your training going?"

"Fine."

He stepped closer, and no matter how strong I wanted to be, his eyes made it clear I was not ready to face him.

Brand? I wasn't sure what had happened yesterday, but I'd called inside my mind, and he'd come. Would he come today? The things he'd taught me were not enough to stop a repeat of yesterday from happening all over again. The way my body ached would give

Adamos supreme advantage over me once more. The dead couldn't get stronger.

"Why don't you show me what Brand taught you?" he said.

I bit down on my cheeks. The staffs were on the far wall and even thinking about walking over to get one, shot pain through every part of me. The muscles in his arms twitched in anticipation. He'd touched me before. Yesterday when he'd kicked me, I hadn't had a memorysight, each kick had been too quick, each blow with a weapon that only revealed his true nature in the pain it brought with it. If we fought without staffs would I see a memory? On a list of people whose thoughts I didn't want to see, Adamos was at the top—bolded, circled, and underlined.

I glanced at the doorway. *Brand?*

Adamos took a step toward me, and I instinctively stepped back. Show no fear, Brand had said. Well, I'd messed up that rule. I was sure Adamos knew how terrified I was.

His perfectly straight white teeth gleamed in the dimly lit room. He took another step. *No fear. No fear. No fear.* But I stepped back again. He struck at me, and I blocked his swinging arm with the palm of my hand. His memory took over.

He was in a room, an office. Behind the desk stood an older man, wearing a black uniform with gloves like the ones everyone here wore, only with two gold stripes around the top. Another person stood behind Adamos. Hatred seared out of Adamos toward the invisible figure.

"Soria," the man behind the desk said. His voice was sharp and squeaky, not like a man of his stature should have. "You will be captaining this mission. Adamos will be your second."

Loathing dripped from Adamos through his silent ratings. *She doesn't deserve this. She's the traitor's sister. She should never have gotten this far. She'll turn just like her brother did.* Out loud, he just gave a brief nod of his head. "Yes, sir."

Adamos jerked out of my grasp. My composure returned fast enough to see his next blow coming but not fast enough to move out of his way completely. My left cheek stung even though his contact was minimal.

I got ready for another whack, but Brand spoke. I never knew such relief could come from hearing his voice. "Adamos, Crase is looking for you."

My would-be assailant stopped mid-punch and turned to glare at Brand. Apparently, Adamos hadn't heard him come in, probably too busy working out a scheme to dispose of my body once he was done with me.

"Your training was ineffective," he said. "Soria expects results. See that you're not so soft on her today."

"Acknowledged," Brand said, bowing his head slightly. Even if Adamos was second in command, I couldn't believe Brand would cower to him so willingly. I wanted Brand to go into Adamos's head and show him just what he could do. I wanted Brand to use his power in the exact way I'd scolded him for using it–to change Adamos. More importantly, I wanted him to tell me what he saw there. Why did Adamos think my father was a traitor?

Adamos moved past us, satisfied for the moment. He didn't look at Brand again, but he looked at me, and a creeping sickness moved in. This wasn't over.

My knees didn't shake until he'd left the room completely. The darkness from him was the exact thing I'd been trying to avoid since my memorysights began. It was worse than I imagined—but then again, real emotions always trumped the ones in a memory.

Brand watched me but didn't move. He didn't pat my back or tell me everything was okay. He didn't wrap his arms around me and hold me—and I wanted him to. No, not him—Eri. Eri had the power to calm me, to keep me from falling apart. Eri wasn't here. He was most likely dead. I bit my lip, trying to keep my tears from falling.

"He is Rhaevian," Brand said. "His one mission is to kill all Tallisians."

I hadn't felt him in my mind, but he knew my thoughts. I hoped I wasn't losing the ability to tell when he invaded my brain. It was my only defense against him. And I needed to defend against him–to defend myself against everyone. Besides, it was Brand who left me all alone in this room. Brand who put me in the position to be confronted by Adamos. He wanted me to hate Eri, but he wasn't innocent himself. It was time to give Brand a piece of my mind—one he didn't already have.

"What difference does that make?" I snapped. "You would rather Adamos kill me?"

"Adamos will not kill you," he said assuredly. He was wrong. Adamos wanted someone to die, and I was the easiest to sacrifice.

"He wants me dead." And not just dead—tortured, broken.

"Did he tell you that?"

"He didn't need to."

Brand didn't say anything, just studied me. Interrogations should be his specialty. He didn't need to talk; all he had to do was look at me, silently, with those eyes, deep, dark, dangerous. I closed my own eyes and tried to feel him in my mind. He was there, going through my memories with a fine-tooth comb. Maybe because he studied me so precisely, I could almost see each thought he looked at. I opened my eyes, and he looked scared and astonished all at once. He'd seen everything now, and not only seen, but taken the time to analyze what he'd found. I should have been angry about what he'd done, but I wasn't. His eyes held the answer I'd been searching for. Brand knew what I was. My first step to knowing the real truth was here.

"You know what I am, don't you?" I asked. "What my mother was?"

He shook his head, but he looked again, with more concentration in his eyes. I let him, even trying to open memories to help him.

"You really can feel that. You can tell when I'm in your mind."

I nodded.

His face paled, and he started to say something, but then he walked over to the rack that held the staffs we'd sparred with the day before.

"What?" I yelled.

Brand tossed a staff to me. He placed one foot in front of the other in a defensive pose and waited.

"What am I?" I snarled through gritted teeth.

"I was instructed to train you, not to converse with you."

He was mad at me? I started to laugh, though not from amusement. He continued to glower.

"You have got to be kidding me." After everything I'd been through, after he trampled through every thought I'd ever had, my most personal memories, he was going to give me the silent treatment?

Brand nodded toward my staff. I looked at it clenched in my hands and then threw it to the ground.

"Pick up the staff," he said.

"No."

"Do it."

We'd had this conversation before. I could challenge him to make me, and he would, and then where would I be? If he had to go in my mind anyhow, why not ask him to do something useful with his skill?

"You're supposed to make me strong. If you want me trained, then train my mind first. Tell me why I can do the things I can. Explain my ability to me. Tell me who I am. You're the mind guy. You want me to learn? Teach me. You have to know I could be stronger if I knew the truth. This is ridiculous. I just found out my whole life has been a lie, and here you are—you know the truth—I know you do—and you're mad at me? You want me to learn? Then teach me—tell me who I am."

"I don't know who you are!"

"Liar." It wasn't a word I used often but was one I'd become too familiar with over the last few days. Was it really surprising Brand would lie to me when so many people I knew and actually trusted already had? Probably not, but it still hurt, maybe even more so now, knowing there was one more person that knew me better than I knew myself and yet refused to share that knowledge.

Brand seemed keen on keeping my abilities a secret. He hadn't even let me tell Soria. But he knew what I could do and why I could do it. I was positive.

"Where was my mom from?" I asked again.

At first, I wasn't mad when he didn't answer. It hurt too much to be mad. A minute passed—then two. He wasn't going to tell me anything. My speech had been in vain. As my mind realized just how exhausting this was, my body remembered its own pain. I moved toward the door. What I needed was to take off these stupid gloves and get a decent rest—not on the floor.

"Wait." It was only a whisper, but I froze. I turned slowly until our eyes were locked onto one another. He looked at me as intensely as before but almost as if he were seeing me for the first time.

"Please just tell me."

"I can't be sure, but..."

I waited. He sighed.

"I have traveled with Soria since I was twelve. I have seen hundreds of worlds, met countless people. Many have abilities, some small, some more important. Some can use their minds for great things; others just have the ability to tell which crops will yield the most nutritional value. Not everyone in every world has an ability, and those who do usually become important to their worlds in one way or another." He took a deep breath. I wasn't sure why he was telling me all this. I didn't need a history lesson right now, just a bit of information about my family tree.

"There are a few gifted ones who prefer to remain recluse. I tell you this so you understand I can't be sure of what your mother was. I only know this, of all the races, and all the abilities, only one group of women can do what you can do." He looked away. I wanted to reach out and see what he thought for myself. When he flinched before my touch, I stopped.

"What can I do?" I asked.

He paused again. Did he not realize his little interludes were killing me? No, it wasn't that. I couldn't read his mind, but he was confused, worried. He looked toward the door of the room. It was the first time his eyes had left me, though they flickered back almost inhumanly fast. He opened his mouth, about to give me the answer, and then shut it again, shaking his head. "It's impossible."

I felt him in my mind. "Stop it. It's not fair. Not if you're going to keep things from me."

You shouldn't be able to feel that. His lips never moved.

Well, I can. I shouted back silently at him.

I closed my eyes and took my own deep breath, not to calm my nerves like he seemed to be doing but to keep myself from wanting to reach out and strangle him. "Brand, tell me." I tried to sound calm, authoritative.

No one else can feel this, can talk like this.

"No one besides who?"

"A Priestess of the Sight," he said reverently.

"Where are the Priestesses of the Sight from?" I asked, nervous and excited at once.

"Darkothia."

Darkothia? Like Brand? "But my dad came here eighteen years ago. And I'll be eighteen next week. Doesn't that mean my mom had to have come with him?"

"Yes, she would have been on Tallis with him."

"Like you, working for them?"

"Yes, like me."

"Then she was on the ship, a technician or something?"

"I do not know why or how your parents came here. That is of no concern. What matters now is you must never tell anyone what you can do. Especially not Soria."

I was a half-Tallisian, half-Darkothian child who was raised as an Earthling. Okay, I accepted that, but why couldn't Brand? He said it like it was the only possible answer, and yet he looked like it was the worst conclusion.

"Why is this bad?"

He gave another nervous glance at the doorway and then a

pleading look toward me. He couldn't expect me to stop asking questions now. Not with the floodgates finally opened.

"We should begin training," he said.

My hand immediately reached for the pole, and all the questions I had were gone. I still knew I had questions but couldn't ask any of them. It was like when I have a memorysight, but this time I saw myself, what I was doing, what I was feeling, but just like I couldn't change a memory, this time I couldn't change my own actions. I held my staff out and attempted to fight.

I was better than the day before, but not much. I blocked the first two of Brand's strikes, but the third one came dangerously close to knocking me senseless. He took my pole and began strength exercises again. The only times we stopped were for water or some awful form of protein crackers. When I finally collapsed on the floor, he let me stay there, but this time he didn't leave the room. Instead, he went to the corner by the door and sat.

21

When you don't see the sun, when darkness or artificial lights are all you know, time takes on a different meaning. There is no longer day or night, only times when you sleep and times when you're awake. I wanted to sleep all the time, but Brand wouldn't let me. Every time I fell asleep, suddenly there he was, waking me to start training again.

It had to have been at least a week since Soria had left. A week without any news, a week of sleeping on the space room floor, a week of eating protein crackers and taking a bitter pill that was a supplement Tallisians needed—the same one chocolate had provided for me until this point. It had been a week of wanting a Snickers bar so badly I thought I would die, discovering so much pain in my body at times I wished I could die, and learning to hate a group of people so badly I refused to die before finding Joe and Claire and avenging my parents.

During the day, Brand kept me occupied with enough physical training I didn't have time to think about anything. And yet, for all the bleeding and bruising my body had endured, it was worse when we stopped. When I trained, at least I was doing something. I felt strong. When the training stopped, I realized how weak I was.

At the end of the week, I finally made it to my room. I didn't make it onto the bed, but collapsing in the privacy of my own quarters lent me a sense of accomplishment that made the hard rock floor luxurious. I wanted to relish that moment, to savor the sweetness. I couldn't.

I'm not sure if it was the fact that Brand was no longer sitting across from me, and therefore possibly no longer in my mind, or because pain and exhaustion took a break from ruling my every thought but, laying on the floor of my room, my mind turned back on.

Brand! He'd stopped me from thinking about everything. Now, I remembered how Eri was before this all happened. I hadn't been able to recall anything good about him when I was awake during training. I also remembered I was Darkothian, that I had as many questions about my mom as I did about my dad. I'd been blind for the past week and now had sight.

Remembering hurt. Knowing if I opened the door and confronted Brand about any of this that he would take everything away again was almost unbearable. I closed my eyes and let the memories come. Joe and Claire and the home they'd given me when I'd lost everything. Soria would find them. She had to. Ryan and the friendship that had sustained me over the last six years. What was he doing now? Wondering why I'd left on some Canadian adventure just weeks before graduation? Wondering why I hadn't come back? Why I didn't bother to write or call? My memories of Eri were the hardest.

I pictured him laughing at the song I belted as we drove down the highway, his eyes sparkling, changing hues with every mood. I thought of his fingers brushing against my skin, his lips tasting mine. How could I think this way about him when we were supposed to be mortal enemies? Brand told me just as many horror stories about the people who had murdered his family as Eri had told me about Tallisians. Who was right?

Here alone, thinking of Eri, my head clear for the first time since I'd lost him, I still wanted him, enemy or not. Our first kiss came to mind—the vision I'd seen. What had that been about? Was it one of my seer powers? Brand would never tell me. Would I ever know why I'd seen such a promising future when the present only showed it as a scam?

Where was Eri? Soria acted like he was too important to kill, but she also said it was unfortunate he didn't have more information. Had they tortured him? Was he somewhere nearby, hurt? Would I ever see him again? Was I only hoping he wasn't dead because hope was all I had? Hope that she would find Joe and Claire. Hope that I might get out of here. Hope that maybe one day I would see Eri again—and we wouldn't only know hatred for each other.

Tears fell to the ground. Would this hurt be with me for the rest of my life? Anytime I thought of Eri—which would be anytime Brand wasn't in my head making him disappear—would I hurt like this?

I crawled to the door and leaned my cheek against the coldness. The way to stop the pain could be just through this wall. The past several nights, Brand hadn't gone more than a few feet away from me. Did he now sit close by? I couldn't imagine him leaving me alone—should I be grateful or hate him for that?

He told me he wouldn't take away the physical pain. He said that was what made me strong, but if I were to ask, would he take Eri away from me? Would he erase every look, every touch, every word? Would he take this pain away? Because it was worse than any physical pain I could ever feel.

I need you, Brand.

He opened my door, picked me up before I could speak, and carried me to my cot. The stubborn side of me wanted to ask if this went against what he'd taught me. If I'd learned anything over the last several days, it was that there was strength in humility. I kept my mouth shut.

Having Brand kneel over me, looking at me with undeniable compassion, made me want to close my eyes and drift into a sleep I wasn't sure I wanted to wake from. Knowing Eri would replace him if I closed them kept me awake. For the longest time, neither of us spoke. Brand stayed, inches away, stroking my hair from my face. I didn't know if I had memorysights with him or if he was taking them away as fast as they happened. I didn't care. It was soothing, hypnotic, but while I didn't have a memorysight, my memories didn't leave either. I tried several times to broach the subject of what I wanted, but no sound moved past my lips.

"You're not supposed to love him," he finally said.

I nodded.

"You should hate the Rhaevians by now." A frustrated concentration crossed his face.

"I do." That was true. I hated all the things I'd learned about them. I hated the vivid mental pictures from Brand's story. I imagined what he must have seen, what he must have felt. My intuition was strong enough to know the people who'd done those things were the enemy. If I truly was half Darkothian, then it wasn't just Brand's hurt consuming me, but the hurt of my own people as well.

I hated the Rhaevians. I hated that Joe and Claire were with Eri's people. People who could do horrible things to them. People who had killed my parents–killed Brand's parents. If Brand had anything to do with the thoughts in my mind, then he'd done his job. I hated the Rhaevians—all but one.

"It would not be good if your aunt found out," he said.

I'd seen Soria's eyes when she spoke of the Rhaevians. He was right. If she knew how I still felt, even after learning the truth about my parents' death, my life would be in danger—and Eri's too.

"Is he alive?" I asked.

Brand nodded.

"She would kill both of us if she knew, wouldn't she?"

He nodded again.

"Make me forget him," I said.

"You would want that?" Brand frowned.

I nodded slowly. "I'm supposed to hate him, but I can't. I saw the future once. With him. I saw what my life could have been like. How can I forget him when I can't forget that?"

Brand stiffened as my tears started to fall.

"I would rather forget I ever wanted him," I went on, "than live with the fact that my wanting him will hurt him."

"Soria will hurt him anyway."

I hated his honesty. I hated knowing he was right.

"But I wouldn't have to know if I didn't remember him." How had I become so selfish? I hated myself but still asked. I couldn't do anything for Eri but worry—and possibly make his fate worse. Wouldn't this be better? Maybe Brand could find a way to erase Eri's memories of me as well. If our relationship never existed, we would never be able to hurt each other.

"That life with him. Would you want that?"

I nodded without hesitation. Did Brand know something? Had that really been the future, not just a mirage?

"Even if it meant losing everything else you love."

The hope left. "Why? Why would that be the price?"

"You don't understand the war. You can't. It's too old, too much hate." His eyebrows furrowed.

"But my futuresight? What was that?" I needed hope, even if only just a shimmer.

"It was wishful thinking. That's all." He looked away from me. So much for hope.

"But he saw the same thing." I don't know why I argued with Brand like I wanted his blessing or something. It wasn't like he told me anything I didn't know. Maybe I hoped he would tell me what I'd seen would come true. That seeing the future set it in stone.

He didn't.

"If we can never be, if that future can never exist, then why are you asking me permission? Why won't you just go in my mind and take him away?" I stood and paced the room, frustration raging through me. "Just make me forget."

"No." He almost whispered.

"Why not?" I yelled, throwing my hands in the air.

Brand stood from the bed and stopped me mid-pace. He grabbed both of my shoulders, forcing me still, forcing me to look at him. "Catelyn, knowing makes you strong. There are many things in my life I would want to have erased, but if I let them go, then I would not remember who I was," Brand said. "Erasing a moment or two—that is one thing, but..." He stopped and closed his eyes as if he didn't want to say anything else. "If I take away more, you will change. I won't do that."

It sounded so true, so sincere, and yet he had already changed me. He'd already been in my mind. He'd let me go a whole week without thinking about anything but my training. I didn't know what he'd done. I didn't know what thoughts were mine or what I might have forgotten already. He wanted me to stay the same, but what did that mean? Was I to be the Catelyn I was before or after crossing his path?

I didn't need to say anything for him to respond. "I'm sorry. I just thought it would be easier for you if you only had to concentrate on your training. But we're here, having this conversation. I didn't take anything away from you; I just made you not think about it. You are the same Catelyn."

"No, I'm not." I didn't say this because I was mad at him. Brand tried to help in the only way he knew how. But I would never be the same Catelyn. I couldn't be. "I can't do this." I sighed, shrugging out of his grasp.

"Yes, you can."

"How? I don't know anything about myself, about my world, about the universe, and most of the things I do know I wish I didn't."

"Would you be happy if I took all those things you know away?"

I shrugged but shook my head in defeat. "No. There is only one thing that will make me happy."

Brand turned away, but I caught the change on his face before he moved from my view.

"He's here, isn't he?" Had Eri been this close the whole time?

Brand's head tilted slightly.

"Take me to him," I demanded and pleaded at once.

"I don't have that type of clearance."

"You can control people's minds. How can you not have clearance? Why is honoring the chain of command so important to you? They don't even treat you well." Enough people, including

Adamos, commanded Brand, yelled at him, looked down on him, but I didn't understand why. How could the one person who could make everyone do his will be so afraid? I couldn't have him be scared. I needed him to get me to Eri.

"It's because..."

"Because what?" I softened my voice. Now wasn't the time to be pushy. Brand had secrets. I still didn't know why he insisted I keep my own secrets so hidden, but it had something to do with his, something about us being Darkothian.

"I'm not like the others here on the base." His shoulders slumped as he sank down onto the cot.

"Because you're Darkothian?" I asked, sitting next to him but not daring to touch him.

He nodded.

"Why does that matter? Why is it so bad that we're Darkothian? Why can't you just go into every one of their minds and make them do what you want?" The last question was full of anger for all the things I had no control over. Even earlier tonight, I'd chastised Brand for controlling minds, and now I wanted him to. How had I come to this?

He leaned forward, and his long braid fell to the side, exposing a scar that ran down his spine and disappeared under the collar of his shirt.

"What is that?"

He tried to answer, but he couldn't seem to come up with the words. I hesitantly reached out my hand to him. Maybe trying to see would be easier on both of us. He didn't take away the memory this time; instead, he led me to exactly what I needed to see.

He was younger, just a few years, maybe eleven or twelve. And he was scared—for his life. He hid in the shadow of a room, curled in a corner, trying to melt into the blackness. The door opened, and a silhouette appeared.

"Are you ready to come out yet?"

I knew Soria's voice. She held the same small device I'd seen in her hand here. She pressed her thumb down on the button, and the pain came—ripping, tearing, death-like pain. Agony coursed through his body, and with my hand touching the scar, it pulsed into me. A sudden, sickening realization came with that pain. Brand didn't do what he did out of loyalty to my aunt; he wasn't her lackey–he was her slave.

22

"It wasn't the Rhaevians who killed your family, was it?" He'd never once blamed the Rhaevians. I'd just always assumed. But I couldn't shake what I'd just seen, what Soria had done.

He shook his head, then sighed, and then, his eyes never leaving mine, the pain left my hand. The memorysight melted away.

"What are you doing?" I asked.

"I'm taking back my memory."

"Stop."

The cruelness I'd just experienced hung in my mind like a cloud that would be whisked away with the smallest breeze.

"What exactly did she do to you?"

Brand looked like he would close up for a moment. He didn't seem to want to talk, but he did. "There is a device implanted along my spine that, when activated, secretes a poison. When given in small doses, it causes severe pain, when given in full strength, it will kill me."

I thought of the scar on Brand's neck. "But how did they do that—why didn't you stop them?" Brand could silence me when I wanted to speak, make me walk when I could no longer move; he could make me forget old memories, change new ones. How could a person who could do all that let someone surgically implant a death device on their spine?

"How old were you when you first saw?"

He was talking about my memorysight. "Just before my twelfth birthday."

"We are born with our abilities, but most of them only show themselves as we mature. Some may lay dormant for years until another of our kind opens them for us. The Tallisians came to Darkothia in the time of my great-grandfather. At that time, we used our gifts for healing. That's the reason the Creator gave them to us. That was all we could do. We were never meant to control minds. With a Priestess of Sight, a healer could use the silent speech." He stopped and looked at me. I nodded in understanding. I'd been talking to him in our minds more and more this week. He went on, "But he couldn't read minds; he couldn't do the things I can do.

"Darkothians were once a trusting people. When the Tallisians came and offered us the stars in exchange for the help of our healers, the opportunity was too great to pass up. They kept their promise, they took my—our—people to the stars, but as slaves.

"My great-grandfather was on that first ship of people. The Tallisians studied him and did things to him, things that would increase what he could do. He was one of three who survived the process, and when the scientists were done with them, they could do more. The Tallisians changed them genetically, and then they were brought back to Darkothia and bred.

"The genetics were weak in the first line. In my family, only my grandfather retained all the abilities his father had been programmed with, but my father and five of my uncles were stronger. By the time my cousins and I were born, the Tallisians had exactly what they had originally hoped for. I'm not just a healer—I'm a weapon."

Not sure what else to say, I asked, "And the device?" I'd always hated telling people my parents were dead, waiting for their awkward reply. Here was a story a million times worse than anything I'd had to live with, and I was the one who had no reply. How do you say "I understand" to something like that?

"All Darkothian males are implanted when we turn five. The Tallisians keep track of each family that stems from the original line, but they take no chances. Using the poison is an effective way for them to weed out males with no abilities. They are using Darkothia as an "evolution of the greatest" project. You either prove yourself useful to their cause, or you die."

"So, everything has been a lie." My stomach wanted to be sick, but I kept it down. "My kind did this to you."

Brand shook his head. "It was the Tallisians. Not you."

"I am Tallisian," I said, feeling the bitter taste that word now left in my mouth.

"You're more Darkothian," Brand said with fierce pride.

I thought back to the memory I'd seen in Adamos's head. Maybe Brand was right. I might have Tallisian blood in me, but I was not one of them. Maybe my father wasn't either. "When Adamos thought of my father as a traitor, what did he mean?"

"Your father was a great leader on Tallis. When he left, when he took the ship that..." Brand paused, and I nodded. He didn't need to tell me more of what the ship could do. "The ship itself was something no one had ever imagined. Part machine. Part living tissue. It was beyond artificial intelligence. It was beyond anything anyone had ever known. It was beyond power. It was enough to make the Tallisians gods among all the races. To have that power in their grasp and then lose it—your father became the most hated fugitive on Tallis.

"That is why Soria needs you so much. If she brings you back, ready to fight the cause, it would be proof the rumors are wrong. She can spin his leaving as a horrible accident, turn him into a martyr, and she can gain the respect she lost the minute his ship blinked out of existence."

"Why would he have left?" All these answers and they just created more questions.

"I don't know why your father came here. We may only know if Soria finds Joseth." He said it like that was the last thing in the world he would want to have happen.

"What?" I asked. What wasn't he saying?

"Joseth knows where the ship is."

I frowned. The ship. The weapon. Soria wasn't looking for Joe and Claire to save them. She wanted the ship. Everyone wanted the ship. And then I knew. I knew why my dad had never said anything to me about all this. I knew why we had found bits and pieces of the ship scattered around the desert.

"My dad didn't want the ship to be found," I said.

Brand looked at me, and I felt him go into my mind. He looked for a memory and then nodded. "I think you're right."

"What am I supposed to do now?" How could I keep training when the people I'd vowed to hate were now my own people? How could I hope Soria would find Joe if finding him meant finding the ship? Or did the Rhaevians who took him already know where the ship was hidden? What would happen if anyone found it?

Brand brushed the strand of hair falling in my eyes behind my ear. His eyes held so many more emotions than I'd ever seen in them. His fingers brushing against my cheek were warm and familiar. I thought I would have another memorysight, but if I did, he took it away just as quickly.

"Nothing," he said.

"What do you mean?"

"There's nothing you can do. You have to just keep training and learning. You have to forget everything I just told you."

"I can't do that," I protested. "I can't just act as if I want to be Tallisian."

"You don't have any choice."

"Why? Why can't you just go into Soria's mind before she has a chance to use that thing on you? Why can't you just stop them, and we can leave?" It wasn't possible. If Brand could, he would have. There was more to the device then he'd told me.

"Soria's is the one mind I can never go into," he said. "The master is implanted with a device as well. You can feel me in your mind because of what you are. She can feel me because of her device. The minute I go into her head, she will know and be able to block me. We are linked like that."

"But you could go into Adamos' head, make him stop her. Take control of the others here, couldn't you?" Soria couldn't fight against her whole crew if Brand controlled them.

"I could," he admitted. "But..." He closed his eyes and looked away.

"What?" I asked gently.

"I defied Soria once before. I went in her head, and I almost paid with my life. She has new precautions now. If I ever defy her again, she will...she has my sister."

"Your sister?" I said, feeling the pressure close in on me.

"Jacia. She's seventeen. Soria has her. I'm allowed to see her once a year, just to know she's all right. She is always brought to me, so I never know where Soria keeps her, but I do know if anything ever happens to Soria, the orders are to kill my sister."

"But what if something happens that's not your fault?"

"It doesn't matter."

"But—"

"Catelyn, it's better this way. Not only will I never defy Soria, but she also knows I will defend her with my life."

Any words would be inadequate, so I found myself putting my arm around him. He stiffened at my gesture, but then he allowed me to rest my head on his shoulder, and his own arms came around me.

A strange thing happened. There were no memories, not even ones I knew he was taking away. The only thing between us was a sense that somehow Brand and I were linked, that together we could do more, be more. I liked the way that made me feel. I feared it as well.

23

I dreamed about Eri. I couldn't see him—I couldn't see anything—but I could smell cinnamon and cloves. It seemed like years since I'd been surrounded by that scent. His hands ran down my arms, his lips nuzzled my ear, but when I turned, Eri wasn't holding me, caressing me. Brand was.

I awoke with a start. Brand lay on the cot next to me, his arm brushing up against me, but nothing more. Nothing like I'd just dreamed. His breathing was long and deep, and he looked at peace for the first time. I pushed myself up gently to avoid disturbing him. He sighed once and rolled onto his side.

Nothing had happened. We talked. About his sister. About Joe and Claire. About how Soria was my only hope of ever seeing them again and all the ramifications that her finding them would bring. And then we must have fallen asleep. Nothing happened, but the dream seemed so real. There was a part of me that wanted it to be real. It would be so convenient to use Brand to help me get over Eri, but that is exactly what I would be doing. Using him.

I moved away from the cot and paced the small room. I hadn't spent much time in here, but my clothes were still in a pile over in the corner. I picked up my shorts. My cell phone was in the front pocket, dead. I wouldn't be able to get service in the mine anyhow, and who did I plan on calling?

I pushed the phone back into the pocket, and a piece of paper scraped across my fingers. I pulled it out and unfolded it, seeing the forgotten list I'd found in Eri's room. Brand snored softly. I sat on the chair next to the nightstand and read the list again.

CATELYN

*Doesn't like to touch things but does it to help people

*Does good acts almost unconsciously

*Smile is infectious

*Bites her bottom lip when nervous

*Sings along to the radio

*Is loyal to those she claims as family

~~*I'm falling in love with her~~

I ran my hand over the blue orb on the stand next to me twice. It brightened enough to keep the room in shadow but allowed me to interpret that final scratched-out sentence. I stared at the words, reading them over and over, at first confused, then hopeful, then frustrated.

"What is that?" Brand asked.

Tears brimmed in my eyes. Brand sat up on the side of the cot. He didn't have to ask. He could have gone into my head and seen everything. We'd discussed that invasion of privacy last night. Now, he waited for me to respond.

I handed the paper to him. "I found this at Eri's house."

He scanned down the list. His eyes must have settled on that last line because he squinted for a second to make out the crossed-out words. He shook his head and sighed.

"What?"

"You know this can never be."

I leaned forward and took the paper away from him, carefully folding it back up. I didn't answer as I put it into the pocket of my pants.

"What are you thinking?" he asked, his frustration at not just being able to get inside my head and find out was written on his face.

"Why can't we be? Why can't he and I just be us? Why do we have to be Tallisian or Rhaevian? My parents were not from the same world."

"And they had to leave everything they knew to come here—and even then, they weren't safe. You know who he is. You saw the markings. He's from one of the high families. He's probably got his whole life planned out for him, and I guarantee you are not part of those plans."

His honesty didn't make it hurt any less.

"What did you see in his mind?" Brand had been in there. He could tell me what Eri thought.

"It doesn't matter," he said flatly.

Of course it mattered. Because I'd seen a vision where we clearly were each other's plans.

"He is still Rhaevian. You are still Tallisian."

"You said I wasn't."

"You know what I mean. Bloodlines run deep for these people. The two of you can never be." The way Brand looked at me sent a chill down my spine. This wasn't the look one friend gave another. It was a look of desire. I thought of my own dream—the one that had woken me. Did I feel something for him beyond friendship? It didn't matter. He wasn't Eri.

"And who am I supposed to be with?" I scoffed. "You?" It wasn't fair; I knew we couldn't always choose who we had feelings for, and I didn't hate him for the way he looked at me. But I also didn't want to give him any indication of hope.

Brand blushed fiercely, but he didn't look away. "No, we could never be either. You are Tallisian. The only one you will ever be allowed to be with will be Tallisian as well."

"That will never happen." I might have to stay and pretend to be my aunt's puppet until she found Joe and Claire, but I wasn't going to just go to Tallis with her and let my entire life be another big lie. Brand had a good reason to do my aunt's bidding, but that didn't make me her pawn.

"Catelyn, Soria is extremely strong. She hasn't made it this far—with all the negative stigma your father left for her—without learning how to control people."

"Just because she controls you doesn't mean I'll be as easy a target for her," I said without thinking.

Brand looked like I'd slapped him.

"I'm sorry."

He nodded, acknowledging my apology, but I still saw the sting in his eyes.

I sighed. "I know you have every reason to do what she says, but I don't. Everyone I love is already gone. She can't hurt me."

I waited for his reply, but none came. He stood unexpectedly fast and walked to the door. It slid open, and he stepped out, looking both ways before turning and glancing back at me. "It is time for training," he said.

I looked at him blankly.

She's back.

"How do you know?"

He looked down the hallway again and then brought his finger to his lips. *Just because I don't control people here doesn't mean I stay out of their heads.* He turned and walked down the corridor. I followed him, running my hand along the side of the door to close it behind me.

Where is she?

Close.

Close was right; we turned the corner and walked right into her. She looked worn and crumpled like a dishcloth left in a heap. Her eyes were red and bloodshot, but not from tears, more from lack of sleep. Still, she held that air of superiority she always had.

I'd thought acting around her would be hard, but even though I loathed the person I now knew she was, I asked, "Claire and Joe?"

She shook her head. "We found a Rhaevian woman, but she gave us nothing. She ingested poison before we could get anything out of her. It's possible the other man has him. If he does, we will find Joseth."

I hated how she left Claire out of the equation but didn't say anything. I had to act like a good Tallisian. But what would a good Tallisian do in a case like this?

Ask to see him. Brand's voice echoed in my head. I was used to it enough by now that I didn't turn to look at him in shock—even if his words made me want to. I wanted to see Eri more than anything, but how was I supposed to broach the subject? Why would I ask to see him now?

"Maybe Er...the one from before is holding out on something," I said.

Soria's eyes narrowed. "There is nothing he knows, is there Brand?"

Brand shook his head. "No. He did not know the whereabouts of the ship."

I wanted to glare at Brand. He told me to suggest this. But Soria couldn't know I had any more connection to Brand than I did to Eri. I understood what he meant when he said he and I could never be together either. A good Tallisian would know without being told that Darkothians were not friends—they were servants.

"Of course, I could look again and see if there are any places that were of interest to them," Brand added quickly.

He obviously had a plan. Still, she would have expected him to look for things like that before. He was putting himself on the line for me, and I didn't know if I could repay him. Soria didn't scold him. She nodded as if the idea were acceptable.

"Come," she said and turned back down the corridor she'd come from.

I was about to see Eri, but I wasn't as excited as I should be. Soria had given in too easily, and it didn't feel like a trick. There was no evil flicker in her eye, nothing that made me question her motive. We went because she had no other options. We were going to see Eri because she had no clue where Joe and Claire were.

We went down a corridor I hadn't even known existed. My knowledge of the facility consisted mainly of my room, a bathroom, and the space room. Even the room I'd first woken up in was off-limits to me. I'd been too busy, too much in a state of forgetfulness—thanks to Brand—I hadn't questioned how big, or for that matter, how safe, an abandoned mine might be—even if it was reinforced with strange technology I couldn't even begin to understand.

We stopped at a door at the end of the corridor. This one required more than just a hand waving to open. A scanner read Soria's handprint and then allowed her to punch in a numerical code. The door opened, only to reveal another corridor. At the end of the hallway, Adamos emerged from the last of several small alcoves that lined the corridor. He looked up as we approached and frowned.

"Is it wise to bring her here?" he asked.

Soria glared at him. Tired or not, she didn't like having her authority undermined so openly. "She is Tallisian."

"She's a security risk." He looked back into the cell. Eri's cell. I wasn't sure how they kept him in, there were no bars, no door, but there had to be something that kept him in there. I doubted Adamos had been standing in the entryway this whole time.

I didn't have time to worry about that right now. There was a fine line I needed to walk. I needed to see Eri and know what they were doing to him. I couldn't save him—at least not now, maybe not ever. But if that time were ever to come, it would be because of whatever happened next. I needed to perform like I'd never done in my life. I needed to convince not just my aunt but Adamos as well that I was Tallisian. That bringing me here hadn't been a mistake.

"Trust me," I said to Adamos. "I'm not here to show him any kindness."

He glared at me. I shouldn't address him so informally. He was too far up in the chain of command. But Soria *was* my aunt, and I got the impression she would approve of any anger shown toward Eri.

He sat on the floor in the corner, looking up at us. For every bump, bruise, or cut I had from the previous week, he seemed to have ten. A large gash ran across his forehead, and one eye was red and swollen. The other eye had a dark purple bruise running from the eyelid around to the inner corner. His lips were cracked, the blood dried as if he hadn't even been conscious enough to wipe it off when the wounds occurred.

I'd been prepared to see him tortured. I wasn't prepared for the way he looked at me when our eyes met, for the deep green with yellow spots that I knew meant emotional pain.

"I thought you were dead." His voice was dry and scratchy.

I clenched my teeth to keep from biting my lip. It was my tell; if he saw it, he wouldn't believe, and he had to believe—everyone had to believe. I was a good Tallisian. "Sorry to disappoint you." I glared down at him. Taking a trick from Adamos' book, I kicked Eri straight in the gut. I didn't allow myself to think about it. I had to show complete disdain. "That's for my parents."

Adamos gave me a shocked but approving nod. He was my biggest critic. If he believed I hated Eri, anyone would. I kicked Eri again before he even had time to look back up from his clutched stomach. "That's for Joe and Claire." I wondered if I should go for a third blow just to be safe—even if the thought killed me. Brand stopped me.

Don't overdo it.

I stepped back, trying not to show my relief—and sorrow. Soria smiled smugly. "She is Tallisian," she said again. Adamos didn't reply.

"Brand," she said, nodding toward Eri. Brand went into his mind, and Eri's eyes became void of any free thought. At least I knew he wasn't thinking about my betrayal for a moment.

Everyone watched Brand. I didn't expect him to find an answer but hoped for a miracle nonetheless. Even if Eri and the Rhaevians weren't bad, it didn't mean Joe and Claire were safe.

"There are several locations in his memories of places they went looking for the ship." Neither Brand nor I had mentioned the fact that pieces of the ship had been scattered.

Soria's eyes shot up. "Where?"

"All near the town. Some closer to here, some a little farther. They didn't find it." Brand looked apologetic, but Soria must have been desperate.

"I want to know every place they looked." She didn't look relieved, but there was the glimmer of something I hadn't ever seen on her face—hope. She couldn't find them. She had to. So many conflicting emotions that when Brand came into my mind, I didn't stop him from making me stand straighter, making me scowl at Eri.

Soria turned to leave, and Brand followed her. Only Adamos appeared to be staying behind with his prisoner.

I wanted to catch one last glimpse of Eri. He remained silent. I couldn't tell if Brand was still in his mind or not. I wanted to look in his eyes and hope that, as an empath, he could feel the apology in me. To let him know I hadn't given up on him—on us. A good Tallisian wouldn't have spared him another thought, so I followed Soria and Brand, not looking in Eri's direction again. He was alive, and he was here. Right now, that was enough.

I SIDESTEPPED a punch from Brand as we skirted around each other in the space room. We'd left the staffs for hand-to-hand combat a few days before. Touching him wasn't an issue. I didn't get memorysights from him unless I sought them specifically. Apparently, it had to do with my being a Priestess of Sight and him being a Healer. When I asked him about not being able to see memories from Joe and Claire, he confirmed Ryan's theory that it had to do with me trusting them completely—which is why I had finally seen one on our last day together, when my trust had wavered. If we found them, if they were still alive, I had to wonder if I would still see their memories. And when I asked if I would see Eri's memories again, he didn't answer. We didn't talk about Eri.

I stuck to topics he would answer. It helped alleviate some of the frustration. "She's been gone five days this time," I said as he lunged at me again. Two and a half weeks had passed since she'd changed her hunting strategies to focus on my father's ship. We hadn't gone back to see Eri; there was no reason—even though I'd tried to invent one. I saw him all the time, whether I was asleep or not. His face haunted the corners of my mind. Sometimes smiling, laughing, loving. Other times broken, tortured, hopeless. When doubt got the best of me, I conjured up what look he would give me if we met again. Surely not loving, but dark, bitter, betrayed.

"The longer she's gone, the more we can hope she's not successful," Brand said, barely needing to move to miss my swing. I punched again in frustration and missed—again.

"I don't know how much longer I can keep on pretending." I lowered my arms, admitting defeat. Brand grabbed my wrist and pulled me to him, my back against his chest, one arm at my waist, the other at my neck. The position meant he could snap my neck if he wanted to, but it felt too intimate—more and more, our contact took on that sort of feeling, although Brand never said anything or did anything overly suggestive. It was just there, and I could tell it frustrated him as much as it did me—if only for different reasons.

I stiffened in his grasp, and he let go immediately. He never lingered with his touch, which in a way, only made things harder. He tried not to act on his feelings—feelings I now wondered if I might have been able to return if not for Eri.

"You can continue," he said. I took it as implying I had no other option. He was right; I didn't. In just weeks, I'd grown in strength not humanly possible. Brand reminded me I wasn't human. My Tallisian genetics made me a lot stronger than even I knew.

I hated thinking of myself as Tallisian. Until I found Joe, I would never know why my parents came here. I would never know if it was an accident or if my father really left on his own. I could speculate all I wanted, but it did no good, so I tried not to think about it. I focused on being Darkothian—that was where my abilities came from.

"Tell me more about my memorysight." This was my favorite

distracting subject. Brand told me stories his grandmother told him about the Priestess of Sight. There wasn't a lot of information; it was one of the few things the Darkothians had been able to hide from the Tallisians. Since Brand had left for Tallis when he was only five, most of what he recalled were sketches or things he'd heard. But some were detailed memories that helped me realize just what I might be able to do.

"There's not much more to tell," Brand said. He wasn't as keen to talk about the subject as I was. He worried the more I focused on my differences, the harder it would be for me to act the part I had put myself into.

"Then can I practice on you?" I asked. Brand had taught me to use my memorysight to seek for specific memories, to block memories I didn't want to see, and the right way to touch an object to either get a memory or not. For the first time in my life, I had an ability and not a disability. But the only person to practice on was Brand—and he didn't love it.

He gave me the look, the one he'd given me the first time I'd asked if I could practice on him. I knew the conditions that look implied. I rolled my eyes. "Yes, you can make me forget," I said.

I hadn't loved the idea of allowing him to take away things he didn't want me to see, but it was worth it. If the time ever arose that my ability could help me out of this mess, I wanted to be able to use it to my advantage. I don't know if he had taken away anything I'd seen so far. I guess I never would, but there were a lot of things I'd seen that were still with me. I felt like I knew Brand better than almost anyone.

I took his hand in mine, interlocking my fingers through his, and concentrated. The first thing that came was a distant memory of his time in a Tallisian prison camp. At first, his memories of that time had fascinated me, but now I knew they were mostly filled with pain. I decided to practice stopping this memory without tearing my hand away from his.

I used my mind to push the memory out of the way, just like

Brand had taught me. Almost instantly, the memory was gone. I smiled. My speed had improved a lot. I attempted to pull a different memory from his mind, but Crase, the same man who had taken me to my room my first day here, came in. Brand loosened his grip on my hand, but I hadn't had time to pull my fingers free of his when the memories started.

They weren't Brand's. In a split second, every detail of Crase's life enveloped me, thousands upon thousands of memories. A hundred firsts—first kiss, first job, first fight—a list of favorites—color, food, people—a world of hatred—Soria, this place, Rhaev—what he thought right now—he hated being Soria's message boy, he was terrified of Brand and what he could do, he wanted to be back home on Tallis with his wife.

My fingers broke free of Brand's. We looked at each other, both wondering what had just happened. Brand recovered quicker than I did.

"Crase?" he said.

"Soria would like you to report to the monitoring room," Crase snapped.

Brand nodded, and Crase left the room.

What was that? Shock stole my voice from me.

Brand went into my head for the first time in days—at least that I could recall. I let him see everything I'd just seen, and then I sank to the floor.

"Catelyn?" He knelt above me, his hands on my shoulders. He shook me gently. It felt like a meteorite had hit me. I sat up slowly, cradling my aching head in one hand.

"Is that what you meant when you said you see everything?" I asked.

"Yes." He nodded. "How do you feel?"

"Overwhelmed, confused, a little sick to my stomach."

Brand frowned. "After a while, you get used to it."

"I did what you can do," I said, more to myself as if trying to understand.

"Yes," Brand said.

"Was I in your head or Crase's?" I'd been playing around in Brand's mind, looking for a memory. Was this the memory I'd gotten? Or had I really just harnessed his power?

"I'm not sure."

24

Anger burst from Soria like solar flares. She used to at least force a smile when I came into her presence, now her gaze had turned volcanic. Her anger told me all I needed to know—she hadn't found Claire and Joe.

She held a picture in her hand from the bookshelf in Joe's study. My dad and mom were younger, my mom just starting to show in her pregnancy. Their arms were locked around each other's shoulders, and they smiled as if they didn't have a care in the world. They were in Zion. I knew from asking that Joe had snapped this moment. His back must have been to the lodge because behind them was the trail to Emerald Pools and, from the angle of the picture, Angels Landing rose high to the left of them.

I loved hiking in Zion, but more because of this picture than even the immense beauty of the area. In Zion, I felt closest to my parents. They'd been there once, and they'd been so happy, so full of life. In Zion, their spirits called me to them, like they were there. Or if not them, a piece of them: the ship.

Except the last place you would hide a spaceship was in the most visited National Park in the state.

"Where was this picture taken?" she asked, thrusting it at me.

"Zion National Park," I said, wishing I could read her mind.

"Where is that?"

"Just northwest of Kanab. It's a major tourist spot. Over a hundred thousand people go there every year." The last bit sounded like a tourist brochure, but it had to be said in case she was desperate enough to think my dad had hidden his ship in Zion of all places.

"Did Joe go there often?"

Lie. Brand's voice came into my head, but he didn't need to tell me. Gut instinct said Soria shouldn't be anywhere the ship might be, even if she was crazy to think it was in Zion.

"Not really." He'd only built his career around being able to hike there on a weekly basis. Did that mean something? Maybe Soria wasn't that crazy.

She threw the picture on the computer terminal next to her. "Brand, is she telling the truth?"

The few times I wondered if my aunt might be skeptical about my behavior, she had always ended up giving me the benefit of the doubt. If she had ever not trusted me, it had never been to my face.

Brand looked at me, his eyes blacking over as if intently searching, but he wasn't in my head.

"Yes," he said to her after a moment.

She looked at him as skeptical as she looked at me. "Catelyn, you are dismissed." Her words were final, and I knew better than to try to argue with her. I left the room, glad to be away from her while she was in such a foul mood but hating to leave Brand.

Halfway to my room, he screamed. I froze. I'd seen his memories enough to know she used her controller on him. I could imagine the poison secreting through him with every cry of agony. She'd done it many times when he had first come to her service. She didn't do it as often now, only when she wanted to teach him a lesson—or if she found he'd lied to her.

Brand?

He didn't answer. Death wasn't an issue; Soria depended on him too much. But if he wasn't able to answer me, he had to be pretty bad off. I went to my room. She was just frustrated. She didn't know Brand was lying. He was always the one she took her anger out on. Knowing that didn't make me feel better and didn't mean I believed it.

I lay on my cot, my knees curled up against my chest, my eyes staring at the door, waiting for someone to come. No, not someone—waiting for my aunt to come and tell me she no longer had any need for me. I waited for her to kill me. My imagination had gotten much more active over the past month. I could easily picture Soria coming in here and shooting me. I could also picture a lot of worse things she could do to me. After the things I'd had to accept, nothing seemed too far-fetched.

I'm okay. Brand's voice brought me to a sitting position.

What did she do?

She hasn't found Joe or the ship. Brand ignored my question.

Does she suspect us?

He didn't answer. I'd spent more time focusing on my memorysight than on our telepathy. I wasn't sure if he couldn't hear me or if he was just ignoring me. Or maybe he couldn't answer.

Brand?

We need to be careful.

I sighed but didn't push the topic further. For now, he was okay. One thing was certain from this whole experience: it was time to find a way out of this place, with or without Brand's help.

I HATED THE MINE. I hated the smell. I hated being stuck with no means of escape. I hated not knowing exactly where I was. I hated protein bars and sephrum pills. For all the material things I really hated, the hydro showers made up for it.

Technology has its advantages, and this one came in the form of perfectly heated water that sprayed—with just the right amount of pressure—on you from every angle—like a human car wash. I was on the spot-free rinse cycle when Brand called to me.

Catelyn?

It had been almost a day since I'd seen him. Soria hadn't come to my room; no one had. Brand had barely answered the few times I'd tried to call him. He was scared and still hurting, but the fact he would choose now to ignore me made me angry. I thought about telling him I was busy. I had to think of an escape plan. He would probably try to talk me out of that. I sighed, turned off the water, and grabbed a towel.

Yeah?

Soria is coming for you.

What does she want?

He didn't answer me.

Brand?

Still nothing. I had a sinking feeling his silence wasn't his own choice this time.

Putting on clothes while wet is awful. Facing Soria in nothing but a towel and my hair dripping all over the place would be worse. I wrapped the towel around my hair and pulled on the clothes I'd set aside previously. The shirt stuck to my back, uncomfortable, but not as uncomfortable as looking up into the face of my aunt.

"How do you feel about the Rhaevians?" she asked.

"They killed my parents. They deserve to be destroyed." It was always easiest to sound bitter if I threw my parents' deaths into the equation. She'd asked me this question several times before, but this time my answer wasn't being received as well as in the past.

"And Darkothians?" she asked. She'd never asked this. What did she mean? Brand?

"Darkothians are our allies." It was what I should have been taught to believe.

She nodded. "Good, then your next decision shouldn't be too hard. Come with me." She turned and walked out of the room.

I followed her down the corridor we'd taken to see Eri, ditching my towel for a hair tie. What did she mean about my next decision? We went toward Eri's cell. What did she expect from me? And what did Brand have to do with it?

Brand? I called again. Still no answer.

I saw Brand first. He slumped lifelessly against the wall just outside the cell that held Eri. His eyes were closed. Adamos emerged out of the cell when we approached. He saluted Soria, though he lacked the desire to do so.

"It's time to prove your dedication," Soria said to me. From the side of her belt, she pulled out a gun and handed it to me. I took the weapon, my fingers trembling. Adamos pointed his gun straight at my head. "Kill him." She tilted her head toward Eri.

The gun sat heavy in my hand. Heavier than it should be. Eri's eyes found mine, and he didn't look away. Could he feel my terror?

"Shoot him," Soria said. She pulled out Brand's control. "It's time for you to choose, Catelyn. Your enemy or one of your own kind." The way she referred to Brand bothered me. She'd never called him that before. I looked up at her. She smiled her cruel smile, the same one I'd seen when she talked of killing anyone from Rhaev.

"I know, Catelyn. I know who your mother was. I recognized her in that picture. A Darkothian slave. She'd gone missing after Aden had, but I never suspected the reason. She never was one to be compliant. I figured she'd spoken against the wrong person. Now I know what became of her." She spat the raspy choke of loathing out in her words. That was why she brought back the picture. That is what caused her anger.

I shook my head. I couldn't kill Eri. She pressed Brand's control, and although he already appeared unconscious, his body writhed with pain. Soria laughed—but Adamos groaned.

"This is pointless," he said. "She won't do it."

"I'm in command here," Soria said.

"I know. Every single minute we waste on this useless planet, every single Tallisian who dies while you mess up again and again, reminds me of who is in charge."

In Adamos's memory he'd believed he should be in charge. I wasn't sure what made him snap now, but it couldn't be good. My aunt didn't need one more thing to fuel her anger.

Soria stiffened. "You will regret that little outburst when I present the ship to the council," she said coldly.

"You don't have what it takes to find the ship. You never have; it's not in your blood. You're weak, a coward, just like your brother. The council should have tried you for his treason long ago. They know, they all do, and they have been playing you this whole time." He grabbed the gun out of my hand and pointed it at her along with his own.

Soria's weapon, the rodwhip she used to torture Eri the first night I'd met her, came cracking down on Adamos's hand. His look of shock proved he hadn't been prepared for her to do that. It reverberated loudly off his skin. He flinched and backed off into a defensive stance dropping one gun as the other flew out of his hand and down the hall.

"This is my mission," Soria said. There was a tone to her voice scarier than anything I'd ever heard. Adamos had obviously found an old wound and pushed too hard. Soria glared at him and then removed her gloves. She dropped them to the ground. "And we both know you don't have what it takes to be a leader."

"Wake Brand," she said to him. Adamos didn't move until she brought her weapon up again.

He dropped to his knees, pulled out a syringe of liquid, and pushed it into Brand's chest. Brand's eyes shot open at once, and he gasped as if he'd held his breath underwater for too long and had finally come up for air. That painful gasp had the opposite effect on me. All the air left my body. We were going to die. Eri. Brand. Me.

"You will never get them to talk," Adamos said, standing and glaring down between Eri and Brand, but much of the defiance had left his voice. As much as he hated her, whatever my aunt did with her whip scared him more.

Soria took her weapon and traced it across Eri's cheek. He didn't move, but he felt something coming from her. I could tell by the way his eyes squinted, and his jawbone tightened. I'd been so concerned with my own power I never asked Brand to clarify what the Tallisian touch was. I hadn't seen her use it since that first day at Eri's, but I knew it wasn't good. "I will," Soria said to Adamos. "Your problem is you're too angry. Hate won't get you anywhere. Love is the answer."

Adamos grunted and landed a kick into Eri's gut. "Love is weakness."

Soria's whip came across Adamos's thigh before he had the chance to land another kick on Eri. Like I'd seen her do before, she let this one linger for just a moment.

"You are ignorant," she said as he fell to his knees. "Someone is going to tell me where that ship is." Her eyes flickered from Eri to Brand and back. "It's simply a matter of finding out who loves my niece the most."

I looked at Soria, and my stomach clenched. From the glazed expression in her eyes, I could imagine too well just how she planned to determine if Eri or Brand cared more for me. There was no time to close my eyes, to flinch away. I stared straight into my aunt's eyes and learned exactly what the Tallisian touch was.

25

The first crack came across my arm. There was no denying the pain, but I stood my ground. I wouldn't think about how this was my aunt—the only family I had left—hitting me. I would stand tall and take it. I wouldn't react and let Eri or Brand try to save me. I'd known pain. I could do this. It's what Brand trained me for.

She struck again and again and...

My teeth clenched so tightly that I thought they would shatter. With each whip, I felt not only physical pain but also mental pain. I relived my parents' deaths over and over. The thought of losing them. The sorrow and heartache. It tore at me, twisted my heart until it ached to stop. But then an image came to my head: a picnic with my parents. I would have been five. I wore the yellow sunflower hat my mom had bought for me at the farmer's market. I'd worn that hat all summer long. The memory was so clear, so real. The pressure of Soria's weapon dug into me, but I was safe.

A noise startled me. The image left, and my torturer came back into view. Soria had her metal whip, and Adamos looked on, surprised but pleased. Eri stared up at me with deep concern. Brand lay on the floor convulsing. In Soria's other hand, her finger pushed on the round device she used to control him.

She stopped and looked me in the face. "He will not be helping you again anytime soon."

The sting Brand had tried to take away when he'd put that image in my mind returned. I waited for her to hit me again, not knowing how long I'd be able to take it. She wanted information about my father's ship. It wasn't going to work. Neither of them knew anything. Soria decided to try another tactic rather than whipping me bloody.

"I have to admit, I didn't expect Brand to risk being the one to save you. He's always been so...scared. I'd heard you two had grown close over the past weeks, somewhat intimate. I assumed it was just physical. I didn't realize how deeply he cared for you."

With each word she said, more and more confusion crossed Eri's face—confusion and hurt. She knew the exact right words, the exact right tone to inflict pain in him without a single touch. Although I wanted to deny it, to tell him her words were lies, Soria also knew exactly what to do to get me to confirm it all.

"I wonder if you feel the same way." She pushed the button down again, causing the most horrific scream you could imagine. I didn't have time to think about hurting Eri with my actions. I launched myself at Soria, grabbing for the remote.

"Stop it," I yelled as I smacked into her. Surprise was on my side because she didn't have time to move before I pounced. Skill, strength, and numbers were on her side because Adamos pulled me from her, and the whip ripped across my arm once more.

The previous strikes were enough to slash the cloth of my shirt, leaving skin exposed. This time her strike lingered, and her *touch* intensified the moment the metal whip came in contact with actual flesh. Physical pain can be unbearable, mental pain can be agonizing, emotional pain—the type that coursed through my body at the touch of steel against flesh—was all-consuming.

Adamos caught me before I slid to the ground. There was no memorysight, only heartache. Her whip came again—and sadness took over, so intense my heart skipped beats. I gasped for air as my lungs closed.

"What are you doing?" I asked in a mere whisper.

She drove the steel into my ripped flesh harder. "This is what we do, Catelyn. The elite on Tallis, those of us who are destined to become something, can emit emotional energy. This is a transistor rod. It helps intensify the feeling." She let the rod drop from her fingers and fall to the floor. I gulped in air as my lungs reopened.

"I don't need help to intensify my feelings," she said. Her hands came up and cupped my face in them. The sadness came back. I wanted to be dead. My organs began to comply with that wish. "This is what I felt when Aden and Joseth abandoned me." The feeling changed to fear. "This is what I felt when I was tortured for months for the crimes my brother committed."

She moved her hands down my face. I shook my head, pleading with her to stop. She grasped my jaw. "This is what I felt when I found that picture and knew he'd betrayed me for a Darkothian." I gasped for breath, and then the last beat of my heart thumped before the nothingness overcame me.

I WOKE WITH A GASP—NOT sure how long it had been—positive I'd just been brought back from the brink of death. Breathing hurt—each gulp of air burned my throat. Adamos kneeled over me, from the empty syringe in his hand I could only guess that whatever had been in it now coursed through my veins instead of the need for CPR.

Brand still lay on the ground. I didn't have the strength to turn my head and see where Eri was. I didn't hear him–not a good sign.

Soria's face appeared before me. She seemed concerned. Good, let her worry that she'd almost just killed her only blood relation.

"Catelyn?" I thought about closing my eyes, ignoring her, making her worry more. I just stared back at her. "Where is your father's ship?" she said, but not as harshly as she had the time before.

"Tell...nothing," I said. I meant Eri had told me nothing, but Soria interpreted my reply differently. Her scowl returned, and her hand came up to slap me across the face. So much anger. I wanted to be angry, but I couldn't let it consume me. If I died, if she killed me, then what would happen to Eri? What would happen to Brand?

I tugged at her shirtsleeve, trying to get her to come closer. I couldn't move toward her. I couldn't lift my head at all. She leaned in.

"Nothing...saw...no...ship," I tried again. My throat burned. "No...ship...found." Soria lifted her hand, and I flinched. She didn't hit me, but she used her thumb to brush away the tears involuntarily seeping from my eyes. It was the first touch of hers I had control of, and I grabbed at a memory.

I was too weak to search for anything specific, and it was a lot harder to have a memory when I wasn't touching the person with my own hands. But vulnerability at the moment let me glimpse a portion of her past. She was younger than I was, maybe by a year or two. She sat in a dark room, her arms tied behind her back, her cheek cut and bruised.

"I want to know every word he said to you, every action, everything." A man's voice filled the room, only his shadow visible.

"Nothing," she said. "He said nothing. He loved Tallis."

The hand came across her face, and pain—the same one she'd produced in me when she'd smacked me–shot through her. "He's a traitor."

She shook her head, and the man hit again.

I flinched, and she pulled her hand away. Did she know what I could do? Her look said she knew something had happened, but she didn't say anything else to me. Standing, she turned to Adamos. "Leave Brand. He's no threat to me. Bring the other one."

"I don't think—"

"That's right," Soria interrupted him, "you don't think. You do what I say, or you will end up like them."

Adamos didn't argue this time. Perhaps he heard the same authoritative sound in her voice that I did. He stepped over me, and when he came into view the next time, he had Eri's body draped across his shoulders, blood dripping from somewhere.

Soria punched in her code, and a blue flash came across the opening. A force field of some type. Brand and I were prisoners now. And Eri was alive, but for how long?

"Brand?" I whispered. I'd slept after Soria left. It seemed like I'd only dozed off for a moment, but when I woke up, my throat was no longer scratchy, and my head seemed clearer. Brand must have healed me, but now he didn't respond. Only the occasional groan and the low, raspy breathing were signs that he lived.

I looked around the cell. I hadn't noticed the surroundings when I first visited Eri. The main walls were rock—the same rock that made up most of the structure of the mine. The force field over the front wall was clear; only the slight wave of electricity could be seen if you were really looking.

I threw my shoe at it. The shoe bounced off and flew back toward me, lighting the doorway up in a bright spark. I moved so it would slam against the back wall and not the side of my head. The laces were singed. I didn't know how much or how little electricity it took to cause that to happen, but I didn't plan on sticking my hand through to find out.

I went back and sat next to Brand. So much for my training. Not much fighting I could do against an electric wall. I should have focused on what to do next, on a way to get out, but with a clear moment to think, only Eri occupied my mind.

He'd been conscious before my heart gave out. He'd been limp and broken when I'd been revived. What happened in that time? Had he tried to stop Soria? Was he unconscious again because of me? The last time he'd seen me, I'd thrown myself at Soria to keep Brand safe. Did he believe the things she said? Would he die not knowing how I felt?

"Catelyn?" Brand startled me out of my self-pity. My head snapped up, and I reached for his outstretched arm, helping him sit.

"Are you okay?" I asked.

"I think so. How long was I out?" He rubbed his forehead and winced in pain.

"I'm not sure. I was out for a while."

He closed his eyes and put a hand on the back of my neck. My remaining pain melted away; it took all he had.

"Stop," I said.

He opened his eyes.

"I'm fine. What I need now is for you to get your strength. If we're going to get out of here, we need to work together."

He sat up, trying to act as if he didn't hurt over every inch of his body. "I will do whatever I can to get you out of here," he said.

"We will do whatever we can to get us both out of here," I corrected him.

"You know I can't. You know she can kill me with just the push of a button."

"Then we'll get the controller from her. We'll make sure you never have to be subject to her again."

He didn't respond, and I couldn't make him agree. He had his sister to think about.

"Do you know where they took Eri?" he asked.

I shook my head.

"You won't leave without him." Brand knew my mind even without entering.

"I can't." I couldn't leave Eri here, and that would complicate things.

Brand nodded, more in resignation than in agreement. Risking his life for me didn't seem to affect him, but for Eri, that was another matter. "If we're lucky, he is in one of the other cells," he said. "If not, she will have taken him to the monitoring room—put him on display while she tortures him. I will be able to control most of the crew before she realizes and stops me." His voice caught.

"I can't ask you to do that. If she is with him, we'll have to come up with another option."

"There may not be another option. I'll do whatever you need me to do." He put his hand on mine. I'd dismissed Brand's affection as convenience—we were together constantly. But convenience didn't make you risk your life for someone.

"When you asked me to make you forget him, I wanted to," Brand said. "You have no idea how much I wanted to. It would have been so easy to take him away and let me be the one you loved. But you have the bond oath."

I looked at him questioningly.

"The vision, the way you can read his eyes, the way you feel. You have chosen each other. If I had taken that away from you, I would have been living another lie. Your lives are tied to each other—if you want them to be, you are still free to make your choice."

He looked at me as if waiting for an answer. My vision had meant something. It could come true, but Brand said I had to choose to want that future. I did. I chose Eri. I would only ever choose him, even seeing how Brand looked at me now. "Brand, I can't..."

"I know," he interrupted.

I didn't have to ask what he knew. Every thought, every feeling I'd ever had for Eri was etched across the pain in his eyes.

"We can't help who we love," he said. "Don't feel bad. I don't regret for a minute the feelings I have for you. I never thought I would feel this way. For so many years, I've tried to eliminate all emotion from myself. It became easier than feeling hate and pain all the time. I never thought I could love because I never expected to find someone like you."

I looked away from him. He reached out and pulled my gaze back to his. "I'm not going to stop loving you just because of your bond with him. I'm a better person because of these feelings. I was wrong when I taught you emotions were what would get you killed. Maybe hate and anger, but never love. If we are going to get out of here—any of us—then I have to love you because that is what has given me the strength to go against every emotion, every act I ever vowed to steer clear from. It is the only way I could ever have the strength to defy Soria. And I need to, for me, for you," he took a long deep breath, not of resignation but more of realization, "for Jacia, because as long as I'm Soria's slave, my sister will never be free. I know that now. I have to be free so I can find a way to make her free. I will only be able to do that if I love you."

My tears were falling now.

"Don't cry," he said.

"I wish things could be different," I said and, for a moment, I really did wish that. It didn't seem logical to push away someone who loved me enough to die for me, for someone who may not ever be allowed to love me. Just because I would choose the bond oath, as Brand named it, didn't mean Eri would.

Brand smiled. "Right now, we need to come up with a plan." He brushed away the water that streaked my face. "And who knows, maybe by the time everything is said and done, you will start looking at me the way you look at him."

I began to protest—not wanting to hurt him, not wanting to give him false hope—but one look from Brand and I couldn't seem to say the words.

26

I *have a plan.* Brand's words echoed in my mind, bringing me back to consciousness. I slowly opened my eyes. I'd been dreaming of happier times, dreaming of Eri. I sat up, stretching my arms and legs, arching my back to alleviate some of the pain that had flared while I'd been asleep.

"How long have I been out?" I asked.

"A few hours," Brand said.

My mouth was dry, and I had an unpleasant taste that let me know my breath may just be classified as a chemical weapon. The small amount of light coming from the hallway allowed me to see Brand's shadowed features.

"Would you like to hear the plan?" he said.

I nodded, still achy, still thirsty, and ready to get out of this hellhole.

"I can control every mind on this base except for Soria's," he said. "You know she has the ability to feel when I'm in her head, but the others don't. It won't be easy, it will take a lot out of me, but I can control them all."

"What good would that do?" I asked. "The minute she sees any of them acting differently, she will use your controller. You said so yourself."

"True, but she won't use it if her mind is also being controlled."

I looked at him, confused. He couldn't control her mind. The last time he'd tried to do that, he'd spent eight months in a hospital. I could feel Brand in my head because of our Darkothian link. Soria could feel Brand in her head because of the surgical implant every master of a Darkothian Healer is given when they receive their slave. The second he went into her head, she would be ruthless—and this time, given everything that had happened, she might not stop at almost killing him.

"You can't go in her head," I said.

"I didn't mean me."

"Is there some other Darkothian Healer hanging out here you haven't mentioned?" My sarcasm was thick, but his cryptic attitude drove me insane.

He smiled. "Remember when you were practicing using your memorysight, and Crase came in?"

I nodded, his idea dawning on me instantly. "That won't work," I protested. "We don't even know if I was in Crase's mind or yours."

"I've been thinking and have determined it was Crase's mind you were in."

"How can you be sure?" I asked.

"Whose memories did you see?"

"Crase's," I said slowly. "But Brand, we don't even know how that worked or why it worked."

"I think I do."

There was a faint skittering sound. We listened, but nothing else could be heard. Still, he moved his head closer to mine and lowered his voice.

"When I see in someone's head, I see everything they know, everything they are. Most of the time, I dismiss it as fast as I've changed their memories. It's the one blessing I have, not to have to hold onto everyone forever. It's as if the Creator knew we would need that reprieve. It would be too much. But I also can save what I've seen if I want to. It isn't as easy as dismissing thoughts, but it is possible." He looked at the opening to our cell and then back. "I've seen into the mind of a Priestess of Sight, just once, but I saved that moment. When you saw Crase's memories, I recalled her memories, but in order to access them, I have to go into a deep meditative state. I don't do it often because it leaves me vulnerable, plus there hasn't been time. But I think you can do it. Just like you saw what was in Crase's head through me, perhaps you can use my ability to seek my saved memories out. If I'm right, maybe you can use them to control Soria's mind."

I leaned back, shaking my head. Even if what Brand said was true, I wasn't really a Priestess of Sight, at least not a trained one. Until a few weeks ago, I was just a teenage girl.

"I can't," I said. "I wouldn't even know how to."

"Yes, you would, you would know exactly how to," Brand said.

"How?" This wasn't something Brand could walk me through as it happened. The plan had so many flaws I didn't know where to start naming them.

"You've been in my mind before. You can find it. It's there, hidden behind a barrier, but if you pull on my powers, you'll be able to see everything, and I'll make sure you remember."

"But then—"

He nodded. "I would have no secrets from you. I couldn't risk taking away anything you may need to help you."

I would know everything about him, even the things he'd erased in the past. Eventually, he could erase things again but changing one memory at a time was a lot different than changing a million—and that is what I would have, a million of Brand's memories in my mind. And every memory he'd ever chosen to save, for that matter. There was also one other set of memories Brand had that I would see.

"You have Eri's memories," I said. It was selfish. It shouldn't have mattered when it came to finding a way out of here. Anyone would understand if I saw all their memories for that reason. Eri would understand. I couldn't bring myself to see them.

Brand shook his head. "I've dismissed his as much as I am able. There isn't anything specific there." The look in his eyes told me it hadn't been for me. He'd erased them because he didn't want to remember Eri's memories.

Would there be something in his mind I wouldn't be able to

forget? "Could you—could you do the same for yours, so I don't have to—"

He took my hand. "No. You need my memories—all of them. If you are going to use my ability, you need to understand every part of me."

It made sense, but it still scared me. This couldn't work. I barely understood my own ability. How could I even start to comprehend Brand's?

"You should do it now. We don't know if we will get another opportunity to try." Brand pushed my hesitation toward action. This was the best plan we had. There wasn't time to think of another way or an excuse about why this wouldn't work. I gripped his hand tighter and closed my eyes.

I searched for a memory, just as I'd done several times before. Brand as a child on Darkothia, running through a field of tall grass, a boy—his spitting image, but taller—chased him and laughed. His brother. I tried to hold on to this memory, to make it something more. Brand helped the process along because the next memory came almost instantly.

This same brother, older now, was in a cell. He was sick, half-starved, half-naked. Brand tried to heal him, but he was too young, so he didn't have his full ability yet. His brother was older, though; he should have shown signs already. He didn't inherit his grandfather's ability, and they were going to allow him to die because of it.

Then everything grew light. Brand was outside. He looked down on a freshly covered grave. There was no marker, but I knew it contained his brother's remains. The pain was like when I'd seen my parents' fresh graves, but there was an anger that could only have come from Brand's memory.

He pushed his power through me again, and the memories started pouring in faster. Brand as a child—the destruction of his home—the death of his parents. Brand as a prisoner on Tallis—the disease—the abuse. Brand being implanted with the device—his time with Soria—the things she'd forced him to do. Brand here on the base

—with me—his feelings for me—the desire—the want. I almost pulled my hand away. The other stuff was hard to see, but it was like a movie. The intense feelings he had for me were reality—my reality.

"Now you know exactly how I feel about you," he said. I tightened my grip. If it was hard on me, it must have been excruciating for him to allow all this out. I had to see it. And I did—everything. When Brand's memories were done, the others came. The ones he'd saved, hidden away, they were open now as if he'd held them behind a door he only now unlocked. There were fighting techniques, cures and remedies, languages and cultures. Everything he'd saved seemed like something he thought would be of use to him one day. And then I found her memories.

She was older than I expected, probably in her late seventies. She was the most beautiful person I've ever seen. Her eyes were the color of cornflowers, her hair, like white silk, trailed down her back. Physically, she was perfect, but it was her memories that made her breathtaking. There was more goodness and light in her soul than was possible in one person. I ached to know her, to be near her, to be like her.

I focused on her ability, on the things she'd done with her gifts. Instantly I knew exactly how to use Brand to control Soria's mind. I knew how to erase another person's memories, how to create a whole new mindset for another person. I would be able to make Soria move, make her speak, make her act however I wanted her to. I knew how to be Brand—and all it would take was the touch of his hand.

"You've found it," he said, and I nodded. I knew how to make myself all-powerful, and it terrified me. With Brand at my side, I could do anything, and no one could stop me. But there was more—something I'd almost overlooked. It couldn't last forever. I could use Brand's gift, but it would take all my strength to do it. We would have to be fast. The moment I took control of Soria's mind, I would need to know exactly what I wanted to do, and I couldn't allow anything to break that focus.

The scuffling sound from earlier came again, louder, drawing me back to the present. Everything had flickered through me in a matter of seconds. I lived Brand's entire life in five beats of my heart.

"You see this for every person you meet?" I asked.

"Yes," he said sadly. It wasn't a godlike power. This was a curse.

The noise came again—closer. Someone was coming.

"I didn't expect her this soon. Are you ready?" Brand asked.

"Yes," I said, feeling anything but. I looked up, waiting for my aunt to stop in front of our cell. I would see her thoughts, and no matter how horrible they were, I would have to ignore them. I would find where Eri was, make her turn off the force field, and then I would make her give me the remote. The minute she no longer had control of Brand, he could take over. A minute, maybe two, was all I needed. It seemed like an eternity.

The figure making its way down the hall came into view. My grip loosened. Brand would get to do his part first. Whoever was coming wasn't Soria—it was definitely a man. I expected Adamos.

I got Joe.

I wanted to speak, but I started to cry. What was Joe doing here? Relief and nervousness mixed, making me want to scream. Brand had seen inside my head so often introductions were not necessary for him.

Joe shot the control box, and the force field quit with a definite zap. He grabbed me into a big embrace. Joe had never been much of a hugger, but now he seemed to be making up for years of that. "Are you okay?" he asked.

I muffled my answer into his chest but nodded enough so he wouldn't need me to translate. Joe's grasp lessened as he eyed Brand skeptically. He needed an introduction.

"This is Brand," I said. "He's a friend."

"He's Darkothian?" Joe asked. I hadn't expected the prejudice in his voice.

I nodded. "So was my mother," I said. "So am I."

Joe looked shocked, but just for a second, and then he nodded. "True," he said, and it felt amazingly good to hear. Like that admittance of truth was an indicator there would be no more lies. "I'm so sorry I never told you."

I wanted to tell him it was okay. I wanted to make him explain why he'd done it. Why they all had done it. I settled for, "What are you doing here?"

"We're here to get you out," he answered.

"We? Is Claire here?" If I was having trouble picturing Joe on this insane rescue mission, I couldn't even imagine Claire sporting a gun and ready to roundhouse someone.

Then a shot echoed through the hallway. I stepped back into the cell, retreating from any line of fire that might come my way. But both Brand and Joe were out in the hall, and neither of them had been hit; they hadn't even dived from a bullet, for that matter. Brand reached for me, and I took his hand, letting him lead me back to the hall. "We need to get out of here," he said. I knew he'd been in Joe's mind. He had the answers to every question I had. I also knew standing here, holding his hand, drawing from him, I would be able to look in Joe's head as well. I would know everything without having to play twenty questions. It was intriguing, but I couldn't waste any strength on Joe's mind.

Joe raised his eyebrow as I clung to Brand. I'd seen that look a hundred times, and it almost made me feel normal—almost.

"I've got him," a familiar voice yelled. It was too distinct to forget. At the far end of the hallway stood Mathis—Eri's fake uncle. And then Eri limped out of a cell.

I would have looked at Joe in disbelief if I could have taken my eyes off Eri. He stared back, only breaking eye contact to glance at my hand clutched in Brand's. Then he turned to Mathis and took the gun he offered. They moved away from us, and Joe seemed keen on following them.

I didn't let go of Brand's hand.

"They set off a stun bomb. The effects will already be wearing off. People are starting to come around. We need to move fast," Brand said. "It's just the two of them; they thought they could get in and out fast enough. He didn't count on the extra baggage."

I knew that meant Brand. In front of us, Joe stiffened at this assessment. He most likely knew exactly how Brand had come by it. But now we were at the end of the hall, and the opening to the rest of the mine stood before us, as did Eri and Mathis.

"The bomb's effects were not long enough," Mathis said, the accusation in his voice apparent. It looked as if the collaboration between Joe and him wasn't necessarily a friendly one.

"We still have time. All we need to do is make our way back to the Jeep," Joe hissed lowly. "We can take the back hall."

Mathis nodded. It hadn't dawned on me how Joe knew exactly where to go, exactly where we would be, until that moment. Mathis would have known the whole layout of the base. It used to belong to the Rhaevians. We inched toward the back hall where Joe pointed. It was a good, safe plan. If we went that way, we might all get out. All of us except Brand.

"We can't go that way," I said, and four pairs of eyes were immediately on me.

"Catelyn," Eri said, speaking to me for the first time. "We know this base. This is our only chance. We need to go now." He held out his hand, and I automatically reached forward. I wanted to go with Eri, to be with Eri. I stopped before our fingers could touch.

"No. We have to find Soria."

"That is suicide," Mathis said.

"Catelyn, I need you to trust me," Joe said, trying to reason with me. "I know she's your aunt, but..." he looked at Mathis and I was certain he knew what had become of the girl he had left behind. He shook his head as if trying to clear the thought away. "Soria will kill us the minute she sees us." The pain in his eyes was for more than just worrying about us.

Shouting came from another hall. They would be on us in a matter of seconds.

It has to be this way. Brand let go of my hand.

"I won't leave here without you," I said.

"We're going now." Mathis moved again. And Eri, who looked as if I'd just slapped him across the face, followed him.

Eri was an empath; couldn't he tell I was his? That my wanting to save Brand had nothing to do with romantic feelings for him?

"Brand saved my life. I can't leave him, and he can't leave as long as Soria has his controlling device," I said. I tried to emanate all my feelings for Eri. "I can get the control from Soria, but I need you to wait for me."

Eri contemplated my request longer than I liked. I wasn't sure if my pleading or the sounds of men screaming dangerously close made his features soften. Whatever it was, he did more than just agree to wait.

Turning to Mathis, who was not happy with me at all, he said, "Get the Jeep. We'll meet you in ten minutes."

"You can't die for a Darkothian or for this girl," Mathis said. "This is a trap."

Eri looked back at me, studying my face. All I could do was hope he felt the truth. "I said go to the Jeep," he responded. Mathis complained again, but Eri silenced him. "That is an order."

Mathis nodded in almost robotic compliance and turned toward the back hall. I'd almost forgotten Eri was the leader of his group, most likely used to taking charge. He turned to Joe and told him to go as well. "He may need your help."

Joe didn't look like he was about to comply quite so quickly but, he must have realized time was of the essence. "Are you sure about this?" he asked me.

I nodded.

He took one more doubtful look at Brand and then turned to Eri. "Keep her safe," he said as he ran toward the exit where Mathis had disappeared.

It would have been nice to have a moment to strategize the plan with Eri. It would have been nice to be able to communicate silently with him like I could with Brand. But we were out of time. Two men burst through the opposite opening and shot at us. Eri answered back with his own gun, hitting one of the men below the left shoulder before the other man lowered his weapon and slid it across the floor toward us.

He wasn't scared. He was under Brand's control.

Brand moved across the room and picked up the gun. I followed, but Eri grabbed my arm and pulled me behind him, acting as a shield between me and anything that might still be coming. As we neared the doorway, Brand asked, "Are you going to be able to do this?"

"Yes." I sounded confident. If he went in my mind, he would know I was anything but.

27

Joe's stun bomb had landed almost exactly in the middle of the main room. There was damage at every turn. A few bodies still lay by the bomb site. I didn't know if they were dead, and I wasn't going to bother finding out. Those farther from the blast sat up, rubbing at their heads, shaking off the daze that had overcome them. The computers in the room hadn't fared well with the electric pulse the bomb sent. People shouted, trying to check on others, check on themselves. We sent Brand's captive into the room before us. People were so disordered they may not have noticed, but Soria came out of her stupor quicker than some of them; whether it was her position to the bomb or the fact she was just tougher than most of them, I didn't know. But the minute we came into view, she let off a shot. It went right through the man we'd taken.

She fumbled for Brand's remote. I had to do whatever I planned to do before she could hit that button. Brand reached back and grabbed my hand. To get to Soria's mind, I had to wade through Brand's once more. I was grateful I'd already seen a large portion of his memories, and, though there was some new stuff, namely all of Joe's memories he had not had time to dispose of, I knew I didn't have time to contemplate that. I focused on Soria. Searching for her was hard as Brand tried to control all the other minds and leave hers alone. I fell into a million memories from everyone else in the room. A spinning vortex of information pulled at me. I hadn't imagined it would be this hard.

Her finger was almost on the button. I had to stop her. While things went through my head at the speed of light, the physical world seemed to move in slow motion. I gripped hard onto Brand, my nails breaking into his skin. In his head, I felt myself clawing at him. I concentrated harder and found Soria's mind. Then with a mental push that seemed to come from nowhere, I was inside her head.

First order of business was to make her stop reaching for her control. She lifted her hands in surrender, dropping not only the controller but her weapon as well. I let out my breath. In order to maintain this level of control, I needed to delve into her mind.

I grimaced, certain that most of the stuff in there I didn't want to see but plunged in anyhow. I didn't expect the level of darkness in her mind. Unlike Brand's or even Crase's mind, Soria's was like walking into a dimly lit room, and yet bright sparks of light tried to get out through tiny holes. I moved to one light—a memory of my father, only a child, holding his sister's hand. She looked up at him, eyes wide with admiration, as he handed her some type of wooden toy.

Another spark held a picture of them older, Soria—early teens, my father—not much older than me. He handed Soria a paper, and a huge grin spread on his face. The paper welcomed her into the officer training academy. I felt her pride, her joy, her desire to be like her brother—special.

Each spark of light led to a good and happy memory. Most included my father. Soria was a teenager or young child in all of them. Parties, award ceremonies—and then there was Joe. He was quite the looker in those days. Dark wavy hair that hadn't yet started to recede, tall and lean, with a smirk that exaggerated his dimple, and blue eyes that were almost turquoise. The Joe memories overpowered me.

Being inside someone's mind is a delicate art, trying to retain the balance between your own thoughts and theirs. Soria's thoughts on Joe held a lot of emotion. She admired him like she had my dad, but there was more—much more.

A full level of desire threatened to push me away from my

objective. I quickly separated my thoughts from hers on that matter. She'd been young, and Joe was her brother's best friend, handsome, a little cocky, and, in her eyes, perfect. She wanted Joe, and she deceived herself into believing they were supposed to be together.

Her imagination fought her logical mind for control. While she knew Joe never thought of her as anything but a cute kid—his best friend's little sister—the part of her wanting it to be true overwhelmed everything else, allowing the darkness to pull me down. Feelings of hurt, anger, hatred poured into me. Soria being interrogated about what had happened to her brother's ship. Hours turned into days. They didn't let her leave. They barely fed her, barely let her sleep. Days slipped into weeks. What did she know? What had Aden told her of his plans? When they knew she had no clue about what had happened, they switched to what did she know about the ship itself? What exactly could it do? Had she seen any plans? Could she reconstruct any part of it?

They released her. She worked for every promotion ever given. Promotions that should have been hers passed over her head. She hated. She struggled, but she developed the touch, and it gave her an edge. She learned to be ruthless. She learned to trust no one. She managed to get a Darkothian by doing things that ashamed even herself. Having a Darkothian meant power. She loved being in control, but she hated him because he was a slave, and yet he would always be stronger than her.

She tortured him. She forced him to do things worse than she had to do to make herself feel better. Nothing helped. She always felt betrayed. All the light she once held, she lost, hidden behind the layer of filth she'd become. She hated everyone. Joe, Aden, herself.

And then she was on Earth. And she met me, and there was some light that tried to push through that memory, some sense of hope, but her wall stood strong like reinforced steel. There were clues she found in her hunt for Joe. Clues that verified to her the tiny hope she had that her brother hadn't abandoned her were false. Clues that told her he left Tallis, and he left her behind as well.

The darkness was thicker here, but I'd seen enough. Considering all this happened in less than a second I knew it would take me time to sort through, time to figure out where my devotion and feelings for my aunt lay. Right now, I needed to get us out of the mine.

"Give me Brand's control," I said.

She smiled happily and bent over, scooping it up and holding it out for me. Brand and I walked toward her. The only person who was going to stop us was the one whose mind wasn't being manipulated by Brand's and my arrangement.

Eri's arm pulled me back to him, his gun steady in the other hand, pointed directly at Soria's head. I had to tighten my grasp on Brand to keep our connection from being broken. It couldn't be severed. If I let go of Brand's hand, we would all be dead.

My strength diminished. It was harder than I'd even imagined. I thought about going into Eri's mind, making him compliant enough to just let Brand and me take care of things.

I didn't.

I wasn't strong enough to handle more than one mind at a time. Soria's thoughts already took a toll on me physically as well as mentally. But there was more to it than that. I couldn't go into Eri's mind. I wouldn't. What if I changed something in him, what if one of my thoughts got lodged in his mind, what if, in my attempt at providing an easy situation, I got carried away and made him love me just because I wanted him so much? I couldn't risk that. I made the decision right there that I would never go into his head. I would never change a single thing in him. Eri would always be Eri—even if that meant when all was said and done, he wouldn't stay with me.

"You need to trust me." It took deep concentration to speak to Eri and maintain my control of Soria's mind. "There is so much to explain, but all I can tell you now is I'm part-Darkothian, and you need to believe me when I tell you every mind in this room is being controlled by Brand or me." That got his attention. He of course would know Brand could control minds, but the fact I could—well, there was a topic starter for later.

"So, they will all do what you want them to?" Eri asked. The fact he seemed to believe without wading through a series of questions did more to bolster my resolve.

"Yes." All of a sudden, the nagging point inside me that told me we were not out of the woods yet faded.

"So, we can end this right here, right now? You can make them surrender."

Everyone still holding a weapon dropped them to the ground. Some even seemed genuinely happy to do so. Others, like Adamos, were a little stronger and seemed to be fighting against Brand. I knew the fact that he was trying to control so many at once was not easy, but even with his attention divided, no one could resist him.

Eri let go of my arm, more than a little shocked, I think. We walked toward Soria. Brand only stopped to pick up the weapons of those closest to us. He handed me one. I may have learned how to fight someone off if I needed to, but I'd never shot a gun before. My grip tightened as we made our way toward Soria.

Her hand was still outstretched. She grinned happily. For a moment, I wondered what else I could make her do. And then guilt filled me. Having this much power was scary. Brand, who was always being so hard on himself, held this power, and he controlled it so well. I gained a new appreciation for how he'd handled himself over the years. I hoped he could feel that appreciation, or at least see it in my mind. To the right, the mine exit waited—a long pathway that led out to the desert sands. I saw it clearly from Brand's memories. Two hundred meters stood between us and escape. Eri was close by, his back to me, making sure no one tried anything. He was right. We needed to end this. I shoved the gun into the back of my pants and took the controller from Soria's hand. It was surprisingly light and less than an inch and a half in diameter. How could something so small do such awful things? "What do you want them to do?" I asked Eri. He moved his gun from one vantage point to the next.

"Have them all go to the cells, lock each of them up."

"You heard him," I said to Soria. She nodded and yelled at the men. Everyone in the room walked away from us, back to the doorway we'd just come through, certainly more Brand's doing then their respect for her. From the corner of my eye, I caught the edge of a photograph protruding out of the pocket of her pants. I wondered if it could be the one she'd taken from my house. As long as I controlled her, I might as well get my parents' picture back.

I entered the thought straight into her mind without saying a word. She stopped, reached in her pocket, and handed it to me. Everything was going perfectly.

Then I heard the blast.

It wasn't a normal gun, bullets and all. This one was like a pulse of electricity, and when it hit Brand, it surged through our interlocked hands before tearing us apart.

Eri fired his gun toward the opposite opening. The picture Soria and I were in the midst of holding tore in half. Her eyes registered what had just happened. I hadn't had time to change all her thoughts, just make her do what I wanted her to. Now it was too late.

Our plan had gone astray. The man Eri had shot earlier leaned against the wall. I'd been certain he'd been dead. Eri fired again at him, and this time the bullet went straight through his head. He was dead now, but the damage was done. People were rattled by the quick release of Brand from their minds. They scrambled for their weapons. Soria crumpled her half of the picture in one hand and reached for Brand's control, shocked only for a microsecond it wasn't there.

She lunged at me, and my training kicked in. I stopped her hand with minimal effort, pushing her away. She twisted and jumped back. Eri still shot at the others in the mine, but she must have realized her only chance was to have a weapon. She didn't attack again but went for the nearest discarded gun.

Eri shot at everything in sight, but Brand lay limp on the floor. I was too exhausted to fight her, but I still had the advantage. I did the only thing I could do. The gun was out of my waistband and in my hand before she got to the weapon she was reaching for. I shot it, causing it to ricochet away from her grasp. Her hand flinched as the sting of the bullet glanced off her. I turned the gun to her, our eyes met, and her look dared me to shoot. My hand clutched the gun, but my finger wouldn't move again. And then Joe was there, yelling at us. We had to run. But we couldn't leave Brand. Knowing I didn't have the hate in me to shoot my aunt, I shot at everything around her, wildly and madly so she had no choice but to retreat to the other end of the room.

"Can you lift him?" I asked. Eri bent down without hesitation and threw Brand over his shoulder. It was a feat that, given Brand's size, should not have seemed so easy, but Eri already ran toward Joe, who shot his own gun like a madman. I followed directly behind them.

At the entrance, a Jeep waited. Mathis gunned it almost before we were all in. Eri threw Brand on the back floor. The two of us practically sat on top of him. Eri and Joe still shot at the entrance where people swarmed from. Another Jeep was to the side of the entrance, and people were diving in. Eri shot—first the front left tire, then the front right. I hoped that was enough to stop them, but the cloud of dust behind the Jeep, not to mention the blinding sun, blocked my view.

I slid down on the seat, trying to feel for Brand's pulse. Trying to take my mind off the sudden nausea that an abundance of heat and direct sunlight provided me. Dust filled my nose and mouth with each breath. I coughed and held on, since Mathis had no intention of slowing down.

28

The sign said *Welcome to Tropic*. I'd heard of it, but had never been here. After being in the cool mine for almost a month, the air burned hotter than a quasar. It wasn't nearly far enough away from where we'd come to seem like a safe place to stop. But there we were.

Brand slumped half on the seat, half on the floor. I situated him reasonably enough with his head on my lap, then leaned over him to keep the wind off both of us. He was breathing, his heartbeat constant, but he wasn't waking up. I tried speaking to him out loud, shaking him. I tried calling him in our silent speech. I tried slapping him. He didn't flinch, didn't move, didn't even groan. Keeping my own eyes open proved challenging, but I couldn't collapse now.

"He's lucky to even be alive, taking a blast at close range like that," Eri said. He was trying to be comforting. It didn't make me feel better, especially since I could tell he wasn't at all happy with the situation.

I'd tried to project my feelings for him in the mine, hoping his being an empath was enough. He had to know how I felt. The more I told myself, the more I believed it. But now, he sat as far away from me as possible, not touching me, still giving me a despondent grimace whenever our eyes met. I wanted him to look at me like he had that night at Lake Powell. I wanted to erase the last month. Being in this no man's land hurt. Maybe drifting into the exhaustion trying to overtake my body would be better.

I tried to think of something to say, but "Sorry our people want to kill each other," or "Too bad there's an intergalactic war going on, and we happen to be members of the opposing sides" didn't seem like the best ice breakers.

And really, there was no time. There was one reason I forced my body not to shut down. Soria would be coming for us.

"We need to go to your ship," Eri said.

"That was not part of the deal." Joe turned to look back at us. "The ship is off-limits. No one needs to know where it is. It's safe, that's all." His glare seemed like the final word.

Eri frowned. "She's looking for it. When she finds it—"

"She won't," Joe said. "Besides, there is no way he," Joe nodded toward Brand, "would be able to get to where the ship is."

"Well, we can't go back to Kanab," Eri said, and they glared at each other for a long moment. "What do you think we should do, Catelyn?" Eri asked but didn't turn away from Joe.

I looked up from Brand in surprise. I hadn't been expecting to be part of any decision. "You're right; she wants the ship. But she doesn't know where it is." I looked down at the crumpled picture in my hand. I had the side that showed my mom. Soria had the side that showed my dad. She'd asked where the picture had been taken. Her questioning had been so severe. I'd been certain the ship wasn't in Zion, but Joe's memories were in my mind, and they showed that, while it still seemed unbelievable, Zion was exactly where the ship was.

I wished I could talk to Joe. I hadn't realized how convenient my mind talks with Brand had been. Leaning forward, I handed Joe the picture. "She has the other side of this." It was the best way to let him know what was on my mind without saying the words. Joe's response, though silent as well, confirmed this was bad. The ship was in the red rock cliffs and canyons that formed Zion National Park. And Soria had a picture of the exact location.

We needed to go there. We couldn't risk letting her find it first. But Joe was right—the only way to get to the ship would be a hike Brand was in no condition to make.

We also couldn't take him back to Kanab. That was the first place they would look for us, even if they knew we would be smart enough not to go there.

What I needed was someone I could count on unconditionally. Someone who I didn't have issues to work out with. Someone who had my back. What I needed was Ryan. It seemed like a lifetime since I'd last seen him. He thought I was in Canada, thought I'd bailed on the last month of school. He thought I didn't graduate. How did I tell him that trip had been a lie?

"I have a place we can go," I said. "Probably a long shot, but does anyone have a phone?"

Surprisingly, Joe handed me his.

I dialed Ryan's number. Five rings were all I had before his voicemail would pick up. He answered on the fourth.

"Joe?" he said hesitantly.

"Actually, it's me."

"Caty! What the hell! Where are you? What's going on? You were supposed to be gone for a week. The police are going crazy. Someone broke into your place—it was completely ransacked after you guys left. What's up?" He stopped and took a breath, and then, in a softer tone, he asked, "Are you okay?"

"I'm fine, Ryan. I just—" Just what? Eri looked at me expectantly. Mathis glared in the rearview mirror. "I need your help."

"Of course. Anything," Ryan said, just like I'd hoped he would. Just like I needed him to say.

"I need to use your grandparents' cabin."

Not far past the Mount Carmel Junction that led to Zion, Ryan's grandparents had a cabin we'd spent a lot of time at over the past years. It was the best place I could think of, close enough to Zion and whatever awaited me there. And no place Soria would think to look—I hoped.

"Caty, what's going on? What does this have to do with Eri?"

"What do you mean?" I couldn't quite imagine what thoughts had been going through Ryan's head over the last month.

"His family disappeared too, and there was a break-in there as well. The whole town is on high alert." The panic in Ryan's voice was palpable.

"Ryan, I can explain everything to you. But I really need the cabin." I hoped he would hear the pleading in my voice.

"They're still down in Texas visiting Uncle James, but I have a key. When do you need it?"

"Today. We can probably be there in a couple of hours." Who knew what would happen in the next two hours? In that time, Brand could wake up and be just fine, or so I hoped. Soria or Adamos could come racing past us at any minute, and—I hoped that wouldn't happen.

"Okay," Ryan said. "And Caty?"

"Yeah?" His hesitancy was clear, but I couldn't explain things to him over the phone.

"I got tickets to Countryfest. You want to go?"

I had no idea what he was talking about. I hated country music. Ryan knew that. "Like I would be caught within fifty miles of there."

"That's good. I'm glad. I'm taking Valerie anyway." I heard the relief in his voice and knew I'd given him the right answer to his test. But he wasn't quite done with his concerns. "Is Joe with you?"

"Yeah, he's right here."

"Can I talk to him?"

"Sure. Here he is."

I handed the phone to Joe, who answered what I was sure were standard questions based on Joe's replies. Is Caty all right? Where are you guys? Does this have anything to do with Eri? Where is he? Joe hung up the phone just as we left the small town.

"He'll meet us there."

Relief and anxiety came at once. Ryan would help, but how did I explain any of this?

"We shouldn't get an Earthling involved in this," Mathis said. "They shouldn't know about us."

I just glowered at him. This Earthling was the person I needed most right now.

We were almost to the Junction before anyone said something besides directions. The silence wasn't comfortable. At least I could tell Eri wanted to talk as much as I did. But each time he was about to say something, he stopped. I did the same. The conversation we needed to have couldn't take place in front of, or, as the case was, behind Joe and Mathis. Too much needed to be said to just spout off pleasantries to fill the time.

Brand hadn't awoken, but he groaned now along with other noises. I tried talking to his mind but got no response. This bothered me more than the fact he hadn't opened his eyes.

"How long does a stun blast take you out?" I asked finally. I tried to keep from worrying, but we'd left the base over three hours ago. It seemed more like three days.

"It depends," Eri said. "He's taking a long time to come out of it—possibly because of what he is."

"What do you mean?"

"He's a Darkothian Healer."

"What does being Darkothian have to do with it?" I asked for Brand, but also for myself.

"It isn't that he's Darkothian, it's what the Tallisians—" Eri stopped, and we both looked away from each other. "What was done to him. His body and mind have been altered. That could affect the way he's responding to the blast."

Eri appeared to know that some genetic altering had been done to Brand, but his voice still held a fair amount of guessing in it. He wasn't a hundred percent sure what Brand could do. That bothered him. I couldn't go into any full description of Brand's abilities. I wanted to trust Eri, but I didn't feel that same way about Mathis.

"What they did was supposed to strengthen him, make him invincible," I said. "Why would he not be able to take a stun blast?"

"Because he should never have had to worry about that. His mind should have been faster than that of the man who pulled the trigger.

Even with his back to him, he should have felt him the second he was in range," Joe said.

He hadn't felt the man because his mind had been focused on helping me.

"Do you think he'll be okay?" I asked, softer.

"I'm sure he'll be fine," Eri said. But he turned away from me again as the desert passed us by. I wanted to touch him, see what he thought. I feared it might make things worse. No matter how much I tried to emanate my feelings for Eri, he wasn't picking up on them, which left me to wonder if maybe he didn't want to. Eri was a strong enough empath to read anyone's emotions, but if he knew how I wanted him right now and still turned away, the message was clear. I'd been prepared for that, but I'd also kept that piece of paper with me from the moment I read what it said, and I had hoped that it would be true again.

My hopes were for nothing.

Ryan was waiting by the front door when we pulled up. He took off his baseball cap and ran his hand through his hair as he walked over to the Jeep. I jumped out before we stopped moving, throwing my arms around him, practically knocking him to the ground. He definitely wasn't expecting that, but he squeezed me tight before pulling away.

"You sure you're okay?"

"It's just really good to see you." A lump formed in my throat.

"Are you going to tell me what's going on?" He looked me up and down. I was a mess of torn clothing, bloodstains, and a missing shoe.

"I'll get to that, but right now, I have a friend who is hurt and needs some help." Ryan raised his eyebrows when he recognized Eri and then Mathis, raising them steeper when he noticed Brand, still unconscious in the back seat.

"What happened to him?" he asked.

No lies. "He was shot with a stun gun."

"A stun gun? Caty, what's going on?"

I hadn't really planned how to tell Ryan about me—again. Luckily, I knew him well enough to know it was best to just jump right into the water.

"Remember the night we said goodbye?"

Ryan nodded, and then a frown creased his face. "I remember you came over to say goodbye," he said. "But I don't remember much after that. I wasn't feeling too well. I crashed for like two days after you left." His frown increased. "Which was probably for the best since I have barely slept from the moment I realized you were not coming back."

I felt the guilt of not having thought about what Ryan would have done if I had never returned. "Do you remember about my memorysight?" I asked.

He looked shocked, but I quickly realized it was because of the others. When he saw it wasn't a secret to anyone here, he nodded.

"I found out why I can do the things I do."

He looked at me expectantly.

"Ryan, I'm not from Earth. My parents and Joe came here eighteen years ago from another planet called Tallis."

"You're an alien?" he asked calmly.

I nodded. The first time I'd told him all of this, there hadn't been time to focus on what I was. Joe and Claire were missing, and that was all either of us thought about. This time, however, the spotlight was all on me. He'd taken it well before; how would he take it this time?

"And that is why you've been gone?"

I nodded.

"And Eri?"

"He's an alien too."

Ryan frowned. For a brief moment, I was certain he wouldn't take it well this time. But then he said, "Is that a problem?"

"Only that our worlds are at war with one another."

Understanding danced in Ryan's eyes. I really hadn't realized how much I missed him. How well he knew me.

He put his arm around me and squeezed my shoulder. "But you two are obviously not." He looked over to where Eri helped Joe move Brand. "He wouldn't be here if you were fighting."

"It's complicated." I sighed. "Like intergalactic-war complicated."

"Nothing in the universe is so complicated that you can't find a way to work through it. Not if you want to."

I looked at him in shock. "Why are you being so calm about this?" He'd just found out aliens existed and all he worried about was giving me relationship advice? It was so typically Ryan that I smiled.

He smiled back. "Well, apparently, one of us needs to be." He led me into the cabin. "Why don't you start from the beginning?" he said as he sat me down on the couch.

"He can control my mind?" Ryan asked. We were in the back room where Brand lay on the top cover of an old sleigh bed. No longer turning restlessly as he had at first, but still showing no sign of waking up.

"You don't have to worry about that. He won't go into your head."

"Apparently, he already did once. What's to stop him again?" My nice calm friend who had listened to my whole story, who hadn't looked shocked once, had vanished.

"He won't hurt you. And we're not leaving you alone. Eri and Mathis will be here with you." I thought it would be easier to get Ryan to stay with Brand. He'd been fine until the whole mind control thing. Maybe I shouldn't have told him everything.

"We'll be going with you," Eri said. Joe looked up from rearranging a backpack with some canteens and trail mix he'd found.

"Catelyn and I will be going by ourselves," he said sterner than necessary.

"If we are going to stop Soria, we need to work together," Eri said.

It amazed me how he could act so calmly all the time. I wanted to see him act as if he were worried if I left, if he might never see me again. I wanted him to be as panicked as I was. I'd never known how uncaring calm could appear.

"There was a reason we didn't take the ship to Rhaev when we left Tallis," Joe said—definitely not calm. "We worked together earlier because I needed to save Catelyn. You may be right about needing to work together again, but I'm not taking anyone to the only safe place I have left."

"Safe?" Eri asked.

I knew how he felt. To him, the ship that had destroyed the planet, that had killed his mother, was anything but safe. But I also knew the things I'd seen in Joe's head when I'd been in Brand's. I knew the ship was safe—my dad and Joe had seen to that. I needed Eri to understand that as well.

"Joe. Tell them why you came here. Tell them what happened," I said. He looked confused for just a moment, and then he looked back and forth between Brand and me.

"Your mother was a Priestess of Sight as well," he said, fully understanding I knew everything.

I looked away, embarrassed. But Joe came and put his arm around me. "It's okay. I'm glad you know everything now. I should have never kept things from you. I just..." he sighed, and I hugged him back.

"I know," I said. "But they don't." I looked over at Eri, who waited patiently, and Mathis—who did not. "Tell them."

"Eighteen years ago, Aden and I built a ship. She had state-of-the-art everything—the best ship the Tallisian Military could ask for. Due to her unique properties—a machine with living parts, with its own intelligence, she could do things no one had ever seen. She could move like no other vessel.

"But Aden wasn't only a genius; he was also an inventor. He wanted this ship to be better than the best. He wanted to give us something that would end the war. Something that would blow everyone away—and he found that something.

"Inside the ship, Aden created a device that could open a wormhole. Until that point, only natural wormholes had been used. We could stabilize them and make them permanent, but no one had ever just opened one on their own. Aden did that."

"Then what about Sardova? Wormholes—even unstable wormholes—don't destroy worlds." Eri spoke softly, and finally, the one emotion incapable of hiding behind his calm interior burst forth —sorrow.

"They do if you try to open a wormhole inside of a planet," Joe said.

I expected another outburst from Eri or even from Mathis. I only got sickening silence. A wormhole inside of a planet? I'd known from Joe's memories that my dad had tried to stop another man from destroying Sardova. I'd seen the planet burst apart in his memories as well, but I had not explored that moment enough to understand what had caused Sardova's final destruction. Until this point, I still thought my dad had actually built a planet destroyer.

"It wasn't a weapon," I said.

Joe shook his head. "Your father would never have created a weapon. Wormhole technology wasn't meant to destroy, just to let us travel faster, give us a one-up on Rhaev.

"It was Bastile who wanted to test the device within the world limits. Your father tried to stop him."

Bastile? That must have been who my father had been arguing with in the memory I had seen the night Eri had brought the orb to my house. Joe's words mixed with my memorysight and the fragments of what I'd seen of Joe's mind from Brand all connected, and I understood. "And that is why he chose to leave? To remove the capability of allowing that to ever happen again," I said.

"What happened tormented him for his whole life. He never forgave himself. But it wasn't his fault," Joe said.

Tears streamed down my face. I found the courage to look at Eri. It didn't change the fact that we were from the wrong planets, it still didn't mean we could be together, but at least when he left, he would know my dad had not been the one who'd killed his mom. "My dad. He didn't do it."

"He was there. He let it happen," Mathis snarled from the corner of the room. I whipped around and glared at him.

"You don't know that," I said. I turned back to Eri. "It wasn't him. He didn't want that. He tried to stop it." I needed Eri to believe me.

There was conflict in his eyes, shimmering through the tears he tried to blink back.

"It wasn't—"

"I believe you," he said. It was all I needed to hear.

I looked at Joe. "He's coming with us." I was certain if I were to touch Eri right now, I wouldn't see anything. If he could offer me that level of trust, then I trusted him right back—not just with my own life, but with Joe's life. With Claire's, because I knew she was with the ship.

"He is Rhaevian." Joe said.

"And you're Tallisian. And I'm, well, what does it matter?"

Joe didn't answer, but he didn't look away from me. We stood there for ten million microseconds, each a lifetime of their own, before he nodded. "Just Eri."

29

"Are you going to be okay?" I sat on the front porch with Ryan, watching Joe and Eri put the packs in the Jeep. The prospect of leaving my best friend and my comatose friend alone with Mathis wasn't thrilling.

"Well, I wouldn't join a bowling team with the guy, but I'm not worried anymore. As long as your other friend in there doesn't wake up and try any voodoo hypnotics on me, I'll be fine."

"Trust me, Brand won't hurt you," I said. "But what do you mean you aren't worried anymore?"

"While you and Joe filled the packs and changed, Eri had a talk with Mathis. I've been paying enough attention the last couple of hours to know Eri must be the one holding the guns—no pun intended. And given the fact his commander is in love with you, I'm fairly certain Mr. Smith—Mathis—is going to make sure nothing happens to me or to Brand, for that matter." Ryan smiled just as I frowned.

"What?" he asked. "Don't act like you can't tell the guy is crazy about you." He gave me a nudge with his shoulder.

"It's not that." The fact Eri believed me about my dad told me he cared about me to some extent. Were they the same feelings I had for him? Possibly. I'd just given Joe a whole spiel about how it didn't matter what any of us were. But those words were easier to say than to believe. Given the way Eri avoided me in the car, the way he looked away every time I looked at him, made me certain Eri didn't believe in a happily ever after for us.

"Things will work out."

"Yeah." I tried to sound positive because, once again, I didn't have time to have a heart-to-heart with Ryan. I didn't have time to even think about Eri and me because of Soria. I didn't know when she would come, but I'd been in her head and knew my aunt well enough to know we needed to hurry.

Angels Landing is one of the most popular hikes in Zion. So of course that is where the ship was hidden. Smack dab in the middle of the towering red cliff. Luckily, with dusk settling in, most sane people were finishing up the hike for the day, not starting.

We all realized the need to get to Scout Lookout as quickly as possible. Soria had the picture. She'd questioned me about it. I don't know what tipped her off, but that didn't matter. We needed to get up there to keep Claire safe and the ship secure. Claire was the number one reason Joe was going as fast as he was up the trail. I'd also seen his look before he hit the switchbacks, one that told me there was another reason he'd distanced himself from Eri and me.

"What's wrong?" Eri asked when Joe's footsteps grew dim.

"What do you mean?"

Ryan told me I needed to talk to Eri. I didn't want to. It was easier to accept whatever was in my head than to have the possibility it might actually be confirmed.

"You're biting your lip," he said.

"It's nothing." I walked faster. I'd built up quite a bit of endurance over the last month; I could catch up with Joe in no time.

"Catelyn, wait."

I stopped. Eri came behind me and put his hand on my shoulder, turning me toward him. He smelled so good—cinnamon and cloves. He felt so warm—right next to me. I needed to say something. He didn't give me the chance. I didn't hesitate when his hands pulled me closer, and I didn't fight when his lips found mine. The only objection I had was when he finally did pull away.

"I'm sorry. I had to do that," he said, his hands falling away from me.

"Why?" I asked.

"Because I promised myself every moment in that cell if I ever saw you again, I would." He let go and stepped away. Sighing, he rubbed one hand through his hair as he walked away.

"Stop." I commanded him this time. He listened but didn't turn around.

"You don't just get to kiss me and then walk away." Anger flared. At him, at the whole situation, at myself for wanting him to turn around and kiss me again anyway.

He turned, but he didn't reach for me. "I'm sorry. I know things have changed for you, but I—"

"Things have changed for me?" What was he talking about? "Because I'm Tallisian? If you hate what I am so much, why would you kiss me?" I knew no one would let us be together. It was better this way. But I wasn't the one who had kissed him—no matter how badly I'd wanted to.

"What?" He scoffed. "Why would you say that? I don't care that you're Tallisian."

"Then—"

"Brand," he said.

"You're supposed to be an empath. How can you not tell how I feel about you?"

His eyes lightened as he searched my face. "But what Soria said, how Brand feels about you, and there is something between you two."

"I have a bond with Brand, not because I'm in love with him, but because of what we are. We were meant to complement each other. My abilities are all from my mother. She was a Darkothian Priestess of Sight, and so am I."

His eyes went lighter still, but he didn't move toward me.

"Brand taught me about my abilities," I continued. "He showed me new ones I never even knew existed. At the base, I discovered I can talk to him without using words. I discovered I can use Brand's abilities as well. It's what we were meant to do. We've been inside each other's minds, but that doesn't mean—"

Eri stopped my explanation with a kiss. His mouth moved on mine. His arms wrapped around me, pulling me closer to him. I inhaled his scent, shivered as his fingers caressed the back of my neck. It was as if we were standing on that cliff at Lake Powell again, sharing our first kiss, but I didn't see memories or visions. I just knew as long as we could breathe and touch, it would be Eri and me.

"You SAID you could use Brand's ability," Eri said as we continued up the long steep switchbacks. "So, have you been inside my mind?"

"No," I said.

"Why not?" he asked, and the fact he sounded more put out about it than worried made me laugh.

"Because some things are better left alone."

"But you went into his mind." Now we were getting to the root of the problem. I shared a bond with Brand because we'd seen into each other. I had no secrets from Brand, and he had none from me. I'd never stopped to think how that would make Eri feel.

"Brand doesn't just read minds. When he goes into a person's head, he sees everything. And he can change anything. That's how it was for me when I used his gift. Maybe there is a way to control it, but I don't know. All I know is there are some things from Brand's mind I wished I didn't have to see—and he's the good guy. The things in Soria's head are going to haunt me for a long time. I did what I had to do to survive. I would do it again if it meant your life, or mine, or someone I loved. But I didn't enjoy it." Even now, I shuddered, remembering some of the graphic memories of torture I'd seen in both Soria's and Brand's heads. It wasn't easy to discard those memories. Brand had years of practice letting go. My own mind had a harder time, perhaps because I'd held on to memories for so long in the past.

"You could look at my thoughts, you know. I wouldn't mind." Eri stopped and pierced me with those green eyes. The sun had set now, and his features weren't as easy to make out in the shadows of the cliff wall, but his eyes I saw perfectly.

I knew he meant it. He wasn't just throwing out some flippant words. He was willing to share the deepest part of himself. That was a sacrifice I didn't even know if I would be willing to make. Knowing Brand knew my mind so intimately, no matter how much I trusted him, hurt. Eri would be different, but once you have experienced something like that, your perspective changes. It's a good thing most people Brand sees into don't understand the extent of what is happening.

"Thank you. But I like not knowing everything; it makes things more—real."

"How?"

"Sometimes we need our imagination more than we need the truth—even if they are the same thing. Like when you kiss me, it's nice to imagine your heart is racing exactly like mine is."

"Trust me, it is." He took my hand and placed it against his chest, then kissed me again as proof.

"You're biting your lip again," Eri said as we arrived at Scout Lookout.

Joe sat on a rock with a canteen in hand, waiting for us. He looked at our hands and then at me. I knew he understood and was trying to be supportive, but he still had that father's look of concern as well.

I smiled. "It's just that I know things with Soria aren't going to be easy." I knelt on one knee and pulled a flashlight from my pack. It was now officially too dark to go on without one.

I'd had a nagging feeling since we left the base. But I'd had a lot of nagging feelings, and each of those got taken care of—my conversation with Ryan, my conversation with Joe, my conversation with Eri. But as my other thoughts worked themselves out, the knowledge that all would not be well the next time we encountered my dear aunt no longer nagged but downright screamed out for attention.

"It will be okay," Eri said. "We have a lot of things going for us. We all know the layout of the base now, and when the Darko...when Brand wakes up, we will have his help as well. There's nothing to worry about."

Eri's calming presence fell over me, and I tried to embrace it even as every inch of me knew it was not real. I was not calm. None of us should be calm.

"How do we get into the ship, exactly?" I asked. Things would be fine once I ensured Claire's safety. I kept telling myself that. Claire and the ship equaled safety. If we got to them, we could make plans. Everything would be fine.

"Come with me." Joe held out his hand, and I took it. Scout Lookout is a flat area just before you start to climb what is known as the Hogsback, the steepest part of the journey, covered with chains to help pull yourself up the ragged sharp-edged rocks. I wasn't looking forward to climbing those at night, but still, it surprised me when he led me not to the next trail but to the other side of the lookout, where nothing but a straight drop down and a few outcropped trees stood.

"What are we doing?" I asked, hoping the answer didn't include jumping.

Joe shined his flashlight on a device similar to the one Eri had used to put trail mix into a rock and pull a compression coil out from a tree. Just to the side of the cliff, a hidden crevice that would have been difficult to make out even during the daytime caught my eye.

"Our doorway," Joe said and pressed the button on his remote.

I knew what came next, but I wasn't so sure about becoming molecularly displaced. Still, I reached out my hand to the place the light bounced off the rock. It seemed solid at first, but as I pressed, my fingers moved straight through the rock. They tingled like pins and needles but didn't hurt. The mountain enclosed my hand. I pulled it back out, steadying myself on the cliff's edge.

"All you need to do is step through," Joe said and stepped into the mountain. I looked over the edge, not sure what I expected, but he had not plummeted to his death.

As much as I tried not to dissect too many of Joe's thoughts that I'd seen in Brand's mind, I wish I would have taken more time to see this. Joe was literally inside Angels Landing. I stared at the wall for a good long minute until Eri came over and took my hand.

"Don't think too much," he said.

I nodded, but I couldn't think about anything else. I debated recalling Joe's memories when Eri stepped forward and tugged my hand enough that I followed, not wanting to let go of him. And then the wall swallowed me. I felt the same pins and needles effect, though it was more unsettling going through my whole body than for just my hand. I wasn't just inside a cold dark mountain but on an actual ship.

The inside of the ship wasn't quite as posh as anything on the big screen, but it was larger than I expected, with intricate piping along the sides and ceilings and symbols above doorways and panels that mimicked the other Tallisian lettering I'd now grown used to seeing.

"Caty," Joe said. "This is Trilla."

"It's so—" what was the word I was looking for? "Alien."

Joe and Eri laughed.

"What were you expecting?" Joe asked. "The Enterprise?"

I hoped the low lighting concealed my blush. "Well, I don't know. It's just—" Again, I found myself at a loss for words. "Wow."

I ran my fingers along one of the consoles before me, and the ship shuddered into life—glowing brightly under my fingers and vibrating gently. Before I had time to take in the strange wonderment of what lay before me, a memorysight shot through me. Perhaps because the ship wasn't all the way living or machine but a combination, my memorysight wasn't as clear as usual. A culminating mix of feelings and images left me with a tight knot in my gut.

"Soria," I said. Somehow my aunt had been here—or was still here.

"Claire," Joe said, pulling his gun out and rushing toward a doorway before I could say anything else.

Eri had his gun out too and followed Joe as he left the control room we were in and down a flight of stairs through a long narrow passageway. I stumbled after them through the doorway at the end of the hall. This must have been the cargo bay, but I didn't have time to explore. Claire was tied up to a post on the far end of the room.

I turned around, but men had already surrounded us. Their weapons pointed at Joe, Eri, and me. Soria stepped out from behind Claire. She held the crumpled picture we'd ripped in half when I left the mine.

I couldn't see how we were going to get out of this, so I did the only thing I could think of. I didn't know what type of distance barrier limited my telepathy with Brand, but I had to try. I opened my mind and called him as best I could.

Brand, if you can hear me, we need you—now!

30

"There's no sign of the Darkothian," a man behind us said.

Soria frowned but nodded in acceptance. She came toward Joe, her eyes softening a little but turning to cold steel just as fast. "Lower your weapons," she said to Joe and Eri.

Neither of them moved.

"There is a gun aimed right at her head," she nodded toward Claire. "I would hate for my man to get nervous and pull the trigger."

Joe dropped his gun. Eri did not comply as fast, but after a few seconds, he decided not to call her bluff and threw his down as well. Soria came closer, pausing next to Joe, but looking at me. She pulled the transistor rod from her belt and rested it in the palm of her hands. Her intimidation worked well. My body stiffened in anticipation of what she would do.

"Where is Brand?" she asked.

I didn't answer. If she thought he could be close, could be able to help us, it may be to our advantage. She lifted up the rod, and I flinched, waiting for it to strike my skin, trying not to imagine what emotion she might emanate. But when the rod hit flesh, my arm did not burn with pain.

Eri cried out, and my eyes opened to see the rod pressed into his flesh. She looked at me and smiled. Apparently, she'd learned my weakness. I wouldn't talk through my own beating, but I couldn't let her do to Eri what she'd done to me.

"He's injured. We couldn't bring him with us," I said through gritted teeth. She let the rod fall from Eri's skin. He stood lock-jawed, defiant, but his pain was there nonetheless.

"So, the gun worked?" She looked pleased. "I had Adamos rewire several of the stun guns to work with Brand's physiology."

I should have guessed something like that. Brand should have healed faster. I no longer had hope that he would wake soon. Brand didn't hear me call. If he had, he would have responded. We were on our own.

"How did you find us?" Joe asked.

She went back to him, looking into his eyes like a lover at long last reunited with her mate. "I got the right side of the picture." She held up my dad's crumpled face.

Joe cursed.

"Aden hated having his image taken," she said. Which was true. Mom had to practically tie him to the car anytime she wanted to get a family picture. "I knew the minute I saw this there had to be some significance. But it wasn't until Catelyn ripped part of it away from me that I noticed the markings."

I wasn't sure what markings she was talking about, but Joe's face said he understood.

"Once I was here," Soria continued, "it was so thoughtful of the Earthling to be outside, almost as if she'd been waiting for me."

I looked over to Claire. The look of guilt on her face said she blamed herself for all of this. I knew Joe well enough to know he was probably doing the same thing, blaming himself for leaving her. I'd blamed myself more than once over the past month.

"What now? What do you want, Soria?" Joe asked.

"I want what I've always wanted. I want you." She reached up to touch his cheek. Joe flinched, and Soria grasped his chin between her fingers and thumb. Since I'd been in her head, I knew which emotions she would share with him.

"I love you, Joe," she said. "And you loved me."

Joe shook his head. "I never loved you in that way, Soria." He wasn't mean, just truthful. "You were just a kid."

The truth seemed to hurt her more. "I was just a kid, and you and Aden left me behind to be tortured. Do you know what they did to me? Do you want to see the scars they left?"

"Aden would have come back for you. But it wasn't possible. You've seen the ship; surely you checked the engines. We couldn't fix her, not here on this world. We didn't have the resources to get what we would need."

"But you left me in the first place."

"He tried to tell you, but you wouldn't listen," Joe said. He was being patient, but he sounded ready to explode. He wasn't looking at Soria at all as he answered her. His head was turned toward Claire.

"I would have listened if *you'd* asked me to go," Soria said softly. "But that is all in the past." She was back to business. "I have the ship. I've already sent men back to get the parts to restore her controls. I have you—a traitor to give to them. I have my niece, and as soon as I get my Darkothian, I'll have everything I need to return to Tallis, a hero. No more second-rate jobs. I will get the admiralship I deserve."

"Where is Brand?" she said to me again.

I couldn't tell her. If she went for Brand, she would find Ryan. Ryan was strong, but he wasn't strong enough to survive what Soria could do to him.

"Where is he?" she said more forcefully and wrapped her fingers around my arm, pushing pain through me. I could withstand that longer than the sadness, but soon it became so intense my concentration faltered.

When she'd been tortured, Soria had known great physical pain. Now she made me feel that anguish with just one touch. Did they know they were giving her a powerful weapon when they tried to beat information out of her? When I fell to my knees, no longer able to stand, she let go.

"Let me explain to you how this is going to work," she said.

I struggled to control my breathing. Eri fell to the ground by me, holding me in his arms. Soria pointed her gun to his head. "Stay away from her."

"Soria, don't do this." Joe reached for her. She moved away from him.

"Don't touch me," she snarled, her gun still pointed at Eri. He didn't move. She moved the gun in my direction. "I said stay away from her."

"Soria, she's your niece. She's your family," Joe said.

"She betrayed me, just like her father. Just like you did."

"You're right. We should have taken you. We just never thought we wouldn't be back. I never forgot you."

"I wish that was true," she said. "I've wished that was true every day since I lost you. But you came here, and you found someone else. My brother had already tainted his blood by choosing a Darkothian—a slave, a lesser. You always wanted to be like him, so I guess you couldn't wait to find one of these inferiors here."

She pointed the gun at Claire. A static noise indicated someone was trying to speak to her through her communication link. She lifted her hand to her ear, her lips settled into a scowl as she listened. A moment later, her eyes flickered back to me. "When I get back, you will tell me where Brand is, or someone is going to die. And I won't be shedding any Tallisian blood."

She turned to one of the men who had guns on us. "Tie them up."

How could I decide between lives? If I didn't tell Soria where Brand was, she would kill Claire or Eri—probably both. If I told her, Brand would be a slave again, and Ryan would most likely die.

My arms were wrapped around a pole behind me and tied at the wrists. I worked on loosening the rope, but I had no clue what I would do even if I got free. Each time I stretched or rubbed the ropes against the pole, they loosened a bit, but never enough. The skin on my wrists rubbed raw, and soon the dampness of blood moistened the ropes.

Soria had left the cargo bay, but her two men stood guard. Their fingers never left the triggers on their guns. Not being a weapon expert, I couldn't tell if they held bullets or just a blast of electricity. They'd tied Eri to the next pole over. We'd attempted to talk once, but trigger-happy-Jack on the right looked like he barely stopped himself from shooting us in his mad warning to be quiet. No one risked speaking after that. No one wanted to find out if they were meant to kill us or stun us—and the fact that the last person to get hit by a stun gun had still not woken up didn't leave me believing that would be any better than an actual bullet.

I looked at Joe. He caught my eye, but his expression didn't communicate hope. I'd wanted a sign we would be okay. I got just the opposite. My gaze went back to the floor.

"When she comes back, don't tell her where he is," Eri said. His voice was less than a whisper. I turned my head to see if he'd really spoken or if I'd just imagined it.

"Don't look at me." The words were not much clearer than his previous ones. His lips didn't move, and he stared at the ground.

"I have to tell her," I whispered back while looking away. Soria wouldn't kill Brand. He was too valuable to her. She would torture him for what he'd done, just as she would continue to torture me. But Brand would live. She had no reason to kill Ryan. Soria was cold and cruel, but the things she did always had meaning behind them. She would kill Eri because he was a Rhaevian. She would kill Claire because Joe loved her. But Ryan was nothing to Soria.

I kept telling myself that over and over. If I believed even for a moment she would kill Ryan, I wouldn't be able to tell her the truth, and in doing so, I would be signing a death sentence.

"She's going to kill me. Even if you tell her, she will still kill me. Don't put anyone else's life at risk."

"What if she kills Claire?"

Eri didn't answer right away. Had he heard me? I looked at Claire. She was just as innocent as Ryan was in all of this. She didn't look scared. I couldn't stop shaking, but not Claire. She sat up tall. Her short red hair fell limply in her eyes. She didn't even move her head to shake away the distraction. She looked at Joe, so much love in her eyes. She didn't show any fear.

I'd never realized how strong Claire was. She always seemed a little old for her years, not in her appearance but in the way she contemplated things. She was that sweet, gentle figure in my life that had cookies waiting after school and a different pie every Sunday. But she'd also held me up through every burden. She'd been strong for me all these years in such a subtle way that I'd taken it for granted. Now her strength showed through again—for me —for Joe.

"They won't kill Claire," Eri whispered.

"How can you be sure?"

"The guard on the left wants nothing to do with this. He's a maintenance worker at best, I'm guessing. His emotions are all over the place; he takes his finger off the trigger at least every thirty seconds. The guy to the right hates me; he's ready to pull that trigger now, but he keeps looking at Claire, and each time he does, his face softens. She reminds him of someone close to him."

I lifted my eyes slowly so as not to draw attention to myself. Sure enough, the man to the left rubbed one palm against his pants. He didn't want to be here. I would have missed it had Eri not pointed it out. I looked to the one on the right. His eyes were on Claire, and they looked at her with all types of sorrow that, once again, I would have missed.

"How did you see that?"

"I have a lot more training than just my empathic skills. Now listen to me carefully. When Soria comes back, I will calm those two. It won't work in my favor because whoever is behind us hates me more than either of those guys. If I had to guess, I'd say that big guy from the base. He has no compassion, no calmness of his own to pull from."

I couldn't turn to see. How could he tell there was someone behind us? If he was right, then Adamos had come into the room at some point, and I'd been too wrapped up in myself to catch it.

"When they are calm, you refuse to tell Soria. It will not be Claire they aim at."

I turned to him now, almost too quickly, panic sweeping all over. He couldn't mean what he said. He couldn't sacrifice himself.

"Turn away," he said slowly, softly.

I looked back at the ground. Neither guard moved. "No," I said. I'd just gotten him back. I couldn't lose him again. Why was this even a choice I had to make?

"I'm dead already." His voice was strong, steady.

"I won't let them kill you," I said, crying, my voice no longer a whisper.

"Quiet," the man to the right hissed, and his finger pulled the trigger of his gun.

Things really do go in slow motion when you think you're about to die. No bullet flew toward me. When the pain first hit my body, it felt like being electrocuted. The impact on my leg burned painfully, but it wasn't as bad as I expected. My whole body tingled. Only a small piece of charred cloth showed on my pant leg. Not a bullet.

I heard yelling. I thought it was Adamos. Eri said my name—he was still alive. Why was everything going so slow? Everything got blurry, and then nothing.

Maybe the electricity running through my body made my dreams wild and vivid. They were all about Joe. Memories I'd seen from Brand played like a movie. I lived the motion picture of his life. He'd done a few stupid things, most before he'd come to Earth, but all in all, Joe really was a good person. The light his memories contained blinded me.

There were moments of him working on the ship with my dad. He gave up his whole life to help my parents be together. I saw when they left Tallis, and all the workings of Trilla. There were so many intricate parts to her, so many things she was capable of. It was amazing. He fell in love with Claire. She'd turned him down nearly twenty times before she accepted that first date.

All the decisions about not telling me who I was consumed him. There seemed to be moments in his memories when one of them wanted to tell me—but those moments never coincided with each other. His pain when the news of my parents' deaths came was almost unbearable. Most of all, I knew how much he cared about me. How proud he'd been at each moment in my life. I could never doubt Joe's love for me after seeing all that.

When I came to, the post was still pushed into my back. My neck was severely kinked, and it hurt to move. My head pounded, and I had to blink several times to bring things into focus. The guard who shot me had left the room. Adamos stood in his place.

Claire, Joe, and Eri were all still here too. But Joe's eyes were closed, though I could see him breathing. It only took a moment to see the burned piece of shirt near his shoulder. Claire looked at him full of worry, but when she saw me wake up, I sensed her relief. Whatever they'd hit us with hadn't knocked us out in the same way Brand had been.

Eri had a red mark across his face that had already started to turn purple. He smiled at me, but he didn't say anything. We'd gotten lucky, but Adamos's gun didn't look quite like the other one had. If he shot at us, I didn't think luck would be on our side again.

When Adamos saw me awake, he turned and left the room. He was likely going to get Soria. My choice on who to sell out would need to come soon, and I hadn't made a decision. Maybe when Soria came into the room, my gut instinct would tell me what to do. Maybe she would kill me first—that would be easier than watching her destroy everyone I loved. I knew she wouldn't, though.

I looked back at Eri. With Adamos gone, he risked talking softly. "You know what you have to do," he said. I did know. I knew right then Soria would never let him live. And if she didn't kill him, Adamos would. The only way to protect anyone meant I had to remain silent. I also knew that meant when Eri died, I would be at fault. I tried to ignore that. Why should I have to do what was best? Why should I have to lose him?

I nodded. Soria came into the room with Adamos. If my tears had any effect on her at all, she didn't show it. I felt Eri trying to calm those in the room who he could. It had no effect on my hardened aunt.

"Untie the Rhaevian," she said to Adamos. Using much more force than necessary, he threw Eri at her feet. Eri didn't struggle. He knew what he had to do as well.

Soria turned him so I could see straight into his eyes. They were the same deep intense aquamarine I'd seen the first time he kissed me. She took her gun and held it to his head. This one was also not just a stun gun. Apparently, I *was* turning into a weapon expert—a skill I didn't want.

"Where is Brand?" she asked.

I didn't answer.

"Where is Brand?" she said again, her grip tightening on the trigger just barely.

"I love you." Eri met my tear-filled eyes. I tried to capture his face in my memory. I wanted to touch him once more. I didn't want to do what intuition told me to do.

"Will you let them go if I tell you?" I asked.

Soria laughed. I tried again. There had to be some way to appeal to her. Some way to soften her. In the past, talking about my dad had worked a little. Now that she thought he had really betrayed her, I wasn't sure it would.

"Soria, I know you're angry. I know what my father did hurt you. You've shown me," I said. She'd shown me just how awful her torture had been when she turned it on me. "You don't have to do this."

"Where is Brand?" she asked a third time, ignoring my plea.

"I'll tell you. Just please don't hurt him."

"You are worse than your father." I'd tried to soften her, but I'd just made her more eager to kill Eri. "He chose a slave, but you, you would choose the enemy?"

I tried another approach. His life for mine. She wanted to take me back, to convert me to her cause. "I'll go with you back to Tallis. I'll give him up. Just don't hurt him."

"I will take you back to Tallis no matter what. Now tell me where Brand is." Her finger tightened, not enough to fire the gun but enough to cause me to flinch. I had no other options. My dad was our only common link.

"My dad loved you," I said.

"Your father never even told you about me," she hissed.

I really wished Joe were awake. He would have something to add; he would help me out of this mess I was making. I wanted to stop her but just seemed to be prolonging Eri's death scene. At the thought of Joe, my dream came back to me. Only it wasn't a dream. Everything I'd seen while I'd been knocked out had been what I'd taken from Brand's mind at the base. A realization hit me. Soria would never bargain with me. In her hands, we were all dead, but there was someone who could help us. Someone I knew had loved my dad, loved Joe. I don't know why I hadn't thought of it sooner, possibly because the idea was so foreign to me.

Trilla.

31

Trilla was more than just a machine. There were parts of her that were living. Her intelligence may have begun as artificial, but I'd seen it evolve. Trilla was alive, and she was smart. She could do a hundred different things with one command. I'd learned all that from Joe's memories. However, the only person who had ever been able to command her had been my dad. Joe could program her to do what he wanted. He could use her controls to turn on the lights, open and close doors, and make her fly. For my dad, she did all those things if he simply asked. No matter where in the ship he was, he'd had complete control of her, and she'd obeyed.

I remembered the way she'd moved under my touch when we first walked in. I was my father's flesh and blood. Could she possibly know that? Would she respond to me if I asked? How did I ask her? Did I have to talk to her in front of everyone? What if it didn't work? What if I asked for help and didn't get it? It didn't matter; things couldn't get much worse.

"Trilla," I said quietly. "You loved my dad." My post shuddered.

"What?" Soria asked. I needed to state my plea out loud. I hoped Trilla knew I spoke only to her.

"You loved my dad," I said loudly. "There was a time when you would have done anything for him."

"That time is past," Soria said. I ignored her. She wasn't part of this conversation anymore.

"I'm his daughter. My dad isn't here, but I need your help. I need you to do for me what you would do for him."

Soria looked at me, baffled. "If your father were here, he would be my prisoner too," she said. She frowned, and her grip loosened. If nothing else, my frantic plea confused her.

"My dad loved you. He wanted to keep you safe. I want you to be safe also," I continued.

Eri's eyes caught mine. He wasn't as confused as Soria was. He smiled at me encouragingly, and suddenly, everything felt like it would be okay. He knew what needed to be done, and he did his part by calming me.

"Tell me where Brand is," Soria said, but her voice wasn't rising as much anymore.

I looked at Eri. He focused on emitting calmness. Unfortunately, my aunt caught our exchange and took on her rigid stance again. She pushed away any calm she might have allowed to seep in. I didn't have any more time.

"I need your help," I yelled, squeezing the post as best I could to create a physical connection with the ship. "I need your help now, Trilla!"

I think Soria's eyes widened, but I can't be sure. As if someone threw the switch, every light went out, and the ship rumbled, shaking things from side to side. Screams penetrated the air, echoing off the walls around us as shots were fired. I grabbed the pole with my hands to better steady myself, but my hands burned, and I quickly let go. I'd loosened the ropes enough earlier to lean away from the searing heat that now came from the pole. The smell of burned rope frightened me until I realized that the heat came from Trilla to help me. I pulled the ropes against the pole, and the heat took only a moment to burn through them. Some of my skin suffered as well, but the broken ropes kept me from dwelling on the pain that seared through my hands and arms.

"Catelyn, we need light," Claire yelled.

"Trilla, lights!" I commanded. The room grew bright once more, and the scene before my eyes shocked me. Somehow Claire had gotten free of her binds as well. The pole she'd been tied to glowed with the same heat mine did. Joe must have been woken in the commotion because he was in the process of pulling his binds away from his own overheated pole. Claire managed to get the stun gun off the man on the right and used it on him. He lay in a slumped mass at her feet. I threw my head back and knocked the guard behind me to the floor. Claire took aim and shot him in the chest on her first try. She wasn't helpless.

Soria yelled. Eri held her in his grip, her own gun now to her head. She struggled, but his grip wouldn't loosen. My eyes searched both Eri and my aunt, but neither had blood on them.

"Where's Adamos?" I asked. Eri nodded behind me, and I turned to see Claire standing over Adamos, a pool of blood spread across the floor under her feet. "He's dead," she said, feeling for a pulse.

Soria struggled, and Claire looked at her with an expression of exasperation. She walked to her. "Don't ever mess with my family again," Claire said—stronger and fiercer than I'd ever seen her. She then whacked Soria across the head with her gun, much like Soria had done to Eri the first time we'd met. She fell limp in Eri's arms.

With Joe's help, Eri used the burned ropes, which were still smoldering, to bind her hands. Even though she was out, I still had a memorysight as my fingers brushed her face. There were others. She'd sent three people back to the mine for parts to fix the ship. She expected them to surprise us. Even in her unconscious state, she spewed hatred toward every one of us. She expected them to avenge her. Too bad she didn't quite understand just what I could do.

I calculated the whereabouts of all the people I remembered from the mine with me. Some dead, some knocked unconscious here with us. If I was right, the three she'd sent off were the last ones. "They're coming back," I said.

"Who?" Eri asked.

"The ones she sent to retrieve parts to fix the—"

Catelyn?

I turned around, expecting to see Brand behind me, before realizing only I could hear him.

"Brand?" I said, and Joe looked at me with one eyebrow raised.

We're coming.

Where are you?

There wasn't another answer, but a brief flash of the switchbacks entered my thoughts. "They're here," I said, running for the doorway. Eri grabbed me by the arm and stopped me.

"Who's here?" he asked.

"Brand, Ryan, and Mathis. They're at the switchbacks. But something's wrong. He's not responding to me." I tried to break free of Eri's grip, but he held tight.

"The others," he said.

My stomach tightened in fear. How had they found them? She'd sent them to the mine. How had they gotten to the cabin?

"Stay here," Joe said. "If anyone you don't know comes onto this ship, shoot them."

Eri nodded.

Joe had only been gone for a few minutes when we heard a commotion. Someone had come back. From the sound of it, more than one someone. Eri held his gun and stepped in front of me. On the other side of the room, Claire still had her stun gun. She motioned to me to turn away so they wouldn't see her. I turned back to the doorway just as Joe returned, followed by Ryan, three Tallisians, Brand, and Mathis.

Brand looked about to collapse. He didn't even look at me as Joe led him and the three men—whose minds he obviously controlled—down another hallway. I ran to Ryan, throwing my arms around him in a fierce hug. "What happened?" I asked.

"We're inside a freaking mountain!" he said.

"I know, but—"

"Stop, Caty, I deserve a moment to marvel." He looked around at the ship before his eyes stopped on Adamos.

"What happened here?"

"I asked you first," I said but gave him a quick rundown of the events that had just taken place.

"He heard you calling for him," Ryan said when my story ended. "Brand woke up screaming that you were in danger, and we needed to get to you. We tried to calm him down, but he was up and making me tell him where Angels Landing was, that he needed to get there. He tried doing that mind thing you two have going on, but you didn't answer. We got him to my car, and he went unconscious again, but Mathis said we couldn't stop. He woke up as we were pulling into the parking lot and insisted on coming with us."

Ryan looked down the hallway where Mathis and Eri had followed the rest of them. "By the time we were done with the switchbacks, Mathis practically carried him. Then these guys came, and the minute they saw Brand, they pulled out guns. But then there was that earthquake—did you feel that too?"

I smiled, thinking of how Trilla saved us.

"Anyway," Ryan continued, not really waiting for an answer, "he took control of their minds instantly, but that was all he could do. He needed the cliff wall to hold him up, but he made them all give their guns to Mathis. I thought he would black out again. We couldn't do anything, so we sat there, Mathis with all these guns, Brand looking like death, those guys staring off into space like they were high or something. If anyone would have come along, I didn't know how we were going to explain any of it—and then Joe stepped out of the freaking mountain."

I laughed, imagining Ryan trying to just go with the flow of all of this while he freaked out.

"I heard Brand call to me, but when he didn't answer, Joe went to see what was up."

"Yeah, by walking out of a freaking mountain. I've never seen anything like that." He looked around the ship, and then his gaze stopped on Claire. "Were you as wigged out about this the first time?"

She laughed halfheartedly, filled with fatigue and sorrow. "About aliens? I didn't believe Joe until he walked through a wall." Her smile got a little bigger. "But yeah, it did take a while."

✦ ✦ ✦

"Thank you." I patted my bandaged hand on one of Trilla's walls. After Claire had applied a salve and determined the majority of the burns I'd received were first degree with only a few blisters on the palm of my right hand, she cleared Joe and me to come and clean up the cargo bay. She helped stop the bleeding on Eri's arm from where Soria had whipped him. Brand had collapsed on the infirmary room table.

Trilla vibrated in response to my stroke. Joe looked up and smiled. "I should have thought of using Trilla before," he said.

"You couldn't have known she would have responded to me. You didn't think she would respond to anyone but my father."

"You pretty much know everything about me now, don't you?"

I nodded, looking away. I had feared Joe or Claire would think I had messed with their minds for years. It was why I'd kept my ability a secret—and back then, I hadn't even been able to read his mind. Now that I had, I couldn't look in his eyes.

"I guess I'm going to have to change the location of my chocolate stash then."

My eyes flickered up just in time to see a broad smile stretch across his face. "You're not mad at me?"

"Caty, I could never be mad at you. It's nice not having any more secrets from you. I've had them for too long. I just hope you didn't see anything that would change your opinion about me."

"Well, there was this green sweater vest thing I wanted to ask you about." I let a grin spread across my face as relief and gratitude warmed me.

"I don't care what you think you saw. I deny ever owning that." He laughed again but then turned and looked down the hall toward the infirmary.

"He is going to have to take them back to Rhaev," he said, frowning.

I nodded. Soria and her crew needed to be tried for their crimes—and they needed to be taken as far from Earth as possible.

"I just hope Soria wasn't able to contact anyone from Tallis," Joe continued.

"She hadn't before we left the base," I said. "I would have seen it in her mind."

He nodded. "Communications through wormholes are nearly impossible, especially as far as that one is from Earth. According to Mathis, their people who had followed us here sent a ship back through the wormhole; they would not have known about it otherwise." Joe's face grew rigid for a minute. I knew he was thinking about my parents. He sat down on a nearby crate, and I followed suit, sliding next to him.

"When I was in the mine, Soria had Brand use my hatred for the people that killed my parents as a way of making me want to fight for her. I wanted to see them destroyed. But then I learned the truth, and I couldn't hate the Rhaevians."

"I thought when we came to Earth, we would be free of the prejudices. I've held them for far too long. But Mathis helped me save you from the base, and Eri saved us when he killed Adamos. I think it's time to stop blaming people just because of their differences," Joe said.

I squeezed his hand.

"You can take Trilla with you," he said after a moment of silence.

"What?"

"When you go with him. You can take the ship. She's yours."

"Joe I..." I didn't know what to say. Of course, the thought had crossed my mind. Eri couldn't stay here; he needed to get back, needed to return to his grandfather. If I wanted to be with him, then I would have to leave. But that meant leaving Joe and Claire and Ryan.

"It's okay, Caty. I wouldn't be saying this if I didn't believe that he loves you."

"Could I come back?" I asked. Eri had gotten here once. Soria had found her way here. Maybe traveling across the universe wasn't quite as big of a deal as it seemed.

"No," Joe said, squeezing my hand as his answer squeezed my heart.

"Why not?" It could be done. I knew it could.

"You need to destroy the wormhole. When Soria doesn't check in, another ship will be sent. And the more who come, the greater the chance that Earth gets pulled into all of this. Leaving needs to be a one-way trip."

Joe was right. I couldn't let anything happen to this planet—my adopted home. The wormhole needed to be destroyed. But how could I choose to leave everything knowing I could never come back?

"I can't take the ship. What about the wormhole device? What if someone tried to use it again like they did on Sardova?"

"You know they can't." Joe scoffed at my excuse. Of course I knew that. I'd seen in his head. He and my dad had dismantled the device and scattered it—not only here in southern Utah but all across the country. Trilla no longer proved a threat to anyone.

"He hasn't even asked me to go." I tried another excuse, less convincing, because we both knew that if Eri walked in right now and asked me to go with him, I wouldn't be able to say no.

"Stop making excuses, Caty," Ryan said, coming into the room. "You know you have to go with him."

Now I looked at him in shock. "But—"

"We will all be just fine here, but you don't belong with us," Joe said.

"You belong with him," Ryan added, grinning at me, even though the pain of goodbye lived in his eyes.

32

After Ryan and Joe finished ganging up on me, telling me I'd better go find my happily ever after with Eri or else, one more conversation needed to take place.

Brand still slept when I walked into the infirmary. Claire stood over him, checking his vitals. She looked up at me and smiled.

"How is he?" I asked.

"He's going to be fine. They told me he took a stun blast to the back, but there are no signs of a burn at all. In fact, the only thing he seems to be suffering from is fatigue and a little dehydration. Is he capable of healing himself?"

"Yeah."

"Will he go to Rhaev with you and Eri?" she asked.

Had they all plotted to get rid of me? "How did you know?"

"Because you finally found someone you can't take your eyes off of." She smiled but looked behind me. I turned to see Eri standing in the doorway.

"I better go see how Joe is doing," Claire said as she leaned over and gave me a hug. "This is the right decision," she whispered. "I knew the minute he defended you against Soria. I couldn't let you go if I didn't know he loved you." She pulled away and gave me a quick kiss on the cheek before sliding out of the room.

"Take good care of her," she said to Eri.

"I will," he said and smiled when she gave him a hug of his own before leaving.

Eri came to my side and took my hand. "Is he going to be okay?" He nodded to Brand.

"Yeah."

"And is he coming with us?" Eri said and grinned when I looked up at him.

"Does everyone know I'm going?" I asked.

"Do you not want to?" Eri looked worried. "Joe said you'd already decided when I asked his permission."

"You asked Joe?" I don't know why that meant so much to me, but I blinked back happy tears.

"Of course. I couldn't take you from your family without—"

I put my arms around him and kissed him. "Thank you."

He responded by kissing me back.

"You know he loves you," Eri said when we parted and tilted his head toward where Brand still lay in a deep sleep.

"He knows how I feel about you," I said, a stab of guilt piercing my heart.

"I know." He kissed my forehead reassuringly. "But it will be hard on him. And he finally has his freedom. Are you sure he will want to come with us?"

It was true. Brand was free. I had destroyed Soria's device. She couldn't hurt him again. But as hard as it might be to have Brand see Eri and me together, there was a good reason why he would be coming with us.

"He has to come with us. There is something he has to do."

"What?" It wasn't Eri who asked. I looked down to see Brand's eyes flicker open. I almost let go of Eri's hand, feeling the guilt rise in me as we stood like this in front of him. But Brand stopped me.

"It's okay, Catelyn."

A conversation we'd had in the mine entered my head—how he had known it was Eri and me all along. How he had still wished somehow it could be him. His look now told me he knew his wish wouldn't come true.

I'm so sorry.

I'm okay. I promise you. Just give me some time.

"You said there was something I had to do?" he said out loud, looking at me with eyes that said right now, that was all he could give me.

I nodded. I hated seeing Brand hurt because of me. But I could do one thing for him. I had seen in the one place he never could see, and I had the answer he'd sought for all his life.

"I know where your sister is."

It was dark when we left Angels Landing. It had been just over a day since we'd come to the mountain. Since I'd discovered my father's ship, now mine. One minute we were inside the mountain, the next the pins and needles effect brought us safely out. It felt like mere seconds before we arrived over the base camp. Trilla landed just outside the secluded mine site.

Mathis and Brand would take the Rhaevian ship and follow us. Brand had been fine with the arrangement. Just because he'd let me go to Eri didn't mean he enjoyed seeing us together. Mathis was anything but fine, but in true soldier fashion, he obeyed the order.

The bodies of the casualties were placed in the mine, and the doorway was sealed shut by an explosion. I went from event to event, keeping my mind on each task as it happened, not thinking of what was still to come. And then we were done. The mine sealed beyond recognition. The mass of rocks displaced to look like nothing more than a natural landside.

We stood outside of Trilla. I hugged Claire first. She was crying already, and I knew I'd better just get it over with. "There's a box of chocolate bars in one of the mess hall cupboards. It's not much, but Joe says it tastes better than those pills you have to take while traveling. Apparently, in that part of the universe you can get the supplement in your food." That was Claire—always feeding me.

I hugged her again.

Joe didn't come to me first. "I'm trusting her with you," he said to Eri.

"I won't let anything happen to her." Eri promised.

Tears clung to the corners of Joe's eyes, and he blinked, trying to keep them back while he pulled me into a tight hug.

"A Rhaevian," he whispered. "I should have locked you in your room until you were thirty." He laughed and kissed the top of my head before letting me go.

Then it was Ryan's turn. I didn't even know what to say. I hugged him. "You could come with us." I don't know why I hadn't offered before. Now it seemed like the best idea ever.

Ryan laughed. "I think I've had enough adventure over the past few days to last a lifetime." He released me from the hug. "I'm going to miss you, but I am so happy for you."

I leaned over and kissed his cheek. "Thanks for everything. You'll always be my best friend."

He pulled out his wallet and opened it, handing me a long stream of photos we'd taken at the beginning of the school year. "I never got around to taking these out. Sorry they are kind of crumpled."

"I love you, Ryan." I smiled.

"Ditto."

I STILL HAD a lot to deal with. Sooner or later, I'd have to go to the cells and face my aunt. Almost more frightening to me would be stepping off the ship in Rhaev and facing a group of people of whom I was their sworn enemy.

I watched out the window until the Earth was nothing but a pinprick in the distance. Eri came and put his arms around me, pulling me to him from behind. "Are you ready for this?" he said in my ear as the first shimmer of the wormhole came into view. His lips found the side of my head and then my cheek.

I was ready. For years I believed I would never leave Kanab. Now here I was, and the sky full of stars surrounded me. Eri's arms held me tight, his breath warm on my skin. There was no place I'd rather be than here, on my way to learn about a past I could never have imagined, with the future I had always dreamed of.

Acknowledgments

Once upon a time I had a dream about a boy who could move things with his mind (he can no longer do that) and so began Caty and Eri's epic journey. None of this would have been possible with the strength and support of too many people to name, but I'll try.

A huge thank-you to Beth Buck for putting a heart next to my Twitter pitch and requesting a rewrite of my manuscript which made it all the better. And to Holli Anderson who agreed that Eri and Caty should have an Immortal home.

To Lindsay Flanagan. How often can you say that your editor is also one of your favorite people in the universe? Thank you for cheering and encouraging and pushing me to be my best.

To my Critiki girls–Juliana Hacken, Heather Clark, Janelle Youngstrom, Rebecca Butler and Kristin South–who have read this book more than maybe even their own books. Thank you for loving Caty's and Eri's story and never letting me give up.

To Orson Scott Card who taught me the editing skills that opened up a future for me I never would have dreamed of.

To my first writing group, who met at Barnes and Noble and read such a rough first draft that they probably won't even recognize this one, but it is what it is because of you all...Alyson Ingebretson, Sarah Beard, Ami Chopine, Terri Barton, Garret Winn, Kylee Parry, and Darren Eggett.

To my mom, my sister Heidi, and my niece Savannah, my original number one fans. Love you all so much!

To everyone at Immortal Works who has helped and encouraged me.

To anyone I missed because so many people read parts and drafts and listened to my stories. Thank you!

Finally to Dustin, Marina, Cali, Luke, and Hertha! You are my everything. I love you more than there are stars in the sky.

About the Author

Sabine Berlin spends her days working in higher education and her evenings imagining what the world would be like if aliens, alternate realities, and all things science fiction were real. She has degrees in higher education leadership, history, and editing and document design. She loves to learn, travel, and watch K-dramas. Most of all she loves spending time with her amazing husband, three awesome kids, and the world's best chocolate Lab. She lives in Provo, UT.

This has been an
Immortal Production

CPSIA information can be obtained
at www.ICGtesting.com
Printed in the USA
BVHW041725091122
651603BV00001B/30